W. CLEMENT STONE'S

THE SUCCESS SYSTEM THAT NEVER FAILS

EXPERIENCE THE TRUE RICHES OF LIFE

AN OFFICIAL PUBLICATION OF
THE NAPOLEON HILL FOUNDATION

MANJUL

Manjul Publishing House

First published in India by

MANJUL

Manjul Publishing House

• 7/32, Ansari Road, Daryaganj, New Delhi 110 002
Website: www.manjulindia.com

Registered Office:
10, Nishat Colony, Bhopal 462 003 - India

ISBN 978-93-88241-09-0

Cover design by Eileen Rockwell.
Illustrations by Jan Ross

This edition is authorised for sale in the Indian Subcontinent.

Printed and bound in India by Thomson Press (India) Ltd.

Publisher's Notes: Not all references to economy and conditions have been updated from original writing. We think you'll agree that the messages contained in this book are timeless.

While efforts have been made to verify information contained in this publication, neither the author nor the publisher assumes any responsibility for errors, inaccuracies, or omission; it is not intended to be legal or accounting advice. All readers are advised to seek competent lawyers and accountants to follow laws and regulations that may apply to specific situations.

The reader of this publication assumes responsibility for the use of the information. The author and publisher assume no responsibility or liability whatsoever on the behalf of the reader of this publication.

CONTENTS

PREFACE

Can There Really Be A System For Success?

"A small drop of ink makes thousands, perhaps millions. . . think," wrote Byron in *Don Juan*. And foremost in the thoughts of these millions has been the search for success in their personal, family and business lives.

At this moment, in every part of the world, there are those who wonder what they can do to get further along toward some shining goal, and to their own self-improvement.

Many will snatch a secret from the depths of their hearts and souls that will drive them on to high achievement. But most of them will continue to wonder, dream, and wish. Then, one day, they will awaken with shock to find themselves standing in the same spot from which they dreamed as young men. Only, they have lost their dreams and they wonder why.

Everyone Wants Something

No matter what it is: money, position, prestige, some special achievement, the opportunity to be of service to fellow men, love, a happy marriage, or a happy home, everyone yearns for some kind of fulfillment, success in some form. To be happy, to be healthy, to be wealthy, and to experience the true riches of life—these are universal desires. These inner urges inspire us to action.

You are no exception. You have the same opportunities as other men and women, in high or low places, to succeed or to fail in this land of unlimited opportunity where many have brought their good desires into reality, and where others have fallen by the wayside of life.

Why does one man succeed and another fail? There is an answer, and it will be found in this book.

For there are formulas, prescriptions, recipes, rules, principles, systems, even treasure maps which, when followed in proper sequence, bring the good things in life to those who seek them. Often the rules for success are so simple and so obvious they aren't even seen. But when you search for them, you, too, can find them.

During the search something wonderful happens: you acquire knowledge, you gain experience, and you become inspired. Then, you begin to recognize the necessary ingredients for success.

In This House

I accepted an invitation to visit Kentuckiana Children's Center at Louisville, Kentucky. I had heard that Dr. Lorraine Golden, its director, had given up a large income from her private practice to use her talents, experience and the help of a Higher Power to help crippled children walk.

As I toured the clinic, I noticed everything was spotlessly clean. I stopped when I saw a little girl seated in a chair.

"What's your name?" I asked gently.

"Jenny," she replied.

The girl's mother was seated nearby so I asked her to tell me about Jenny.

The mother's eyes looked into mine as she said, "Jenny is six years of age. For the first four years of her life she was a cripple, unable to walk. We didn't have money, so I brought her to the clinic. Dr. Golden told me that Jenny had a nerve blockage. Now, Jenny can walk."

The mother hesitated. From her expression I felt she had something more to say—something personal. So I waited.

"Mr. Stone . . . I want you to know that . . ." She hesitated again. And then she said, ". . . outside my church this is the only house in which I feel the presence of God."

When she finished, her head was bowed as if to hide her emotions and, perhaps, a tear. Jenny, the little child who couldn't walk for the first four years of life, walked over to her mother, put her arms around her and kissed her.

And as I continued my tour through the clinic I realized that it was the driving desire of Dr. Golden which had made Kentuckiana a reality—a generous, dedicated, self-sacrificing desire that could not be held down. But to move one to action, desire must be joined to ambition and initiative.

Desire Is the Beginning of All Human Achievement

How does one develop ambition when he isn't ambitious? How does he develop initiative when he doesn't have it? How do you motivate yourself or another person to action? These are questions I have often been asked by persons in all walks of life: parents, teachers, ministers, salesmen, sales managers, executives, and high school and college students.

"First, develop the desire," I respond. But how do you germinate a desire? How do you begin? These answers will become self-evident as you read on.

Remember: there is magic in desire. Magic also lies in the skill of the magician. And skill depends upon three necessary ingredients. In fact, continuous success in each human activity always depends upon these three important ingredients. This I learned. And this I proved as I first developed my sales system that never fails which later led me to an amazing discovery . . . *The Success System That Never Fails.*

Prepare for Future Abundance

I have seen the principles of success at work in the lives of hundreds of men and women in every field of endeavor. It was only through continuous study and testing that I found the reasons behind both success and failure, and how to motivate those who had once failed to succeed.

In the belief that that which remains with you when you share with others the good and the beautiful will multiply and grow, I am sharing with you, in this book, the techniques for success as I have found them to be.

And I know from experience that if you will take a journey with me, chapter by chapter, through this book, on a treasure hunt, you, too, will be able to use *The Success System That Never Fails* to bring your worthwhile desires into reality.

A Hindu legend states that when the gods were making the world, they said: "Where can we hide the most valuable of treasures so that they will not be lost? How can we hide them so that the lust and greed of men will not steal or destroy them? What can we do to be assured that these riches will be carried on from generation to generation for the benefit of all mankind?"

So, in their wisdom, they selected a hiding place that was so obvious it wouldn't be seen. And there they placed the true riches of life, endowed with the magic power of perpetual self-replenishment. In this hiding place, these treasures can be found by every living person in every land who follows *The Success System That Never Fails.*

As you read this book, read it as if I were your personal friend writing to you and you alone. This book is dedicated to you, and to all those who seek the true riches of life.

W. CLEMENT STONE

INTRODUCTION

Many self help and motivational books, sayings and principles come and go. Enduring the test of time and demonstrating ongoing tangible results from the principles in the book you are about to read, may be one of the greatest tributes to W. Clement Stone and the ***Success System that Never Fails.***

In 1922, W. Clement Stone borrowed $100 in capital and moved to Chicago where he established a small insurance business. He was 21. Today that enterprise is a billion dollar global insurance company, Combined Insurance, operating under the same Success Principles outlined in this book ... a real testament to their lasting influence and impact.

Throughout the company, his pictures, sayings and memories are known by all who work here. As you walk by the sales classes, you hear loud shouts from new agents repeating several times, "I feel healthy. I feel happy. I feel terrific." – a saying Mr. Stone repeated every day. He lived to be 100 years old, so clearly there is something powerful in those words and the positive mental attitude behind them.

Thousands of agents and employees throughout the years, from 1922 to today, have benefitted from the motivational tenets, Success Principles and teachings of our company's founder. Whether they still work for Combined Insurance or have moved on to other careers, most will talk about how the principles and philosophies have helped them and their family, and have contributed greatly to their success in business and in life. Many challenges people run into daily are not just in the next sale or business decision, but in opportunities that arise in their personal life and the world around them. The book and its learnings apply in all aspects of life and are as relevant today as they were when first published in 1962.

Mr. Stone is known for many things. He was an entrepreneur, a business leader, a friend and advisor to influential politicians and leaders, a philanthropist, husband, father, author and motivational speaker. Those who were lucky enough to have known him light up when they talk about his coaching, teaching, motivation and leadership.

"All I want to do is change the world ... make it a better place for this and future generations." said Mr. Stone. It explains so clearly why he wore so many hats. He always believed there was nothing he couldn't accomplish if he put his mind to it and, as you will learn, approached it with a positive mental attitude. His life, his company and this book are proof that he is a man of his word.

His approach to success is simple: set your goals and never give up on those goals. He believed that whatever is conceivable and believable is totally achievable.

This book has taught thousands of others, like you, the principles to achieve personal, professional and family goals. The positive attitude and confidence instilled by the Success System influence not just those who read it, but also those they meet and thus influence and impact. So, in many ways, he has changed the world and made it a better place.

We are very proud and blessed to have benefitted so directly from Mr. Stone's leadership. We believe that if you read his book with an open mind, develop a commitment to change and begin to understand the Success System, you truly will have a direct impact on your goals and your life in general. We hope you enjoy the experience as much as we do every day at Combined Insurance.

DOUG WENDT
President
Combined Insurance

Part I

THE SEARCH BEGINS

Decisions without actions are worthless

Failure can be good for you

Don't let mental walls block you in

Direct your thoughts, control your emotions, ordain your destiny

1

A YOUNG BOY BEGINS THE SEARCH

I was six years old and scared. Selling newspapers on Chicago's tough South Side wasn't easy, especially with the older kids taking over the busy corners, yelling louder, and threatening me with clenched fists. The memory of those dim days is still with me, for it's the first time I can recall turning a disadvantage into an advantage. It's a simple story, unimportant now . . . and yet it was a beginning.

Hoelle's Restaurant was near the corner where I tried to work, and it gave me an idea. It was a busy and prosperous place that presented a frightening aspect to a child of six. I was nervous, but I walked in hurriedly and made a lucky sale at the first table. Then diners at the second and third tables bought papers. When I started for the fourth, however, Mr. Hoelle pushed me out the front door.

But I had sold three papers. So when Mr. Hoelle wasn't looking, I walked back in and called at the fourth table. Apparently, the jovial customer liked my gumption; he paid for the paper and gave me an extra dime before Mr. Hoelle pushed me out once again. But I had already sold four papers and got a "bonus" dime besides. I walked into the restaurant and started selling again. There was a lot of laughter. The customers were enjoying the show. One whispered loudly, "Let him be," as Mr. Hoelle came toward me. About five minutes later, I had sold all my papers.

The next evening I went back. Mr. Hoelle again ushered me out the front door. But when I walked right back in, he threw his hands in the air and exclaimed, "What's the use!" Later, we became great friends, and I never had trouble selling papers there again.

Years later, I used to think of that little boy, almost as if he were not me but some strange friend from long ago. Once, after I had made my fortune and was head of a large insurance empire, I analyzed that boy's actions in the light of what I had learned. This is what I concluded:

1. He needed the money. The newspapers would be worthless to him if they weren't sold; he couldn't even read them. The few pennies he had borrowed to buy them would also be lost. To a six-year-old, this catastrophe was enough to motivate him—to make him keep trying. Thus, he had the necessary *inspiration to action.*
2. After his first success in selling three papers in the restaurant, he went back in, even though he knew he might be embarrassed and thrown out again. After three trips in and out, he had the necessary technique for selling papers in restaurants. Thus, he gained the *know-how.*
3. He knew what to say, because he had heard the older kids yelling out the headlines. All he had to do, when he approached a prospective customer, was to repeat in a softer voice what he had heard. Thus, he possessed the requisite *activity knowledge.*

I smiled as I realized that my "little friend" had become successful as a newsboy by using the same techniques that later flowered into a system for success that enabled him, and others, to amass fortunes. But I'm getting ahead of myself. For now, just remember those three phrases: *inspiration to action, know-how,* and *activity knowledge.* They are the keys to the system.

The Boy's Search Goes On

Even though I was raised in a poor, run-down neighborhood, I was happy. Aren't all children happy, regardless of poverty, if they have a place to sleep, something to eat, and room to play?

I lived with my mother in the home of relatives. As I grew older, the grandfather of a girl who lived on the top floor of our apartment building sparked my imagination with stories of cowboys and Indians while we ate puffed rice and milk. And each day, when he tired of his story-telling, I would go downstairs in the backyard and live the part of Buffalo Bill or a great Indian warrior chief. My pony, made out of a stick or old broom, was the fastest in the West.

Picture a working mother seeing her young son in bed at night and asking him to tell about his day's experiences—those that were good and those that were bad. Picture him, after they had talked for a while, getting out of bed and kneeling beside his mother while she prayed for guidance. Then you have the feeling of the beginning of my search for the true riches of life.

Mother had a lot to pray for. Like all good mothers, she felt that her son was a good boy, but she was concerned because he was keeping "bad company." And she was particularly disturbed that he had developed the habit of smoking cigarettes.

Tobacco was costly, so I used to roll coffee grounds in cigarette paper when tobacco was not available. Perhaps it made me feel important, for another boy and I smoked only when other boys and girls were around, taking particular pleasure if they seemed shocked. When we had company at home, I would demonstrate how grown up I was by smoking a homemade cigarette. A pattern was being established. But it wasn't good.

Like other kids who get started in the wrong direction, I played hookey. I didn't have any fun doing it; I felt guilty. Perhaps that was the way I tried to show that I was different from the others in my group. But there was one good thing I did do: At night, when my mother and I would talk, I would tell her the truth—and I would tell her everything.

My mother's prayers for guidance were answered. She enrolled me in Spaulding Institute, a parochial boarding school at Nauvoo, Illinois. There, through exposure to a wholesome environment in which the three ingredients of *the success system that never fails* were employed, something happened—something good.

Where can one develop *inspiration to action* to search for self-improvement better than in a religious school? And who has greater *know-how* and necessary *knowledge* to teach character than those who are devoting their entire lives to the church, striving to purify their own souls while trying to save the souls of others? As the weeks passed into months and months into years, I developed a secret ambition to be like my religious father—the pastor whom I admired and loved.

But I also loved my mother, and I missed her very much. Like so many boys living away from home at private schools, I was homesick, and like them, every time I saw my mother or wrote to her, I would beg her to bring me home permanently.

After two years at Nauvoo, she felt I was ready. Equally important, she was ready. Or perhaps it was motherly love, for she too, longed to have me with her. Although there was some question of my ability to adjust to a new environment, she knew that she could always send me back to Nauvoo if it became desirable. I was ready, and she was too.

The Upward Climb

Early in life, Mother had learned to sew, and because she had initiative, talent and sensitivity, she became proficient at it. Shortly after I left for Nauvoo, she realized that a change of home and business environment was desirable for her, too. She was now in a position to do something about it, for she didn't have to be concerned with arranging for someone to care for me while she was at work.

She obtained a position in a very exclusive ladies' import establishment known as Dillon's. Within two years, she was in complete charge of all designing, fitting, and sewing, and she had developed a reputation among the exclusive clientele of being an outstanding designer and dressmaker. Her earnings were sufficiently great to enable her to get her own apartment in a nicer neighborhood.

Within a block of our apartment was a rooming house where the landlady did her own home cooking, and I had my meals there. The food was wonderful—beef stew, baked beans, homemade pies, mashed potatoes and gravy—notwithstanding the jovial complaints of the adult boarders, who were the most interesting people in the world to an eleven-year-old boy: show people. They liked me, too. I was the only child there.

Like thousands of men and women who grasp the opportunity to make *the upward climb* in this land of unlimited opportunity, mother saved enough money to establish her own business. Her reputation as a designer and dressmaker brought good clients, but she lacked the *know-how* to utilize bank credit. (Many small businesses would become big businesses if the owners would only learn that banks are in business to help small businesses become large through sound financing.)

Because of lack of working capital or the proper utilization of bank credit, mother's dressmaking establishment never expanded beyond her personal work and that of two full-time employees. Like most persons who endeavor to establish their own business, she, too, had her financial problems. But these problems brought to us many of the true riches of life, such as the joy of giving.

I made my spending money (which was partly savings money, for I had established a savings account) by building a *Saturday Evening Post* and newspaper route. Although each night mother asked me to tell her about my troubles, she never bothered to tell me about her own. But I could sense them. One morning, I noticed that she seemed to be quite worried. Later that day, before she returned home, I drew out what was to me a big chunk of savings and purchased a dozen of the best roses I could buy.

My mother's joy at this token of love inspired me to realize the true joy of the giver. Often over the years she would tell her friends with a mother's pride about the dozen beautiful, long-stemmed roses and what they had done for her. This experience made me realize that money was a good thing to have—for the good it could do.

January 6 was always an important date in my mother's life and in mine, for that was her birthday. One January 6, when for some reason—perhaps because of Christmas shopping—my bank account was down to less than a dollar, I was very much concerned, for I wanted desperately to buy her a birthday gift. That morning I prayed for guidance.

At the lunch hour, while walking home from school, my ears were tuned to the cracking of the ice beneath my feet. Suddenly I stopped and turned around. *Something* told me to go back and take a look. I walked back, picked up a crumpled green paper, and was amazed to find a ten-dollar bill! (That *something* you will hear more about.)

I was excited, but I decided not to buy a gift after all. I had a better plan.

Mother was home for lunch. As she was clearing the table, she picked up her plate and found a handwritten birthday note and the ten-dollar bill. Once again I found the joy of the giver, for it seemed that this was a day when everyone else had forgotten her birthday. She was delighted with this gift, which at the time seemed to her quite a sum.

Decisions Are Important When Followed Through with Action

These personal experiences will indicate that each new decision that a child or an adult makes in a given set of circumstances begins patterns of thought that later create a tremendous impact in his life. When an adult makes a decision, it is likely to be foolish or sound, depending on his past experiences in coming to decisions. For *the little things that are good ripen into big things that are good. And the little things that are bad ripen into big things that are bad.* And this applies to decisions.

But good decisions must be followed through with action. Without action, a good decision becomes meaningless, for the desire itself can die through lack of an attempt to achieve its fulfillment. That's why you should act immediately on a good decision.

When You Go For Something, Don't Come Back Until You Get It

I was twelve years of age when an older neighbor boy whom I respected invited me to attend a Boy Scout meeting. I went and had a lot of fun, so I joined his troop—Troop 23, under a scoutmaster named Stuart P. Walsh, who was attending the University of Chicago.

I'll never forget him. He was a man of character. He wanted every boy in his troop to become a first-class scout within a short space of time, and he inspired each boy to want his troop to be the best in the city of Chicago. Perhaps that's one reason why it was. Another was his firm conviction: *to get what you expect—inspect,* when you teach, inspire, train, and supervise others.

Every scout in Troop 23 made a weekly report of the good turns he had done each day in the week—the ways he had helped someone else without receiving compensation of any kind. This made each boy look for the opportunity to do a good deed—and because he looked, he found the opportunity.

Stuart P. Walsh imprinted in the memory of each member of Troop 23, in indelible pattern, the principles of the Scout Law: "A Scout is trustworthy, loyal, helpful, friendly, courteous, kind, obedient, cheerful, thrifty, brave, clean, and reverent."

But more important, he *inspected* to see if each scout in his troop knew how to relate, assimilate, and use each of these principles—not just to memorize them like a parrot, but to use them like a man. I can hear him say now: "When you go after something—don't come back until you get it!"

In the next chapter, you will see how this principle taught by my old scoutmaster became so ingrained in me that it formed, at first without my realizing it, another step on the road to the success system that never fails. The six-year-old newsboy about whom you read in the beginning of this chapter had not yet awakened to where he was going—but he was on his way.

LITTLE HINGES THAT SWING BIG DOORS

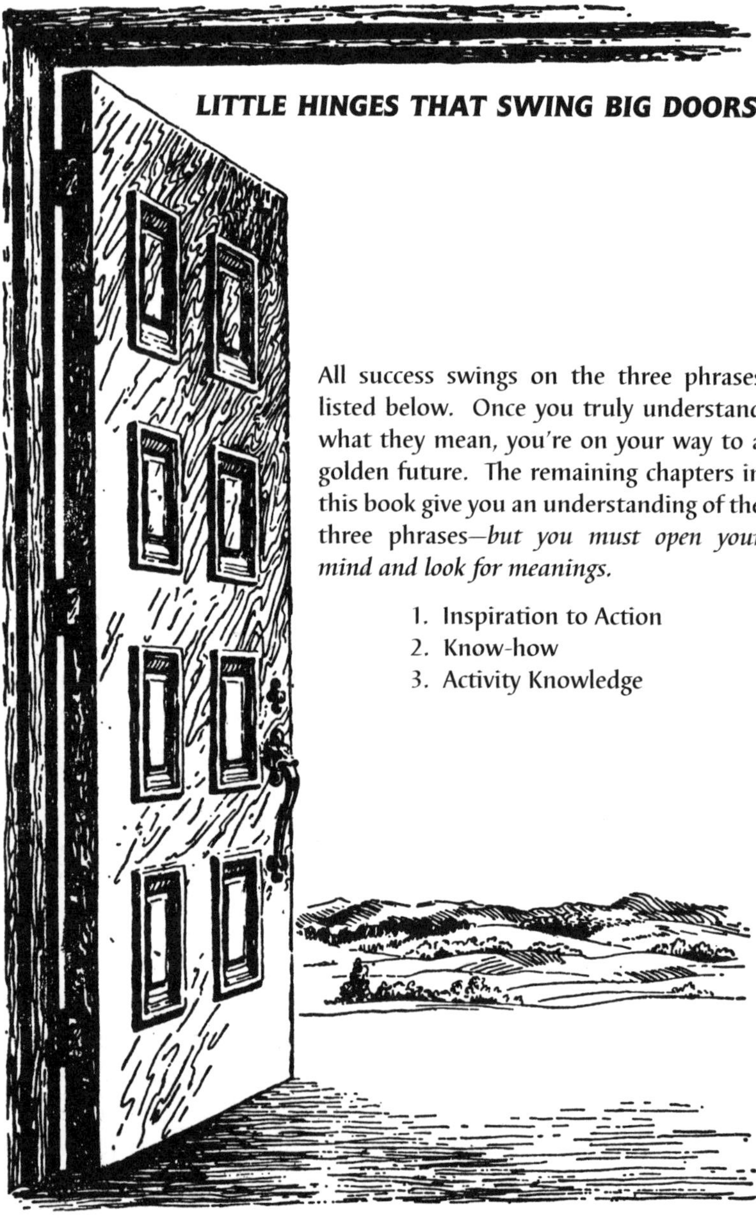

All success swings on the three phrases listed below. Once you truly understand what they mean, you're on your way to a golden future. The remaining chapters in this book give you an understanding of the three phrases—*but you must open your mind and look for meanings.*

1. Inspiration to Action
2. Know-how
3. Activity Knowledge

2

GET READY FOR TOMORROW

One of the most important lessons of my life forced itself on me at about the time I was graduating from grammar school. It was a lesson that turned into a major principle: *You are subject to your environment. Therefore, select the environment that will best develop you toward your desired objective.*

Although I was not then able to state the thought as succinctly as that, I was aware of the principle behind it. When it came time for me to enter high school, I concluded that Senn High was a better school than Lakeview High, which I would have to enter if we continued to live in the neighborhood in which we had our apartment at the time. Because an important change that my mother was making in business required that she move to Detroit, we made arrangements with a fine English family in the Senn district for me to live in their home.

I also decided that I would select my own friends on going to the new school. In choosing, I searched for individuals of character and intelligence. And because I searched, I found what I was looking for: fine, wonderful persons who had a tremendous influence for good upon me.

Get Your Money's Worth

With me in a good home environment and attending a fine public school, mother made an investment in a small insurance agency representing the United States Casualty Company in Detroit, Michigan.

I'll never forget it. She pawned her two diamonds to get sufficient cash to add to the money she did have to buy the agency. Remember: she hadn't learned to use bank credit in establishing a business. After renting desk space in a downtown office building, she looked with anticipation to her first day's sales. That day she was lucky. She worked hard, but she didn't make a single sale—and that was good!

What do you do when everything goes wrong? What do you do when there is no place to turn? What do you do when you are faced with a serious problem?

Here's what she did, the way she later told it to me: "I was desperate. I had invested all the cash I had, and I just had to get my money's worth out of this investment. I had tried my best, but I hadn't made a sale.

"That night I prayed for guidance. And the next morning I prayed for guidance. When I left home, I went to the largest bank in the city of Detroit. There I sold a policy to the cashier and got permission to sell in the bank during working hours. It seemed that within me there was a driving force that was so sincere that all obstacles were removed. That day I made 44 sales."

Through trial and error the first day, my mother developed inspirational dissatisfaction. She was *inspired to action.* She knew Whom to ask for guidance and help in her efforts to make a livelihood, just as she knew Whom to ask for guidance and help when she was faced with a problem regarding her son.

And through trial and success the second day, she acquired *know-how* in selling her accident policies that developed for her a successful sales system. Now she had *know-how* in addition to *inspiration to action* and *activity knowledge.* So *the upward climb* was rapid.

Salesmen, like other persons, often fail in *the upward climb* because they do not reduce to a formula the principles applied on those days when they are successful. They know the facts, but they fail to extract the principles.

Now that she was earning a good living in personal sales, my mother began to build a sales organization that operated throughout the state of Michigan under the trade name of Liberty Registry Company.

Mother and I would see each other on holidays and during vacation periods. My second high school summer vacation was spent in Detroit. That's when I, too, learned to sell accident insurance, and, that's where I started to search for a sales system for myself—a system that would never fail.

Do Twice as Much in Half the Time

The Liberty Registry Company office was in the Free Press Building. I spent a day in the office, reading and studying the policy I was to try to sell the next day.

My sales instructions were as follows:

1. Completely canvass the Dime Bank Building.
2. Start at the top floor and call on each and every office.
3. Avoid calling in the office of the building.
4. Use the introduction, "May I take a moment of your time?"
5. Try to sell everyone you call on.

So I followed instructions. Remember, I had learned as a Boy Scout: *When you set out to do something—don't come back until you have done it.*

Was I frightened? You bet I was.

But it never occurred to me not to follow instructions. I just didn't know any better. I was, in this respect, a product of habit—a good habit.

The first day I sold two policies—two more than I had ever sold before. The second day, four—and that was a 100 percent increase. The third day, six—a 50 percent increase. And the fourth day I learned an important lesson.

I called at a large real estate office, and when I stood at the desk of the sales manager and used the introduction, "May I take a moment of your time?" I was startled. For he jumped to his feet, pounded his desk with his right fist and almost shouted: "Boy, as long as you live never ask a man for his time! Take it!"

So I took his time and sold him and 26 of his salesmen that day.

That started me thinking: There must be a scientific way to sell many policies every day. There must be a method that will make one hour produce the work of many. Why not find a system for selling twice as much in half the time? Why can't I develop a formula that will bring maximum results for each hour of effort?

From that point on, I was consciously trying to discover the principles that have since built for me my sales system that never fails. I reasoned: "Success can be reduced to a formula. And failure can be reduced to a formula, too. Apply the one and avoid the other. Think for yourself."

Think for Yourself

Regardless of who you are, it is desirable to learn the techniques of good salesmanship. For selling is merely persuading another person to accept your service, your product, or your idea. In this sense, everyone is a salesman. Whether or not you are a salesman by vocation, the minute details of my selling system are not really important to you; but the principles may be—if you are ready.

What is important to you is that you reduce to a formula, preferably in writing, the principles you learn from your successful experiences and your failures, in whatever activities you may be interested. But you may not know how to extract principles from what you read, hear, or experience. I'll illustrate how I did it. But *you must think for yourself.*

How I Overcame Timidity and Fear

Before I describe how I overcame timidity and fear when opening up closed doors, entering plush offices, and trying to sell to businessmen and women as a teenager, let me first tell how I faced the same problem as a boy.

Many persons find it difficult to believe that as a youngster I was timid and afraid. But it is nature's law that with every new experience and in every new environment an individual will feel some degree of fear. Nature protects the individual from danger by this awareness. Children and women experience this to a greater degree than men; again, this is nature's way of protecting them from harm.

I remember that as a boy I was so timid that when we had company I would go into another room, and during a thunderstorm I would hide under the bed. But one day I reasoned: "If lightning is going to strike, it will be just as dangerous whether I am under the bed or in any other part of the room." I decided to conquer this fear. My opportunity came, and I took advantage of it. During a thunderstorm, I forced myself to go to the window and look at the lightning. An amazing thing happened. I began to enjoy the beauty of the flashes of lightning through the sky. Today, there is no one who enjoys a thunderstorm more than I do.

Although I called in each office in sequence in the Dime Bank Building, I had not licked the fear of opening a door, particularly when I couldn't see what was on the other side (many of the glass doors were frosted or had curtains on the inside). It was necessary to develop a method of forcing myself to enter.

Then, because I searched, I found the answer. I reasoned: *Success is achieved by those who try. Where there is nothing to lose by trying and a great deal to gain if successful, by all means try!*

The repetition of either of these self-motivators satisfied my reason. But I was still afraid, and it was still necessary to get into action. Fortunately, I struck upon the self-starter: *Do it now!* Because I had learned the value of trying to establish the right habits and the harm of acquiring wrong habits, it occurred to me that I could force myself to action as I left one office if I would rush quickly into the next one. Should it occur to me to hesitate, I would use the self-starter *Do it now!*—and immediately act on it. This I did.

How to Neutralize Timidity and Fear

When once inside a place of business, I was still not at ease, but I soon learned how to neutralize the fear of talking to a stranger. I did it through voice control.

I found that if I spoke loudly and rapidly, hesitated where there would be a period or comma if the spoken word were written, kept a smile in my voice, and used modulation, I no longer had butterflies in my stomach. Later I learned that this technique was based on a very sound psychological principle: the emotions (like fear) are not immediately subject to reason but they are subject to action. *When thoughts do not neutralize an undesirable emotion—action will.*

The sales manager in the real estate office hadn't liked the introduction: "May I take a moment of your time?" Besides, many persons on whom I had used this introduction had answered "No." So I abandoned it and, after experimenting, came up with a new one that I have used ever since: "I believe this will interest you also."

No one has said "No" to this introduction. Most have asked, "What is it?" Then, of course, I have told them and given them my sales talk. The purpose of a sales introduction is solely to get a person to listen.

Know When To Quit

"Try to sell everyone you call on" was one of the instructions my mother had given me. So I stayed with every prospect. Sometimes I wore him out, but when I left his place of business, I was worn out too. It seemed to me that in selling a low-cost service, as I was doing, it was imperative that I average more sales per hour of effort. For it wasn't every day that I sold 27 policies in one place of business.

So I decided *not* to sell everyone I called on, *if the sale would take longer than a time limit I had set for myself.* I would try to make the prospect happy and leave hurriedly, even though I knew that if I stayed with him I could make the sale.

Wonderful things happened. I increased my average number of sales per day tremendously. What's more, the prospect in several instances thought I was going to argue, but when I left him so pleasantly, he would come next door to where I was selling and say, "You can't do that to me. Every other insurance man would hang on. You come back and write it." Instead of being tired out after an attempted sale, I experienced enthusiasm and energy for my presentation to the next prospect.

The principles I learned are simple: Fatigue is not conducive to doing your best work. Don't reduce your energy level so low that you drain your battery. The activity level of the nervous system is raised when the body recharges itself with rest. *Time is one of the most important ingredients in any successful formula for any human activity. Save time. Invest it wisely.*

How to Get a Person to Listen to You

"When you are talking to a person, look at his eyes," I was taught as a youngster. But in selling, I would look at a person's eyes and he would often shake his head "no." And more often he would interrupt me. I didn't like this. It slowed me down. Soon, I hit on a simple technique to avoid this: Get the prospect to concentrate through his senses of sight and hearing on what I had to show him and on what I had to say. I pointed to the policy or sales literature and looked at it as I gave my sales talk. Because I looked where I was pointing, he looked too. If, out of the corner of my eye, I saw a prospect shake his head "no," I paid no attention. Often he would become interested, and I would later close the sale.

Play to Win

In a highly competitive game or sport, you play according to the rules, and you don't violate the standards that you have set for yourself, but you play to win. So it is in the game of selling. For selling, like every other activity, becomes a lot of fun when you become an expert.

I found that to become an expert I had to work, and work hard. *Try, try, try, and keep trying* is the rule that must be followed to become an expert in anything. But in due course, by employing the right work habits, you do become an expert. Then you experience the joy of work, and the job is no longer work. It becomes fun.

Day after day I worked, and worked hard, trying to improve my sales techniques. I searched for *trigger words*—words and phrases that would set off the right reaction within the prospect. And the right reaction meant that he would buy within a reasonably short space of time, for time meant money to me.

I wanted to say the right thing in the right way to get the right reaction. This took practice, and practice is work.

Everything has a beginning and an ending. The introduction is the beginning of a sales presentation. How could I end the sale in the shortest space of time, in a manner that would make the prospect happy?

Because I searched, I made a discovery: If you want the prospect to buy, *ask* him to buy. Just ask him, and give him a chance to say "yes." But make it easy for him to say "yes" and difficult to say "no." Specifically, use force with such finesse that it is subtle, pleasing, and effective.

And here's what I found: If you want a person to say "yes," just make *a positive statement and ask an affirmative question.* Then the "yes" answer is almost a natural reflex action. Examples:

1. Positive statement: *It's a nice day . . .*
   Affirmative question: *Isn't it?*
   Answer: *Yes, it is.*
2. The mother who wants her child to practice the piano for an hour on Saturday morning when she knows that the child wants to go out to play, could say:
   Positive statement: *You want to practice for an hour now so that you'll have the entire day to play . . .*

Affirmative question: *Isn't that true?*
Answer: *Yes*

3. A sales lady offering the customer a lace handkerchief could say:
   Positive statement: *This is beautiful, and it's quite reasonable . . .*
   Affirmative question: *Don't you think so?*
   Answer: *Yes*
   Affirmative question: *May I gift wrap it for you, then?*
   Answer: *Yes*
4. The effective close I found is just as simple:
   Positive statement: *So, if you don't mind, I would like to write it for you also, if I may . . .*
   Affirmative question: *May I?*
   Answer: *Yes*

Why It Was Written

The stories of my experiences in the Dime Bank Building indicate the techniques I used to begin to develop my sales system that never fails, and why I used them. I was searching for the necessary *knowledge* for each step that would comprise the entire sales presentation. I was endeavoring to acquire the *know-how*—the *experience of using this specific knowledge* through repeated *action.*

In brief, I was preparing myself to develop the habit of using a formula that would *consistently* obtain outstanding results in sales for me in the shortest possible space of time.

Although I didn't realize it then, I was in reality *getting ready for tomorrow.* For some years later, I discovered that my sales system employed principles that are the common denominator of continuous successful achievement in every human activity. And thus I made a greater discovery: the *success system that never fails.*

What Does It Mean to You?

Health, happiness, success, and wealth can be yours when you understand and employ *the success system that never fails.*

For *the system works . . . if you work the system.*

Up to this point, you may not recognize and understand the success principles to be found in the stories and explanations you read well enough to adopt them. But as you continue to read, they will become crystal clear.

As you search for *the success system that never fails,* you will make faster and more permanent progress by keeping in mind the three necessary ingredients, which are, in order of their importance:

1. *Inspiration to action:* that which motivates you, or anyone else, to act because you *want* to.

2. *Know-how:* the particular techniques and skills that *consistently* get results for you. Know-how is the *proper application of knowledge. Know-how* becomes *habit* through actual repetitive *experience.*

3. *Activity knowledge:* knowledge of the activity, service, product, methods, techniques, and skills with which you are particularly concerned.

For continuous success, it is necessary to *get ready for tomorrow.* To get ready for tomorrow, you must *be a self-builder.* And to learn to be a *self-builder,* read the next chapter.

LITTLE HINGES THAT SWING BIG DOORS

1. In the end, your environment will control you; therefore, make sure that you control your environment. Avoid situations, acquaintances, associates, who tend to hold you back.
2. Success is achieved by those who *try.* Where there's a lot to gain and little to lose, *try.*
3. *Thinking* will not overcome fear, but *action* will.
4. Never forget: *The system will work . . . if* YOU *work the system.*

3

BE A SELF-BUILDER

"Don, do you know where I can get a job?"

Donald Moorhead hesitated, smiled, and said, "Yes, Jim. See me at my office at 8:30 tomorrow morning."

That's the way the conversation was closed. It began when Mr. Moorhead, an officer of the United States Casualty Company, met a friend one afternoon while walking down Wall Street.

And the next morning, when Jim came up to see him, Don suggested that an easy way to make a large income and render a service to the public was to sell accident and health insurance.

"But," said Jim, "I'd be scared stiff. I wouldn't know whom to call on. I've never sold a thing in my life."

"That's nothing to be worried about," was the response. "I'll tell you what to do. I'll guarantee that you can't fail . . . if you call on five persons a day. And I'll give you the names of five prospects each morning, if you'll make me a promise."

"What's the promise?"

"Promise me that you'll call on each of them the same day I give you their names. It's all right to mention my name if you want. But don't tell them I sent you."

Jim needed a job badly, and it didn't take very long for his friend to convince him that he should at least try. So Jim took the necessary literature and instructions home to study, and he reported back to Mr. Moorhead's office a few mornings later to get his five names and get started on a new career.

It's in Your Mind

"Yesterday was a thrilling day!" he exclaimed, when he reported the next morning with two sales and lots of enthusiasm.

He had better luck the second day, for he sold three of the five prospects. The third morning he rushed out of Mr. Moorhead's office, full of vim and vitality, with five more names. These were especially good leads—he sold four of the five prospects he called upon.

When the new, enthusiastic salesman reported to work the following morning, Mr. Moorhead was in an important conference. Jim waited in the reception room for about 15 minutes before Mr. Moorhead came out of his private office and said, "Jim, I'm in an exceedingly important meeting that will probably last all morning. Why don't you save my time and yours? Get the five names for yourself from the classified telephone book. That's what I've been doing for the last three days. Here—I'll show you how I do it."

Then Don opened the classified book at random, pointed to an ad, picked out the name of the president of the company, and wrote down the name and address. Then he said: "Now you try it."

Jim did. After he had written down his first name and address, Don continued: "Remember, success in selling is a matter of mental attitude—the attitude of the salesman. Your entire career may depend on whether you can develop the same right mental attitude when you call on the five names you select as you had when you called on the persons whose names I gave you."

And thus started the career of a man who subsequently made a real success. For he realized the truth—*it's in your mind.* In fact, he improved the system. To be certain that his prospect would be in, he telephoned and made an appointment. It's true that he had to develop *know-how* in making appointments. But he got this with experience.

And that's how you learn *know-how*—through experience.

Then there is the story of the banker who made one mistake and lost his position but got himself a better job when he took inventory of himself. It was recently told me by Edward R. Dewey, Director of The Foundation for the Study of Cycles.

Take Inventory of Yourself

"Mike Corrigan was a banker friend of mine," said Mr. Dewey, "who misplaced confidence in a customer whom he liked. Mike made this man a substantial loan, and the loan went sour. Although Mike had been with the bank for many years, his superiors felt that, in view of his experience, he had made a stupid decision. So Mike was fired, and he was out of a job for some time.

"I have never seen a more beaten man: his walk . . . his face . . . his bearing . . . his speech . . . all showed complete discouragement and dejection. He had what you, Clem, term a negative mental attitude," Ned Dewey said to me. Then he continued:

"Mike made several attempts to get a job, but they were futile. To me it was understandable, because of his attitude. I wanted to help him, so I gave him a book: *Pick Your Job and Land It,* by Sidney and Mary Edlund. The Edlunds tell how to show your business experience in an attractive manner to the prospective employer of your choice. 'It's a must,' I told him. 'After you have read it, I want you to see me.'

"Mike read the book and saw me the next day, for he needed a job badly.

"'I've read the book,' he said.

"'Then you've noticed,' I said, 'that the book suggests you list your assets: all the things you have done *to make money for your previous employer.'* And I asked him several questions, such as:

1. What profit increases did your bank experience year by year under your supervision as branch manager—increased profits because of something special that you did?

2. How much money did the bank save by eliminating waste through increased efficiency under your administration?

"Mike was smart . . . and he was ready. He got the idea.

"After dinner that night he came over to my house. I was amazed at the transformation! He was a new man: a sincere smile . . . a firm and friendly handclasp . . . a voice of assurance—the very reflection of success.

"And I was equally amazed at what he had written on the several pages listing what he considered to be his real assets. For, in addition to outlining the value he had been to his former employer, he made a special listing under the heading *My True Assets.*"

When Edward R. Dewey mentioned some of the assets listed by Mike Corrigan, I was unable to resist interrupting him with: "Mike Corrigan recognized the ingredients essential to becoming a self-builder!" And you will see what I meant when you read the chapter titled "The True Riches of Life."

Mr. Dewey continued. "Among the *true* assets were:

- A wonderful wife who meant the world to him.
- An only daughter who brought joy, happiness, and sunshine into his life.
- A healthy mind and body.
- Many friends—good friends.
- A religious philosophy and a church that were a source of inspiration to him.
- The privilege of living in America.
- A house and a car, each fully paid for.
- A few thousand dollars in the bank.
- Sufficient youth to have many good years ahead of him.
- The respect and esteem of those who knew him.

"It was fun being with Mike that evening," said Ned. "In fact, he was so enthusiastic that he made me enthusiastic, too.

I felt that he was the kind of fellow I'd hire if I were an employer.

"For the next two days, I could hardly get Mike out of my mind. And when the telephone rang at dinner the second evening, I had a feeling it was Mike. It was.

"'I want to thank you, Ned. I've got a good job,' he exclaimed happily.

"And Mike did get a good job, as treasurer of a large hospital in a neighboring city, a position he has now held for many years," Mr. Dewey concluded.

He Developed a Time Recorder . . . and Became a Self-Builder

You don't have to be out of a job to take inventory of yourself. Those who engage in self-inspection are generally those who are seeking self-improvement—and find it. George Severance, who represents the Ohio National Life Insurance Company in Chicago, is such a man.

It was he who invented the Social Time Recorder, which helped him achieve success in reaching his many worthwhile objectives. The principle he used can be applied by anyone who will take the time to develop and follow his own time recorder.

And should you follow the instructions in designing your time recorder—and use it daily, as outlined in detail in Chapter 19—then you, like George Severance, will become a self-builder.

For you, like him, will use his technique to have peace of mind and happiness . . . get out of debt . . . save money . . . eliminate waste of time and money . . . acquire wealth . . . eliminate bad habits and develop good ones. Its daily use will motivate you to higher achievement. *I guarantee it!*

George is a friend of mine. I know his story well. He found his first excitement in sales when he began knocking on back doors selling industrial insurance. Here's what he says:

"I believe I knocked on every back door in my neighborhood. In fact, I know that at one time or another I have canvassed in every section of the city. As time went on, my sales began to grow in volume; however, I found myself in very serious financial difficulties, for my debts were expanding faster than my income.

"One day, the total amount of these debts struck me like a bolt of lightning. I was faced with a real financial crisis. Then I recalled a statement I had read somewhere:

"If you cannot save money, the seed of success is not in you.

"I wanted desperately to succeed. I wanted to get out of debt. I felt I had the seed of success within me. Then and there, I decided to do something about it."

If you cannot save money, the seed of success is not in you. This statement indicated that George Severance, like many persons who have achieved success, benefited from memorizing and responding to self-motivators.

And, therefore, I once asked him: "In addition to the *Bible,* what self-help book played the most important part in your life?"

*"Authors of Portraits and Principles,"** he replied.

Now, there is something more to success than reading self-help books and extracting the philosophy contained in them, and that is *Action.*

George told me that his Social Time Recorder *helped him* to take inventory of himself—to organize his thinking time, set definite objectives, and select the right track to run on—and *motivated him* to action. And he also said:

"After I had developed the Social Time Recorder, I found that I had been spending as much as 32 hours in a single month drinking coffee with my friends. I was amazed, for I realized that this was equivalent to four working days. And then I realized that my lunch hours were sometimes a full hour longer than they should have been." He continued:

"Travel—like a jack rabbit I hopped here, there, and everywhere, rather than working one territory thoroughly.

"Late hours—I used to go to many night meetings. And when

*Designed and arranged by Wm. C. King, King Richardson & Co., Springfield, Mass., 1895.

the meetings broke up at eight or nine o'clock, a group of us played cards or engaged in idle chatter that would often last past midnight. Now I go home and enjoy the evening with my family. I get a good night's sleep. I have more time to read self-help books.

"Sports—sometimes I used to go to ball games or play golf during selling time. I hate to think of the income lost during this valuable earning time.

"Family duties—I'd take time to run chores for the family during business hours, instead of using my time profitably to do the job expected of me as a wage earner.

"When I looked back, I found that in many respects I was a social success during business hours. But when I developed my Social Time Recorder, I realized:

"If a business day is a social success, it has been a business failure."

So George completed his Social Time Recorder daily. The officials of his company were amazed. For the records indicate that after inventing his Social Time Recorder, George accomplished wonders:

- He wrote over four million dollars' worth of life insurance in a single year.
- He established a company record by submitting over a million dollars' worth of new business in *one* day.
- He consistently sold enough life insurance to become a life member of the Million Dollar Round Table—an achievement every life insurance man seeks, but relatively few attain.

With justifiable pride, George said, "I began to pay off my debts, and eventually, when these were paid, I started a savings account. Finally, I had saved $6,000. A friend of mine and I each invested $6,000 in an enterprise that our bank helped us finance. Within a year, we each received $50,000 out of this project. This was a big step forward in acquiring wealth."

Would you like to see a facsimile of George Severance's Social Time Recorder? Read a detailed report on how it works? Develop a time recorder for your own special use?

You'll have your opportunity when you get to Chapter 19: "The *Success Indicator* Brings Success." But it takes will power to begin the habit—to take inventory of yourself daily. And an inspirational self-help book will help.

POWER OF WILL

Authors of Portraits and Principles and other self-help books inspired George Severance. *Power of Will** helped me. Perhaps when you read of my experience cold-canvassing in the Dime Bank Building in the last chapter, you may have questioned how a teenage salesman on his first assignment built sales techniques based on the functioning of the human mind when older and more experienced salesmen in all fields often failed to do this.

But don't sell the teenager short. As a high school freshman, I had problems that motivated me to purchase *Power of Will,* by Frank Channing Haddock. For one thing, I wanted to develop will power. In addition, I was president of the Debating Club at Senn High, where we debated such topics as, "Is the will free?" It was necessary to engage in research, and *Power of Will* is a good reference book for such a subject.

The training in debating and public speaking gave me self-assurance and confidence. And the necessity to develop quick and convincing rebuttal arguments made effective rebuttal arguments in sales come naturally to me, for the principles are the same. Debater or salesman, you must think logically and be sensitive to every statement that you can turn to your advantage. You must be *persuasive* to win.

I have often wondered why schools don't expose teenagers to self-help books. They're at the age where they are seeking truths and personal help. The Constitution prohibits the teaching of religion in public schools, but there is nothing in the Constitution that prohibits the teaching of the proper attitude toward work,

*Frank Channing Haddock, Ralston Publishing Co., Cleveland, Ohio.

honesty, courage, the building of a noble life, thinking good thoughts, and doing good deeds.

You Reach the Soul Through the Mind

The history of man has taught us that *the best thoughts that are very new are the best thoughts that are very old.* That's the way another friend of mine, Nate Lieberman, expresses it. Countless persons have thought good thoughts and done good deeds to build a noble life through the influence of the church. The moral teachings of the church are to be found in the Bible and other religious writings. In seeking self-improvement, expose yourself to religious philosophy and go to the Bible—the self-help book that has inspired more persons to desirable action than any book written. And when you read the Bible, be encouraged, even though you don't at first have the *know-how* of relating, assimilating, and using its principles. For *know-how* is the product of experience.

Through the Bible and the influence of your church, you reach your soul through your mind. And because of the importance of a healthy mind and the curative powers of religion, ministers of all denominations are beginning to recognize the need for cooperation between the minister and the psychiatrist to obtain most effective results in providing individuals with physical, mental, and moral health.

For 25 years, Dr. Smiley Blanton and the Reverend Dr. Norman Vincent Peale have proved the value of the psychiatrist and the minister working as partners while fulfilling their separate vocations. But most of all, through the American Foundation of Religion and Psychiatry (which they established) with headquarters in New York City, they have trained ministers of all denominations in many parts of the world to better fulfill the mission to which they are dedicated.

I mentioned this philosophy because, as a sales manager, I have taken men who have failed with other companies and, by motivating them to become self-builders, have prepared them for outstanding success. Anyone who wishes to be a self-builder can achieve his objectives by constantly striving to develop physical, mental, and moral health, provided he doesn't build unseen walls.

Tear Down the Unseen Walls

In the third century B.C., Chin Shih Huang Ti, the first emperor of the Chin Dynasty, built two walls—the famous Great Wall of China and, simultaneously, an "unseen wall."

The Great Wall, with its 25,000 watchtowers, stretched 2,500 miles. For more than 2,000 years, it prevented the barbarians from coming in and the world's oldest civilization, with its advanced knowledge and culture, from getting out.

In the third century B.C., China was self-sufficient; it didn't need the rest of the world. But the rest of the world needed what China had to share with it: the art of printing, the use of coal, water clocks, bronze casting, gunpowder, astronomical instruments, the naval compass, drugs, spices . . . and more.

As the centuries passed, the barbarians gained *inspiration, knowledge,* and *know-how* and advanced their civilization so far beyond that of Chin Shih Huang Ti that China today is primitive by comparison.

For like the leaders of nations who fear the freedom of religion, education, and the press, and who have built bamboo or iron curtains around their peoples, the Emperor stultified progress by destroying whatever literature did not correspond to his ideas, concepts, and philosophy.

Now you may not appear to be an emperor, king, or leader in the eyes of others, but you are an absolute monarch when it comes to the control of what you think, feel, believe, and *try* to do. And the literature that you don't explore is as useless to you as if it were burned or destroyed.

So now may be the time to ask yourself:

"What unseen walls have I built?

"Since leaving school, have I exposed myself to ideas, concepts, and philosophies that are different from those I had at the time?

"Am I keeping pace with economic, social, religious, scientific, political, and other important developments of our times?

"Do I read a self-help book as if the author were a personal friend and writing to me and me alone?

"Or have I already learned every fundamental principle that I will ever learn?"

Be a Self-Builder

Build your own life. Be a benefit to yourself and to all mankind. Build from within. But get help from without. You can do this as you search for, find, and follow your *success system that never fails.*

To get help from without, extract the good where you can find it. And this starts from within: the right mental attitude toward persons, places, things, knowledge, customs, beliefs—be they your own or others.

Is your future behind you because of an unseen wall that you have built so strongly within you that it prevents enlightened ideas from breaking through?

Perhaps it is . . . perhaps it isn't. You can tear down these unseen walls if they do exist. The next chapter, "Don't Leave Your Future Behind You," tells you how.

LITTLE HINGES THAT SWING BIG DOORS

At this moment, do you know exactly what your assets are? Are you aware of your true abilities, your potential for growth, your successes of the past, no matter how small? If you're not, *take inventory of yourself.* To know where you're going and how to get there, you must first *know yourself.*

4

DON'T LEAVE YOUR FUTURE BEHIND YOU

Floyd Patterson crashed to the canvas. Seconds later, he was no longer the world's heavyweight champion. Ingemar Johansson had taken the title away from him.

The experts said Floyd was through; his future as a fighter was behind him. And everyone knew that Floyd was faced with one of the oldest jinxes in sports: No heavyweight champion had ever won back the crown. But Floyd had to try—and more than that, he said he would do it!

For Floyd Patterson had developed *inspirational dissatisfaction.* He knew he could succeed, and he was not content to remain a failure; he had taken a fierce pride in being champion.

On reflection, he realized that he must change his mental attitude and work hard to make up for lost time. And he did work hard. He studied. He listened to his trainers.

He listened to the former champion Joe Louis, who said, "The way to get Johansson is to make him miss. Then step inside." And Patterson did make Ingo miss. He did step inside. In fact, from the first second of the fight until he shot his final left hook flush on Johansson's chin in the fifth round, Patterson proved that the motivating power of his *inspirational dissatisfaction* was sufficient to develop in him the (1) *inspiration to action,* (2) *know-how,* and (3) *activity knowledge* necessary for him to regain the world's heavyweight championship crown.

It is significant that when newspaper photographers were taking pictures of Patterson just before the return bout, he said: *"The most important thing you can't get any picture of; because the most important thing for me is my mental attitude."* You see, Floyd had changed his negative attitude to the right mental attitude. And thus his future was ahead of him.

Is Your Future Behind You?

Is your future ahead of you or behind you? Your correct answer may depend on whether you try to eliminate any existing unseen walls—negative habits and undesirable thoughts and actions—and strengthen and build positive habits—good thoughts and deeds. For character is the keystone to true success.

The essence of perfection is never reached, but you gain character by trying to reach it. Good luck or bad luck as the days pass into weeks—success or failure as the weeks pass into months and years—which will it be for you? The choice is yours. You hold the tiller. You can steer the course you choose in the direction of where you want to be—today, tomorrow, or in a distant time yet to come.

But where are you? Now is the time to find out. And now is the time to check your habits of thought and action, for these have brought you to where you are now. The thoughts you think and the things you do *now* will determine your future destination. Are you on the right course to get from where you are now to where you really want to be?

Regardless of what you are or what you have been, you can still become what you may want to be. For as you continue your voyage through life, you, like the captain of a ship, can select your first port of call and then continue until you arrive at the next. You'll experience calm and stormy seas as you go from one port to another, but it is you who must steer that course. Many a ship that lost its rudder and many a person who lost character have become derelicts, lost to the world. This can happen at almost any point in a voyage at sea or in life. For *character is the one common denominator of all personal qualities that will insure a truly successful future.*

He Left His Future Behind Him

My mother loved the theater, music, and the opera, and when I was a boy, she often took me to see one of the great actors of that day. He was a hero to me then. When I was a man, I saw him again years later—no longer a worshipped hero. He still drew large audiences and they still applauded—but no longer for his art and talent. They applauded when he appeared on the stage at the beginning of the play, even when he was late, just because he showed up. They applauded each slip of the tongue, forgotten line, or clever ad-lib. He was no clown—but they laughed. He was no comedian—just a great man who had left his future behind him. For he had become an alcoholic derelict. I didn't know it then, but this brilliant actor's future was behind him when I saw him as a boy. Even then, he knew the direction in which he was headed. But he refused to grab the tiller, turn around and get back on the right course—to eliminate undesirable habits and adopt good ones.

How to Win Over Yourself

What a tragedy it is to have all the necessary ingredients to success but one—the most important: *character.* The development of good *character* is a battle that you, I, and everyone must fight for himself. But victory can be ours.

Although the battle is from within, we can get help from without from good persons and self-help books that motivate the reader to try to become a better person and seek the true riches of life. But remember: *The true value of a self-help book is not what the writer puts into the book, but what you, the reader, take out of the book and put into your life.*

And most important you can pray for help and guidance. Let me remind you:

> *You are the product of your heredity, environment, physical body, conscious and subconscious mind, experience, and particular position and direction in time and space . . . and*

something more, including powers known and unknown. You have the power to affect, use, control, or harmonize with all of them. And you can direct your thoughts, control your emotions, and ordain your destiny.

That's what is says in *Success Through A Positive Mental Attitude.* And that's what I believe. You'll prove it for yourself when you understand and employ *the success system that never fails.* You'll be inspired, and you'll have the necessary *knowledge* and *know-how.* You will think good thoughts . . . and you will do good deeds.

You will keep your thoughts *off the things you should not want* by *keeping your thoughts on the things you should want.* And thus you will begin to *win over yourself* by affecting your subconscious mind through *self-suggestion.*

A thought is the most potent form of suggestion—often more powerful than any received through the sense of sight, hearing, smell, taste, and touch. Your subconscious mind has known and unknown powers, and you must control them to win over yourself. As you continue to read on through *The Success System That Never Fails,* you will gain the necessary *knowledge* and obtain the *know-how* to use the power of suggestion effectively.

Try to Do the Right Thing Because It Is Right

Each time I say to you, "Try to do the right thing because it is right," that's a suggestion from me to you. Each time you think or say to yourself *Try to do the right thing because it is right,* that's self-suggestion. Each time your subconscious flashes to your conscious mind, *Try to do the right thing because it is right,* that's auto-suggestion.

It is important to know:

1. Suggestion comes from the outside (your environment).
2. Self-suggestion is automatic or purposefully controlled from within.
3. Auto-suggestion acts by itself, unconsciously, like a machine that reacts in the same way from the same stimulus.

4. Thoughts *and* impressions from any of the five senses are forms of suggestion.
5. *Only you can think for you.*

Throughout this book I endeavor to motivate you as I explain or illustrate the art of motivation. And repetition increases the effectiveness of any form of suggestion. But it is *you* who must deliberately get into action if you want to have know-how in the use of self-motivators. Therefore, I urge you to prove to yourself their effectiveness.

During the coming week, every morning and every evening—and frequently throughout the day—repeat: *Try to do the right thing because it is right.* Then, when you are faced with temptation, this self-motivator will flash from your subconscious to your conscious mind. When it does—*immediately act. Do the right thing.*

In this way, through repetition, you will form a habit—a good habit—that will help make your future. For your future depends upon character—and character depends on success in overcoming temptations. The world has become a better place in which to live because of persons who have made it a habit to try to do the right thing *only* because it was right. Thus they overcame temptations. Among them are sinners who became saints. They were motivated to become saints because they had sinned. They were inspired to desirable action because they were motivated by remorse—the desire to atone, to make amends . . . to be free of a guilt feeling—and the desire to be esteemed by their fellowmen . . . to thank God for His blessings . . . to make up for lost time.

Perhaps this was the case with William Sidney Porter, whose pen name was O. Henry. During his imprisonment in an Ohio penitentiary for embezzlement, he engaged in study, thinking, and planning. Because he engaged in *soul-searching,* he was inspired to win over himself. *Then* his future was *ahead* of him.

He used his talents to write, and shortly after he left prison, he had several sources of income. One was from the *New York*

World—a hundred dollars a week for a weekly short story. Rapid fame became his. The sale of his books was enormous. "The tragedy of his own life taught him a chivalrous tenderness for the unlucky," says the *Encyclopaedia Britannica.*

Regardless of who you are or what you have been, you can be what you want to be.

From Rags to Riches

Now let's meet another old friend: Horatio Alger, Jr. I first met him at Green's Michigan farm and summer resort. I was twelve at the time, and my mother was still in the dressmaking business in Chicago. She believed it was good for a city boy like me to get out in the country during the summer—and she was right. At Green's I learned wholesome living experienced by those fortunate enough to live in such surroundings.

I learned to swim, row, and fish in the creek. Watching the old mill with its water wheel—hunting turtles in the mud when the creek was low—a corn bake in the woods at night—the fun at a picnic or carnival—being scared after an evening around the fireplace where ghost stories were told—hearing the answers of the Ouija board and rocking table when Mrs. Green, her teenage son Walter, her husband, and I asked questions on stormy nights—sleeping in the hayloft . . . these are treasured memories.

But I'll never forget the first day I went upstairs to the attic, for there I met Horatio Alger. At least 50 of his books, dusty and weather-worn, were piled in the corner. I took one down to the hammock in the front yard and started to read. I read through all of them that summer. The theme in each: from rags to riches. The principles in each: the hero became a success because he was a man of *character*—the villain was a failure because he deceived and embezzled. How many Alger books were sold? No one knows. Estimates range from 100 to 300 million. We do know that his books inspired thousands of American boys from poor families to strive *to do the right thing because it was right* and to acquire wealth.

RMA AND INSPIRATIONAL DISSATISFACTION

Now you may believe, as I do, that most persons are fundamentally honest and good. But a person may have good character, excellent health, and a good mind, yet leave his future behind him.

For his attitude may be negative instead of positive—the wrong mental attitude instead of the right. But what is the right mental attitude?

The book, *Success Through a Positive Mental Attitude,* says: *The right mental attitude is most often comprised of the "plus" characteristics symbolized by such words as integrity, faith, hope, optimism, courage, initiative, generosity, tolerance, tact, kindliness, and good common sense. The wrong mental attitude has opposite characteristics.* On this, you and I can agree.

Yet the most wonderful person in the world will not make progress until he is dissatisfied—wholesomely dissatisfied. For it is *inspirational dissatisfaction* that converts the magic of desire into reality.

Every growing organism grows into maturity—levels off and dies unless there is new life—new blood—new activity—new ideas, says Edward R. Dewey.

All the world's progress in every field of activity has been the result of *action* by men and women who experienced *inspirational dissatisfaction*—never by those who were satisfied. For dissatisfaction is man's driving force. *Inspirational dissatisfaction* is the result of RMA—the right mental attitude. With the wrong mental attitude, the driving force of dissatisfaction can be injurious.

To be dissatisfied, you must *want* something. And if you want something badly enough, you'll *do* something. You'll *try* to get it.

WHERE DR. JOE GOES, GOD GOES

Bob Curran and I were talking about the force of inspirational dissatisfaction and the right mental attitude, when Bob asked: "Did I ever tell you about my brother-in-law, Dr. Joe?"

"No," I answered, and he continued: "Dr. Joe Hopkins of Texas is married to my sister. He has been practicing medicine for over 50 years. It was 33 years ago that he developed cancer of the larynx. Of course, it had to be removed. The delicate operation saved Dr. Joe's life, but it took away his voice.

"Somewhere he heard of an old Cajun country doctor who had had a similar operation. The old Cajun had an overwhelming desire to talk again without artificial gadgets, and he had succeeded in perfecting an amazing technique. First he'd swallow air. Then he'd bring it up again to his throat and mouth. Somehow, with his tongue against the inside of his teeth, he formed sounds from the air pressure. Eventually, he could talk very well.

"When Dr. Joe heard about this, he was inspired. He believed he could talk without a larynx, too. After his throat healed, he tried to make specific sounds. It was discouraging at first, but he kept on trying and praying. It seemed impossible to get the sounds he wanted, but one day he was able to form specific vowels clearly. With new hope, he tried harder and prayed harder. Day by day, he made progress. First he mastered the vowels, then the complete alphabet, then one-syllable words. With more practice, he was able to pronounce two-and three-syllable words—and then, he achieved complete success. Soon he was talking all the time.

"Now it's true that his voice sounds sort of gravelly, but he is easily understood—even over the telephone. At first, when he had difficulty pronouncing a word, he would pause and think, then he'd use a synonym. Now he doesn't have this problem, and he seems to speak with relative ease."

"Has he been able to help others who have had a similar condition?" I asked.

"Yes, indeed," Bob responded. "And Dr. Joe has a most interesting technique to instill confidence. For example, when another doctor refers a patient to him whose larynx has been removed, the patient may find Dr. Joe's waiting room full of people. The new arrival sees Dr. Joe come in and talk to others with that gravelly voice of his. He smiles and laughs. He appears to be happy. And he is.

"Then, when the speechless patient comes into Dr. Joe's private office, Dr. Joe tells the thrilling story of how he himself was inspired by the old Cajun country doctor, and how he taught himself to talk.

"The patient generally becomes excited as he pictures himself talking just like Dr. Joe. He is told he must work hard and practice, practice, practice.

"Today, Dr. Joe is one of the busiest men I know. He is on the staff of three hospitals, and, at the age of seventy-five, works every day. Once he was named Texas Physician of the Year; another time he was given the national Laetare medal; and because of his sympathetic work with the poor, he was knighted by Pope Pius XII. On more than one occasion, I have heard it said, '*Where Dr. Joe goes, God goes.*'"

The Blessing of Work

As you read this chapter, you saw it clearly: To develop good character, *work*. To have good health, *work*. To win over yourself, *work*. To do the right thing because it is right, *work*. To rise from rags to riches, *work*. To fight your way back, *work*. To acquire knowledge, *work*. To acquire know-how, *work*.

When you read the next chapter, you'll see how to make work fun. You'll learn the joy of work when you apply the principles. And you'll find that *it takes less work to succeed than to fail.*

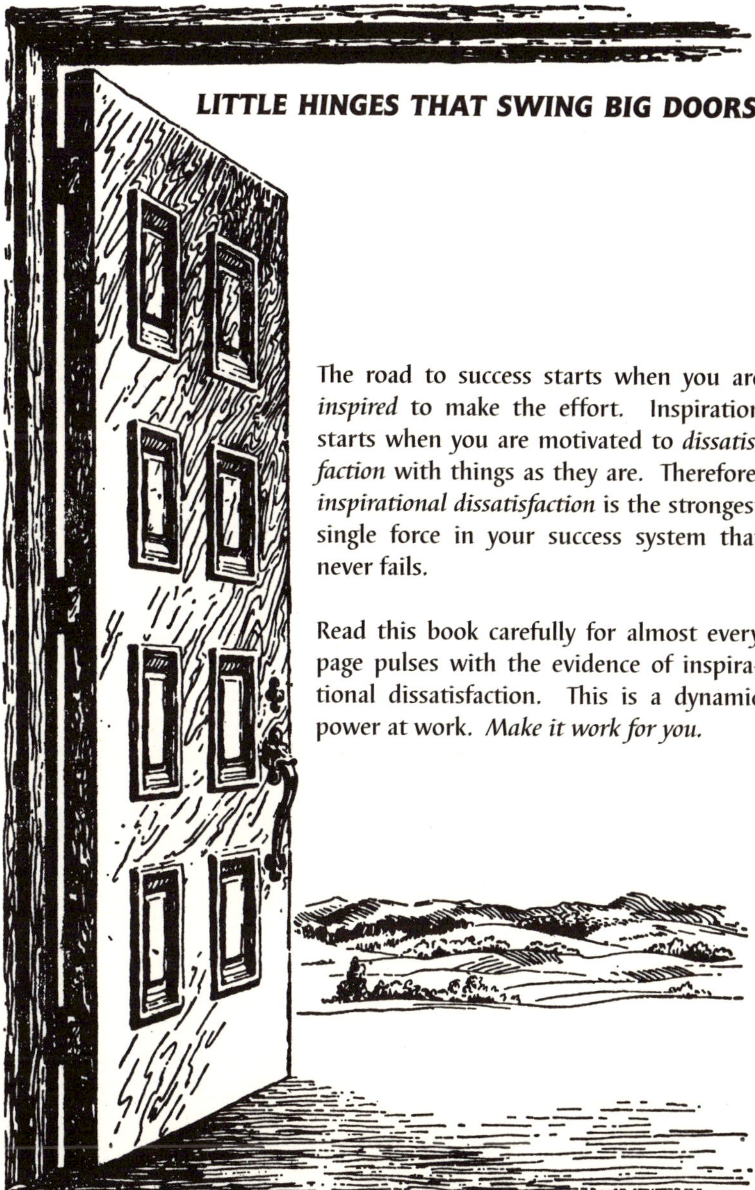

LITTLE HINGES THAT SWING BIG DOORS

The road to success starts when you are *inspired* to make the effort. Inspiration starts when you are motivated to *dissatisfaction* with things as they are. Therefore, *inspirational dissatisfaction* is the strongest single force in your success system that never fails.

Read this book carefully for almost every page pulses with the evidence of inspirational dissatisfaction. This is a dynamic power at work. *Make it work for you.*

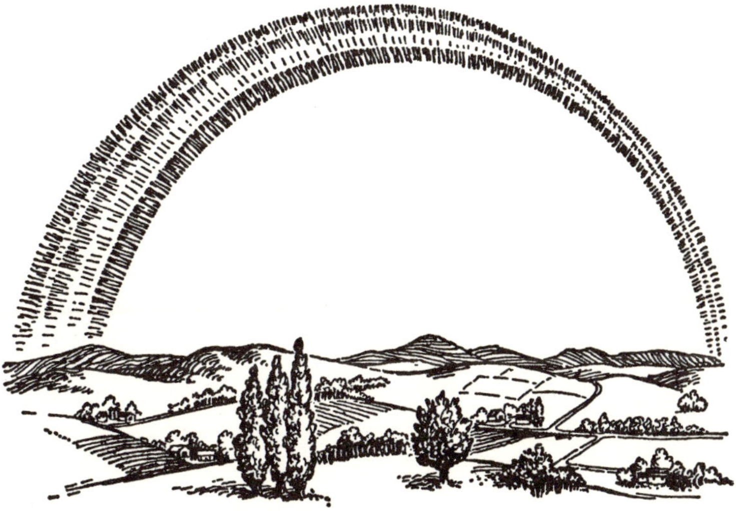

PART II

I FIND THE TREASURE MAP

Do What You Are Afraid to Do!

Believe You Can—and You Can!

Dare to Aim High!

5

IT TAKES LESS WORK TO SUCCEED THAN TO FAIL

Remember that eventful day? Anxiety, excitement, amazement, relief. Explosions of joy and pride!

That's what every American and most of the free world felt when Lt. Col. John H. Glenn, Jr. and his Mercury Capsule, Friendship 7, were lifted from the ground by an Atlas D rocket, shot into space, orbited the globe three times at 17,545 miles per hour, and finally landed at a predetermined destination.

During the trip, Colonel Glenn was forced to take control manually because the automatic devices regulating yaw, pitch, and roll failed. He was ready. And after he landed, it was evident to the world's television audience that Colonel Glenn was a man of character and courage, with a pleasing personality and common sense.

The sudden release of the concentrated energy of an Atlas D rocket can shoot a satellite into space, and it will keep going without the expenditure or use of additional power—all because of the natural law of inertia: *Matter will remain at rest or continue in uniform motion in the same straight line unless acted upon by some external force.* But if the amount of energy that is used to send a satellite into space is expended slowly, its force is dissipated, and the satellite cannot overcome the force of the earth's gravity. Failure, instead of success, is the result.

By now you know the purpose of every illustration in this book is to *motivate you to use the principles of the stories in your own life.* The story of Colonel Glenn and the Mercury Capsule is interesting and exciting—but what principles can we extract from it to assimilate and apply in our own lives?

There are many. Among them: *It takes less work to succeed than to fail.*

And *it takes less time to achieve success when you concentrate your thought and effort on learning a lot about a little* and becoming an expert than when you dissipate your energies by trying to learn a little about a lot. Therefore, focus your attention and effort to acquire the necessary *knowledge, know-how* and *motivation* to become an expert and achieve your specific desired objective.

You are guaranteed success if you do. But you may never have a successful career, achieve your desired objectives, or enjoy continuous success if you are ignorant of these principles or fail to use them.

It Takes Less Work to Succeed Than to Fail

The use of energy is work. When you or I engage in *any activity whatsoever,* energy is used. To concentrate your energy on a given task, focus your attention on it, and don't waste your efforts needlessly.

Simple as this may seem, that's how you acquire *activity knowledge, know-how* and *inspiration to action.* And that's how I developed my success system that never fails. When you do something, put your heart into it. Give it everything you've got—then relax! Concentrated attention and effort, then relaxing, became a habit with me shortly after I started to sell accident insurance. First, I'd get a good night's sleep. Selling door to door in stores and offices and desk to desk in banks and other large institutions used up physical energy. And as a young man I needed lots of sleep.

Next, I made it a practice to make my first business call at a specific time—9:00 A.M. But before making that call, I would condition my mind. I would concentrate. And I would ask for divine guidance and help. I would allow nothing to disturb me. I'd get *keyed up*. Then, I moved fast every working hour of the day. I tried to make every minute count.

At noon, I'd relax with a light lunch and start all over again. If I were working in a city away from home, I would go back to my hotel, have lunch, sleep for a half-hour, and then figuratively start a new day. When I was through working at 5:00 or 5:30, I was through working. I relaxed and got my mind off selling.

I Learned a Lot About a Little

By concentrating my efforts on the sale of just one accident policy, I learned almost all there was to know about that one policy. And I learned from experience what to say and how to say it—what to do and how to do it—to sell in tremendous volume. I gained *activity knowledge* and *know-how*. I learned how to develop *inspiration to action* at will.

In a sense, like a scientist, I learned from trial and error—trial and success. For I firmly believed that I could develop a memorized sales talk and an organized sales plan that would make sale after sale a possibility.

In another sense, like an actor, I could put feeling, emotion, and timing into my memorized talk. When you go to the theatre and see a great actor, it never occurs to you that someone else wrote the lines. You may not realize that his actions as well as his words are the same at every performance. For he lives the part. I not only lived the part when selling, but also developed the script. And, like a good playwright, I improved it at every opportunity. Unlike the playwright, I changed the sales talk to meet changing conditions, but what was said became standardized for such occasions. Thus, if I were interrupted in the beginning of the presentation, I would use one of my standard jokes to relieve tension rather than give the joke later in the talk as I had originally intended.

Work? Yes, it was work. And I had many battles to win over myself—and that was work, too.

But that was good. For I searched for techniques to control my feelings and emotions. There were times when I used to wonder whether I would ever overcome the fear of calling on the owner or president of a large bank or department store. But I found that *conditioning my mind, using self-motivators,* and the simple technique of *keeping on trying* helped me. The day eventually did come when I could call on the head of a large institution in New York, Chicago, or elsewhere without a feeling of fear, for I had become the product of habit.

Like the scientist who finally discovers the success formula for which he is searching and the actor who lives his part, I found that by doing the same thing the same way I developed consistent results. And like the scientist, I found that time was an important ingredient in every formula.

Nothing stands still; there is constant change from within and from without. If you should concentrate the rays of the sun through a magnifying glass on one spot of a fallen log, you'd start a fire within a few minutes. Yet the sun could shine for decades on the same piece of wood and it wouldn't ignite without the glass. In time, under ordinary circumstances, it would merely decompose and become part of the earth. Similarly, with you and me:

It takes time to succeed—it takes time to fail.

But it takes less time to succeed than to fail.

We can clearly understand this when we consider continuous success . . . an entire career . . . the span of a life. For it takes less time to succeed when you do the right thing rather than the wrong—when you work the right way, with the proper *knowledge,* effective *techniques,* and *inspiration to action.* For then you have a success system.

You may work the wrong way or do the wrong thing and temporarily succeed by accident, or by virtue of the conditions at the time. You may even stumble on the right system and momentarily succeed, then lose the system and fail because you don't reduce the principles of your temporary success to a formula.

Short-Term Success and Long-Term Failure

It's quite common for a company or a person to succeed for a time and then fail. Let's take a specific example with which I am familiar.

Since 1900, when insurance man Harry Gilbert made a trip to England and found that insurance companies there were selling what they termed *coupon contract accident policies,* many American insurance companies have sold similar policies. We call them preissue accident policies, for they are written and delivered by the salesman at the actual time of sale. These were sold on a cold-canvass basis. (Cold canvassing, as you know, is making unannounced calls on persons you don't know to sell them something.)

Many agencies for these companies were outstandingly successful for a period of years. Today, however, every agency and every company that handled preissue accident policies has discontinued this selling plan or has gone out of business—with but one exception. Why? The business was unprofitable. They lost money. They either didn't develop a success system, or if they did, they lost it.

The one exception? The companies I manage. Again, why? I developed a sales system that never fails, and with it I was able to sell more policies in a week than salesmen without a system sold in months. There was one reason: I saved time.

That is why I succeeded in the long run and others failed. My efforts were concentrated on one policy, and my attention was focused on its sale. I saved time. I tried to make one hour do the work of many, just as I tried to make one dollar do the work of many.

Often I thought: "If I have to work, I might as well try to earn in one year what others earn in a lifetime." But I realized that this could only be done by operating on the basis of a *success system that never fails.* I eventually achieved many worthwhile objectives, including the one regarding annual earnings, and the basic principles I applied to reach my targets in every instance were:

1. *Inspiration to action,* to be achieved at will.
2. *Know-how,* to be gained through experience.
3. *Activity knowledge.*

But how does one acquire *activity knowledge?*

Do What You Are Afraid to Do

There are many ways to acquire activity knowledge. I learned all I needed to know to sell personal accident insurance in volume *through experience.* I learned by doing.

In particular, I learned this principle: *Do what you are afraid to do . . . go where you are afraid to go.* When you run away because you are afraid to do something big, you pass opportunity by.

During the first few years of my selling career, I was exceedingly frightened when I approached the entrance of a bank, railway office, department store, or other large institutions. So I passed them by. I learned later that I'd passed by doors leading to exceptional opportunity. For I found that it was easier to sell in those places than in smaller establishments where I'd learned to neutralize my initial fears. And I eventually concluded that outstanding success in sales could be achieved in large institutions, because other salesmen were also afraid. They too, passed by the doors of opportunity and, like me, didn't even try.

Actually, the sales resistance of officers and personnel in large establishments is lower than in the stores and offices where many salesmen are not afraid to sell. These smaller places often have five, ten, or fifteen salesmen brave enough to call on them in a single day. With such experience, the managers and employees soon learn to resist salesmen and to say "no." Of course, with the right system the "no" can be turned into a "yes," but this often takes time.

And besides, a big man, a successful man, a man who has built from the bottom up, has a heart. He'll give you a break. He will try to help someone else on his way up. All this I learned. Here's why and how it happened that I first began to develop the habit of selling in large organizations.

The Door I Feared Opened to Opportunity

I was 19 at the time, and my mother sent me on a trip up to Flint, Saginaw, and Bay City, Michigan, to renew established business and to sell new prospects. Everything went fine at Flint. In Saginaw, I was in real selling trim, and my daily sales were outstanding. Since we had only two renewals in Bay City, I wrote to ask my mother to send notices to them so I could continue working in Saginaw.

"Don't run away from good fortune or success" has always seemed a wise motto to me. But my mother telephoned and gave me orders to leave Saginaw and go to Bay City. I didn't want to, but I went. Orders are orders.

Perhaps it was rebelliousness, although I like to consider it righteous indignation, but when I reached my hotel in Bay City, I took the two renewal names and threw them in the upper right-hand dresser drawer. Then I went to the largest bank and interviewed the cashier, a man by the name of Reed.

I didn't know it then, but he'd just been made cashier. In the course of our conversation, he pulled out a metal identification tag and said: "I've had your policy and keytag service for 15 years. I bought it originally when I was working in a bank in Ann Arbor. I was transferred here quite recently."

I thanked Mr. Reed and asked for permission to speak to the others, which he granted. I let each prospect know that Mr. Reed said he had carried our service for 15 years and had granted me permission to speak to him. Results: Everyone bought.

With this momentum, I kept on going, from store to store and office to office. I called on banks, insurance offices, and other large institutions. I called on everyone. I just mowed them down! I averaged 48 policies per day for the two weeks I was in Bay City.

And on the Saturday that I left, in fairness to our policyholders and the company, I opened the upper right-hand dresser drawer, took out the renewal names, and serviced them, too.

The principle became crystal clear to me: *Do what you're afraid to do . . . go where you're afraid to go . . . when you run away because you are afraid to do something big, you pass opportunity by.*

I later realized that I had passed opportunity by for many reasons other than fear. And although you must have experience to develop *know-how,* you can acquire *activity knowledge* if you are willing to learn from those who are willing to teach, from the experiences of others, and from books.

I should have realized this before the age of 19; it seems so obvious to me now. Yet there are many teenagers who, like me at that time, drop out of high school. They have an argument with the teacher, or they don't have the right study and work habits, or they want to earn money, or they feel they're grown up and perhaps resent regimented authority.

But fortunately for me, as you will see, I developed the desire and willingness to learn from those who were willing to teach and from books. And a willingness to learn can turn temporary failure into success in the long run.

Temporary Failures but Permanent Success

The story of Otto Propach is a good illustration of the necessity of acquiring specific knowledge from sources other than experience alone.

With each new activity, even though you may have inspiration, know-how, and technical knowledge for success in a career, it is often necessary to gain additional knowledge to meet changing conditions. America is attracting wonderful people from Europe and from Central and South America. They have inspiration, knowledge, and skill. But, like immigrants of the past, they find it necessary to take menial jobs and learn the language before they can be given the opportunity to employ their knowledge and skills.

Otto was once one of Germany's leading banking executives,

but when the Nazis came into power, he and his family suffered great indignities and eventually imprisonment in concentration camps. All their earthly goods, except the clothing on their backs, were taken from them.

After the war, the Propach family came to the United States, the land of opportunity, for a fresh start. Otto was then 57. He was inspired to succeed. He was an expert in accounting and banking; he had knowledge and know-how. But he couldn't get a job.

After trying for weeks, he took a job as a stock room clerk at $32 a week. He still continued to try employment agencies. And on Saturdays he interviewed the personnel officers of companies he found open on that day, seeking a job in accounting, the work he knew best. With each interview, he received a courteous turndown, for Otto is the type of man whom people respect.

After many weeks, the turning point came when Otto Propach suddenly realized that although he knew accounting and banking and could speak English, he did not know the language of American accounting and finance.

In telling his story to me, he said: "To land an accounting job—or any specialized job, for that matter—you must, in addition to having knowledge and experience of the job, be able to use and understand the technical language. Such technical terms are never included in language courses. I was prepared for accounting and banking in America in every respect but one: technical terminology.

"The next Saturday morning, I went to the office of the dean of LaSalle Extension University here in Chicago," he said. "The dean was very understanding and helpful. I walked out of his office with two consecutive one-semester courses in basic accounting as a gift, for home study, without the privilege of getting correction or credit for my homework. I had further signed up for two *class courses,* one in advanced accounting and the other one in cost accounting. I just had to learn the terms used by Americans.

"From then on, I worked every night at home until bedtime and all day long on Saturdays and Sundays. It was not just reading the texts that took the most time, it was memorizing the words and expressions, which was more difficult because of my limited general knowledge of English. Besides, I had to deliver homework in writing for two courses every week, which sometimes involved a chain of long multiplications and divisions without help of a machine."

Did Otto's concentrated effort in study pay off? Of course it did. Within a few months after he began his studies, he found a job as a minor accountant at $200 a month. Then he moved ahead quickly. As he explained: "I found my work so interesting and found so many points where improvements could be made that office hours weren't sufficient to do all the things I wanted to do. I put in many extra hours. Besides, I took further night courses in business law, taxes, auditing, and similar subjects. My time was well filled with work, but this work was fun. It enlarged my perspective and carried me forward like a mountain stream into a river that leads to the ocean—from minor accounting jobs to accounting clerk, to treasurer, controller, vice-president and director—within a few years."

How to Find What You Are Looking For

Otto Propach turned temporary defeat into permanent success because he knew what he was looking for and he did something about it. He was looking for opportunity to work in a field in which he was an expert, but to do this, he had to concentrate his efforts in intensive study. And this was real work. But after he gained the knowledge, it was his. He could use it as he pleased, and no one could take it away from him.

He knew what he wanted—knowledge of the technical terms used in America in accounting and finance—and he knew he had to learn from others.

Colonel John Glenn and the thousands of persons who worked to develop the Mercury Capsule also achieved success because each knew what he wanted and did something about it. Individual concentrated effort revealed the necessary knowledge for successful achievement. Each learned a lot about a little. Knowledge is found by those who seek it, and when you set a goal, the ways of reaching it become clear.

Activity knowledge is more than facts and figures. A friend of mine, for example, has a photographic mind. He is a page reader—one who can instantaneously read an entire page rather than a few words, phrases, or sentences at a time. He will quote the contents of entire pages of the encyclopedia word for word. I was amazed when he came to me and said, "Clem, you know my gifts. Perhaps you can tell me what to do with them. How can I use the knowledge I have?" Here was a man who had knowledge and skill but he didn't know what to do with it.

Thomas Edison, like my friend, was a page reader. He also had a photographic mind. But he gained *activity knowledge.* He knew what he was looking for, and he found it, because he knew what he needed to get what he wanted. He was able to extract the principles from the facts he learned and to relate, assimilate, and use them.

I, too, knew what I was looking for. I wanted to develop a sales system that never fails. Therefore, I tried to recognize the principles involved in each selling experience, good or bad. I set out to use those that were helpful and eliminate those that were harmful.

You, too, can determine what you want. You can decide on *your* major objectives, targets, aims, and destination. Like Colonel Glenn, Otto Propach, and Thomas Edison, you can concentrate your thought and effort on how you can get what you want by gaining knowledge from those who are willing to teach and from books. You, too, can gain *activity knowledge* from experience, when you are inspired to action.

But in every instance you must try to relate, assimilate, and use the principles that will help you to achieve your objectives. When you develop this habit, you will find that it takes less work and less time to succeed than to fail.

So you see, *knowledge* is important. But as you will see in the next chapter, *know-how* is also imperative to success. Therefore, if you'd like to succeed, learn to acquire *know-how.* Read the next chapter, entitled "Get on the Right Course."

LITTLE HINGES THAT SWING BIG DOORS

Wait a minute! Are you reading the little stories in this book merely as entertainment? If you are, you're missing the point! Each anecdote contains a little particle of unchanging principle. Plant this Principle in your life, and watch it grow!

A startling thought: *It takes less work to succeed than to fail!* Put it another way: Failure means you have worked hard for nothing! With less work, directed systematically, you would have succeeded.

Face your fears, and the death of fear is certain.

6

GET ON THE RIGHT COURSE

You've heard it said: "Mother is a wonderful cook, but she can never tell me exactly how she does it. 'It's just a pinch of this and a dash of that,' she says, but her stews, meatloaf, and biscuits are sensational every time."

Mother has *know-how.*

What's the difference between *knowledge* and *know-how?* It's often the difference between success and failure!

The word *know-how* does not mean knowing how to do something—that's activity knowledge. *Know-how* is doing that something the right way, with skill and effectiveness, and with a minimum expenditure of time and effort. When you have *know-how,* you can do that something successfully again and again. It's a habit, and it comes naturally from experience. *Know-how* is one of the three essential ingredients in the *success system that never fails.*

But how do you develop *know-how?*

Only by doing.

That's the way I developed the *know-how* I needed to sell accident insurance. And that's the way "mother" became a wonderful cook. In fact, that's the way everyone develops *know-how.* The experience must be your very own.

When You Need It, Know Where to Find It

I discontinued high school in my junior year—I'll tell you why later. Shortly after leaving high school, I entered a night law school. At that time, it was permissible to enter the Detroit College of Law with the understanding that four years of high school credits would be completed elsewhere before graduation from law school. So I worked days and went to school at night. I wasn't considered a good student, because I didn't get my homework in. But I did learn. And I made it a practice to learn principles.

Our instructor, one of Detroit's outstanding lawyers in contract law, said in his first lecture: "The purpose of law school is to teach you where to find the law when you need it, and the school will achieve its aim if you learn that." I believed him. I accepted his statement literally. And I doubt if many students with one year of law have ever profited as greatly as I did, for I was able to find the law when I needed it and to use it advantageously.

Almost all the law that a sales manager or an executive officer of an insurance company needs to know can be found in the State Insurance Codes, and that's where I found the law when I needed it. I developed the *know-how* to apply with common sense the knowledge of law gained from the Codes and at law school. I don't recall an instance where a legal problem with which I was faced was not decided favorably. During this time, I was operating my own insurance agency, and the *know-how* became invaluable to me and to the insurance companies I represented.

He Turned Defeat into Victory

This story reminds me of the case history of a boy I know who almost flunked in every grade in grammar school. As a teenager, he was lucky enough to be passed through high school. As a freshman at the state university, he flunked out the first semester.

He was a failure but that was good, for it developed inspirational dissatisfaction with him. He knew he had the ability to succeed, and on reflection he realized that he had to change his attitude and work hard to make up for lost time.

With this new right mental attitude, he entered a junior college, and he did work hard. He kept trying. And on graduation day, he received the honor of being second highest in his class.

No, he didn't stop there. He applied for admission to one of the nation's leading universities, where scholastic standards are exceedingly high and admission is most difficult to obtain. When the Dean of Men wrote in response to his application for admission to the university, he asked, "What happened? How do you account for your success at junior college after failure for so many years?" The boy responded:

"At first, it was real work for me to study regularly, but after several weeks of daily effort, study time became a habit. It became natural for me to study at regular periods. And there were times when I actually looked forward to it, for it was fun to be a 'somebody' at school and be recognized for my scholastic work.

"I aimed to be the best in my class. Perhaps it was the shock of being flunked out in my freshman year at the University of Illinois that awakened me. That's when I began to grow up. I just had to prove to myself that I had the ability."

Because of his right mental attitude and his record of achievement at junior college, this young man was admitted to the university—and there, too, he developed an enviable record.

Here is an instance where a boy who had done poorly at school was motivated to seek the necessary knowledge and discipline to study. He selected the particular junior college he attended because its environment was conducive to the development of good study habits. But it was he alone who gained the *know-how* through his own repeated efforts, and he alone who turned defeat into victory.

Practice Overcomes Handicaps

Raymond Berry was sickly and physically handicapped in his youth. As an adult, he still has a back weakness, one leg is shorter than the other, and his vision is so poor that he must wear strong glasses. Yet, despite his handicaps, he was determined to make the football team at Southern Methodist University. With persistent effort, hard work, and year-round training, he did. Later, he decided to play professional football. But after his senior season, every team in the National Football League passed him by for 19 rounds of the player draft. Finally, on the twentieth round, he was chosen by Baltimore.

Few expected him to make the team, let alone become a starting player. But Raymond Berry was determined. Fitted with a back harness, mud cleats on one shoe to make his stride even, and contact lenses so he could see, he continuously practiced running pass patterns as an offensive end. He became a master at blocking, faking, and catching passes from every angle.

On days when the Baltimore team wasn't practicing, he'd hurry to a nearby soccer field and persuade high school boys to throw passes to him. Even in hotel lobbies he'd often carry a football to keep his hands "used to the feel."

What happened? Raymond Berry became the champion pass-receiver in the National Football League. When the Baltimore Colts won the League Championship both in 1958 and 1959, Berry was a star!

And it's easy to see why Raymond Berry became a champion: practice, practice, practice. *It was practice that developed know-how. Practice makes perfect,* it's said, for practice develops skill by experience or exercise.

THREE WON'T BE THREE IF ONE IS MISSING

It's easy to see that when one number of a combination is missing, you don't have the combination. A trio is not a trio if one of its parts is missing. *The success system that never fails* is a trio, and it will not be a success system that never fails if any one of the ingredients—inspiration to action, know-how, or activity knowledge—is missing.

That's the reason a person who is successful in one activity may be a failure in another. Many men who become outstandingly successful in a business or profession fail in a new venture. They have gained skill through experience, and they have risen to the top in their own work. But on entering another business, they are not willing to gain the additional knowledge and experience required to succeed in the new activity.

At law school, I lacked one or more numbers of the success trio to become a good student. But I was motivated to find and use the necessary three ingredients when I needed them in business.

The student who flunked out lacked one or more of the missing numbers, but he turned defeat into victory when he employed all three in combination.

Raymond Berry was motivated, he sought knowledge, and he gained know-how. Thus, he used the three magic ingredients necessary to become a champion.

From Success to Failure

Richard H. Pickering, one of the most wonderful persons I ever knew, was a gentleman in the true sense—a man of character. He was extremely successful as a life insurance counselor, for his recommendations were always based on the answer to the question he asked himself: "What's best for my client?" Over a period of years, he amassed a modest fortune in renewal equities, for he let his renewal commissions remain with the company.

When he was in his sixties, he decided to move from Chicago to Florida. Restaurants there were flourishing, and he wanted to own one, even though he knew nothing about operating this type of enterprise. His only experience had been that of a customer.

His enthusiasm was so great that he wasn't satisfied to operate one restaurant; he simultaneously established five. He sold his equities in his renewal commissions and invested everything he had. Within five months, he was out of business. He was broke.

Mr. Pickering's experience is little different from that of other successful persons who are unwilling to gain the necessary knowledge and know-how before operating a new enterprise on a large scale. Had he only done the purchasing, handled the cash register, or operated a restaurant for someone else who was an expert in this business, he would soon have gained knowledge and experience, and he would not have failed. For Mr. Pickering was an intelligent man—and he proved it by returning to the life insurance business, in which he did have knowledge and know-how.

This failure was caused by the lack of the necessary knowledge and experience. Now here's the story of another friend of mine who acquired knowledge and know-how for his business career by getting experience while at college. You'll be intrigued by the self-motivator that still inspires him to action.

"You've Got Backbone—You're It!"

"You've got backbone—you're it! That's what inspired me," said Karl Eller, the 33-year-old president of the Eller Outdoor Advertising Company at a breakfast interview recently.

I interviewed Karl and his wife that morning because I had heard that he had purchased the Arizona division of Foster and Kleiser for a reputed price of five million dollars. The interview was pleasant, informative, and inspiring.

"I was a freshman at Tucson High, and it happened like this," Karl said. "I didn't know much about football. At the tryouts, I didn't even have a uniform. But for some reason, when the first team's star runner came my way, I was able to tackle him. I hit him hard and knocked him down. On the next attempt, he tried another end of the line, but again I was there and stopped him. This made him mad. The more he tried, the madder he got. The madder he got, the easier it became for me to stop him. Six times in a row I stopped him.

"After practice, I was seated on a bench in the locker room, putting on my socks, when I felt a hand on my shoulder. As I turned and looked up, the coach asked, 'Have you ever played fullback?'

"'No, I've never played fullback,' I replied.

"Then the coach said something I have never forgotten: 'You've got backbone—you're it!' And then he walked away.

"'*You're it?* What does that mean?' I asked myself. The next day I found out. I was amazed at what I heard: 'Karl Eller—fullback—first team,' the coach called out.

"And then I remembered: 'you've got backbone—you're it.'

"'You're it' meant that he had faith in me and was backing his faith with a key position. I just couldn't let him down. His faith in me gave me faith in myself. Ever since—when I begin to doubt my abilities, when the going is tough, when I'm supposed to do something and don't know exactly how—I say to myself: 'You've got backbone—you're it,' and my self-confidence is restored.

"Ronald T. Gridley, coach of Tucson High, knew how to get a man to do his best. We were undefeated in 33 football games, and we won 14 out of 15 possible state championships in all sports. Why? Gridley knew how to trigger the right inspiration in each and every one of us."

"Did you work your way through college?" I asked.

Karl replied, "While at the University of Arizona, I didn't have to pay for my room. Judge Pickett let me have his coach house for mowing his lawn. It didn't cost me anything to eat, since I served tables at the Kappa Alpha Theta sorority. That's where I met Sandy, my wife."

Then Sandy interrupted: "Karl made more money at college than he did at first on his job after he left school. At school he had 25 students working for him. Karl tied up practically every concession on the campus: hot dogs, soft drinks, candy, ice cream—you name it, Karl did it. He published and distributed *Figi Notes*–600 sales a semester at four dollars each. Publishing the sports programs and selling advertising for them started him on a career in advertising after graduation."

To me this was understandable. Here was a smiling young man with a pleasing personality a football hero. Every businessman in Tucson would welcome a chance to talk to him personally, and when he asked for an ad in a sports program or one of the university magazines or papers, the merchant would buy it willingly. Then, too, Karl was a good salesman. He kept his customers year after year. They liked to see him—and he gave them the opportunity.

After graduation, Karl applied for a job with a leading advertising agency in the big city—Chicago. He was offered $25 a week.

"So instead," said Karl, "I got a job with Foster and Kleiser Outdoor Advertising Company right in Tucson."

His sales were phenomenal—and so was his progress. He was promoted to sales manager of the Phoenix Office, became national sales manager with headquarters at San Francisco, and advanced to vice-president and manager of the Chicago office at the age of 29.

Then there was a change in ownership of the company, and it became a toss-up whether Karl or an older, more experienced man was to become president. The older man got the job. Karl quit and joined another advertising agency in Chicago.

At a national convention, he heard a rumor that the Arizona division of Foster and Kleiser was to be sold. "Here was opportunity," Karl said, "but I didn't know how to go about it. And the amount of money involved seemed fantastic. Again 'you've got backbone—you're it' flashed into my mind."

He continued: "Sandy and I love Arizona. I knew the business. The people knew me. I had an irresistible urge to grasp this opportunity. I knew what I wanted, and I knew I could make a success. But most of all, I had a tremendous desire to do something big on my own. If I could do it for others, I could do it for myself. But I didn't know exactly how I could swing the deal. Actually, I had everything but money: knowledge, know-how, experience, a good reputation, wonderful friends, and business contacts in the Tucson area."

"How about the money," I asked.

"A friend of mine worked in the loan department of the Harris Trust and Savings Bank in Chicago," Karl replied. "He introduced me to the proper officials. A deal was worked out between the Harris Trust and the Valley National Bank in Phoenix for a joint loan to be paid over a period of five years. Then, too, nine of my friends participated in the purchase. The deal provides that I have an option to buy back their interests at any time within five years for the same price they paid. There are many tax and other advantages to them because of the nature of the outdoor advertising business. Thus, even if I pick up my option, the deal is a mutually profitable one."

Karl Eller's story clearly indicates that to solve a problem or to succeed in business, you don't need to know all the answers in advance—if you are on the right course. For you will then meet each problem as you come to it.

You Don't Need to Know All the Answers

To solve a problem or to reach a goal, you, like Karl Eller, don't need to know all the answers in advance. But you must have a clear idea of the problem or the goal you want to reach.

So begin to determine what you really want in the distant, intermediate, and near future. If you are not ready to set distant and intermediate specific, concrete goals, be encouraged. It may be more beneficial at this time to decide what your general or abstract objectives should be: to have physical, mental, and moral health; to gain wealth; to be a person of character; to be a good citizen, father or mother, husband or wife, son or daughter. Whatever these general goals, they must of necessity be immediate objectives as well.

Everyone has immediate, specific aims or objectives. You know, for example, what you intend to do tomorrow, or what you would like to do next week or perhaps next month. And it would be easy for you to write down specific immediate goals that will, when achieved, bring you closer to the health, wealth, happiness, or character you expect to acquire in the intermediate and distant future. But you must want to.

The Most Important Ingredient of Success

There are those who have knowledge and know-how, but they don't succeed. For although they know what to do and how to do it, they don't feel like doing it. They're not inspired to action.

Inspiration to action is the most important ingredient to success in any human activity. And inspiration to action can be developed at will.

The man who is inspired can overcome all obstacles, for he has *go power.* You'll generate *go power* when you follow the directions that will be revealed in the next chapter.

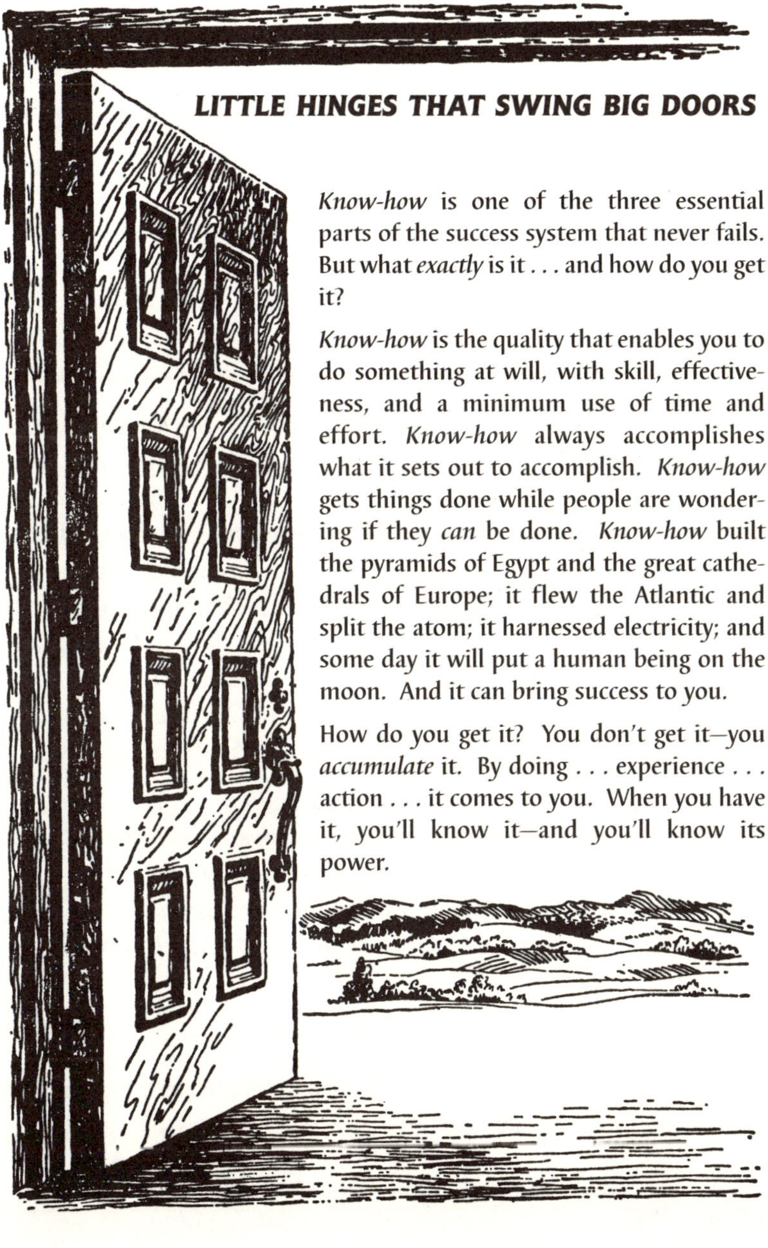

LITTLE HINGES THAT SWING BIG DOORS

Know-how is one of the three essential parts of the success system that never fails. But what *exactly* is it . . . and how do you get it?

Know-how is the quality that enables you to do something at will, with skill, effectiveness, and a minimum use of time and effort. *Know-how* always accomplishes what it sets out to accomplish. *Know-how* gets things done while people are wondering if they *can* be done. *Know-how* built the pyramids of Egypt and the great cathedrals of Europe; it flew the Atlantic and split the atom; it harnessed electricity; and some day it will put a human being on the moon. And it can bring success to you.

How do you get it? You don't get it—you *accumulate* it. By doing . . . experience . . . action . . . it comes to you. When you have it, you'll know it—and you'll know its power.

7

GO POWER

"Go! Go! Go! Go!" came the chant from the Chicago White Sox bench. And the batter did *go!* He slid safely into third, ahead of the outfielder's throw.

"Go! Go! Go! Go! White Sox!" became the chant of their fans in 1959—and it motivated the White Sox team to go . . . go . . . go . . . game after game, to win the championship of the American League.

"Go! Go! Go! Go! White Sox!" motivated each member of the team to try harder than he had ever tried before. But what is motivation?

> *Motivation is that which induces action or determines choice. It is that which provides a motive. A motive is the "inner urge" only within the individual which incites him to action, such as an idea, emotion, desire, or impulse. It is the hope or other force which starts in an attempt to produce specific results.**

Mixed Emotions Intensify GO POWER

When strong emotions such as love, faith, anger, and hate are mixed—as in passionate patriotism—the *go power* they generate is

**Success Through a Positive Mental Attitude,* by Hill and Stone, Prentice-Hall, Inc., 1960.

an intensive driving force which will last throughout a lifetime. This is true of the freedom-loving peoples of the present who are under the yoke of Communism. And it is true of the patriots of the past. Here's the story of one:

The Cossacks came. The child saw his mother and father brutally beaten and killed. He ran from the house, but a horseman caught up with him and he felt the lash that knocked him, bleeding to the ground. And as he regained consciousness, he could see the burning remains of his father's cottage. Then and there he made a vow—a vow to free Poland from the Russians.

Freedom for Poland became an obsession with him. The picture the child saw—the horror and grief of it—was burned indelibly into the mind of the man. It spurred him to action.

That man—Ignace Jan Paderewski, the great pianist—was named Prime Minister and Minister of Foreign Affairs of the New Polish Republic in January, 1919, and he later became President of the National Council of Poland.

Paderewski lived to see the Poles lose their freedom again, but his work was not in vain. Poland is still a nation, and its people have the passionate patriotism that will again release the go power to regain their complete freedom.

Paderewski had *go power* that spurred him to action.

You have *go power,* too.

And in this chapter you'll learn how you can generate, intensify, and release your *go power. Go Power* is the "inner urge" that impels men to all worthwhile achievement. You'll be able to use it to acquire riches, health, and happiness, and to do good for others. Because inspiration to action, when sufficiently strong, motivates you to act.

And the greatest motivator of all is love.

The Greatest Motivator of All

When I was in the sixth grade, I decided I wanted to be a lawyer. That's why, when I entered high school, I was interested in such subjects as mathematics, to help me think logically; history, to help me understand the past and present and project into the future; English composition, to give me the opportunity to express my thoughts and philosophy; and psychology, to give me an understanding of the functioning of the human mind. I joined the Debating Club at Senn High primarily to become an expert in argumentation.

I later entered the Detroit College of Law, but I discontinued after a year because I decided that I wanted to get married when I was 21. And I knew that the girl I was to marry would be the most important influence for good in my life. That's true, of course, of anyone: *A husband or wife is the greatest environmental influence* for any man or woman.

I dropped out of law school because I felt I couldn't make a large enough income as a lawyer until I was at least 35 years of age. It's unethical for a lawyer to solicit clients, but as a salesman I could call on all the prospects I wanted to. My income would be contingent on my ability and its application—and I knew I could sell. Moreover, I reasoned that it was possible to make and save enough money through selling to retire at the age of 30, go back to school, study law, and enter a legal and political career. "Besides," I said to myself, "I can then handle the law cases I want to handle—not those I have to."

Jessie and I had met at Senn High. Our courtship and my love for her can be expressed by the words of Mary Carolyn Davies' song, "Why I love You":*

Why do I love you?
I love you, not only for what you are,
But for what I am when I am with you.
Not only for what you have made of yourself,
But for what you are making of me.

After two years at Senn High, I had moved to Detroit and entered Northwestern High School. We corresponded often. Jessie and her mother would sometimes visit my mother and me, and I

*By permission of the copyright owner. Copyright 1954, Midway Music Company.

made several trips to Chicago. I concluded that it would be best to establish my own insurance agency in Chicago. My mother wrote to Harry Gilbert, who was the officer we did business with for the United States Casualty Company and the New Amsterdam Casualty Company. As you recall from Chapter 5, Harry Gilbert was the father of preissue accident insurance policies in the United States.

Mr. Gilbert responded that he would be pleased to have me represent the two companies in Illinois, but I would first have to get permission to make a home-office connection from the general agent in Chicago, who already had an exclusive arrangement.

If You Want Something, Go After It

I made arrangements to meet with the general agent. I just *had* to sell him. My whole program depended on his permission. But I was a salesman by vocation, and I knew from experience that if you want something, you have to go after it. The general agent was very courteous, and I'll never forget what he said:

"I'll give you permission. But you'll be out of business in six months. It's difficult to sell in Chicago. If you appoint agents, you'll have nothing but trouble, and you'll lose money."

I'll always be grateful to him for not interfering with my opportunity.

So in November, 1922, I established my agency under the name of Combined Registry Company. My working capital was one hundred dollars, but I was debt-free, and my overhead expense was low, since I rented desk space at $25 a month from Richard H. Pickering. Mr. Pickering was a real inspiration to me, and he was most helpful in giving good advice. For example, when it came to having my name on the lobby directory, he asked me, "How do you want your name listed?"

"C. Stone," I responded. At school, and up to that time, that was the way I signed my name.

"What are you ashamed of?" he asked

"What do you mean?"

"Well, don't you have a first name and a second name?"

"Yes . . . William Clement Stone."

"Did you ever stop to consider that there are thousands of C. Stones? But chances are that in the entire United States there is only one W. Clement Stone."

This appealed to my self-esteem. "Only one W. Clement Stone," I thought. And ever since, that has been the way I sign my name.

The wedding was set for June. I wanted to acquire as much cash as I could before then, so I didn't waste time. On my first day, I worked on North Clark Street in Rogers Park, within a few blocks of the place where I was staying. I made 54 sales that day. Then I knew that Chicago would be an easy place to sell in, and that I would be in business for more than six months.

I was motivated to work hard to establish my business and get the money I needed to marry the girl I loved. This is understandable, for you may use reason to motivate yourself and appeal to reason to motivate others, but the *inner urge* of your feelings, emotions, instincts, and ingrained habits gives you the *go power* that puts you into action.

TO MOTIVATE . . . TUG AT THE HEARTSTRINGS

One of the best ways to inspire another person to desirable action is to relate a true story that appeals to his emotions. At a sales meeting, the reading of the following portion of a letter from Jean Clary moved the salesmen to action.

> *Six weeks ago, my six-year-old daughter Pamela came to me and said, "Daddy, when are you going to win your Ruby?" (This was an award given for specific high sales and earnings within a set time period.) "When are you going to write 100 policies in a week? Daddy, I have been asking God every night to help you make your Ruby. I have been asking Him for many nights and, Daddy, I don't think He is helping you." A child's faith in God, a child's faith in her father—so innocent, so honest, so sincere. I answered my daughter*

> *after long thought and consideration, for I realized that she was confused as to why God hadn't helped. My answer was, "Pam, God is helping Daddy, but I don't think Daddy is helping God." In fact, I wasn't even helping myself. I was paying the price of failure. Why? Because I wasn't trying. I was making excuses and alibis. I was blaming everyone but myself. How blind can a man be? I decided then and there . . .*

In the rest of the letter, Jean listed the many achievements caused by the depth of feeling for his daughter that inspired him with *go power.*

Faith Is a Sublime Motivator

Jean got his Ruby, and Pamela's prayers were answered.

Jean had *go power* all the time. Everyone has *go power.* But it was the suggestion of Pamela's prayer that brought about the self-suggestion of inspirational dissatisfaction expressed by Jean in his thoughts: I wasn't even helping myself. I was paying the price of failure. Why? Because I wasn't trying. I was making the excuses and alibis. I was blaming everyone but myself. How blind can a man be . . . ?

This *inspiration to action* sparked the *go power* to performance.

Faith is a sublime motivator, and prayer, an expression of faith, accentuates the release of the driving force of one's emotions. A case in point: It happened in San Juan, Puerto Rico, not long ago, when Napoleon Hill and I were holding a three-evening "Science of Success" seminar. On the second night, everyone in the audience was urged to apply the principles the following day. And each was to report the results he achieved.

Among the volunteers on the third evening was an accountant, and here is what he said:

"This morning when I arrived at work, my general manager, who is also attending this seminar, called me into his office. 'Let's see if a positive mental attitude works,' he said. 'You know, we have that $3,000 collection that is months overdue. Why don't you make the collection? Call on the firm's manager, and when you do, use PMA—a positive mental attitude. Let's begin with what Mr. Stone calls a self-starter: *Do it now!*'

"I was impressed by your discussion last evening of how everyone can make his subconscious mind work for him that when my manager sent me out to make the collection, I decided to try to make a sale also.

"When I left my office, I went home. In the quietness of my home I determined exactly what I was going to do. I prayed sincerely and expectantly for help to make the collection and also a large sale.

"I believed that I would get specific results. And I did get them. For I collected the $3,000 and made an additional sale of more than $4,000. As I left my customer, he said, 'You certainly surprise me. When you came here, I had no intention of buying. I didn't know you were a salesman. I thought you were the head accountant.' This was the first sale I ever made in my entire business career."

This accountant was the same man who the night before had had the courage to ask: "How can I get my subconscious mind to work for me?" And he had been told about setting goals, inspirational dissatisfaction, self-motivators, and the self-starter *Do it now!* He also learned that he must choose a specific immediate goal and start toward it. And he learned these things too:

1. You affect your subconscious mind by verbal repetition. The subconscious mind is particularly affected by self-suggestions given under an emotional strain, or given with emotion.
2. The greatest power man possesses is the power of prayer.

He listened. He took time for reflection. He related and assimilated the principles. He prayed sincerely, reverently, and humbly for divine guidance. He believed he would receive it, and because he believed, he did receive it. And when he did, he didn't forget to give a sincere prayer of thanks.

INSPIRATION BEGETS KNOWLEDGE AND KNOW-HOW

One evening, in a "Science of Success" class, a teacher of music who was also "spinning records" part time at a leading metropolitan radio station jumped up and asked the question:

"How can PMA help me? As long as I live, I can never expect to earn an average of more than $100 a week as a teacher of music. This is true of any other average teacher of music."

I immediately responded: "You are absolutely right! You can never earn more than $100 a week on an average—*if that is what you believe.* But if you choose to believe that you can earn $250, $300, $350, or any other specific sum, it will be just as easy or just as hard as earning a $100 a week. Memorize Napoleon Hill's famous self-motivator: *What the mind can conceive and believe, the mind can achieve.* Repeat it many times throughout the day. Say it with *emotion and feeling* at least 50 times this evening. Then set your objectives. Set them high! And get into action. Let me know what happens!"

Three and a half months later, this teacher wrote:

"I have come out of the maze since I started this PMA course. My health is better than ever. My average income for the past ten weeks has jumped to approximately $370-$380 a week. Despite the many hours I put in, my attitude is very cheerful and positive at all times."

The night that music teacher asked "How can PMA help me?" he did not just *hear* the answer given him—he *listened! To hear* does not necessarily imply attention or application. *To listen* always does. And he listened to the messages that were applicable to him. He began to recognize and understand the constructive force of the right mental attitude in the word *believe.* And he began to use this force.

When he wrote his letter, he was still teaching music and spinning records at the same radio station. He was the same man.

What had happened then? Who made it happen? He responded to suggestion. He used self-suggestion as directed. He changed his belief from "It can't be done" to "It can be done!" He dared to aim higher.

One afternoon, when a famous actor appeared at the radio station as a guest artist, the music teacher decided to get into action. He responded to the self-starter *Do it now!*

He became so enthusiastic in telling about the happiness that comes to one who learns to love music by playing a musical instrument well that the actor urged the teacher to teach him. This actor could afford to pay the tuition charged by an expert who was willing to fit his time to suit the convenience of the student.

Because of his new mental attitude, the teacher recognized the principles and developed know-how from this experience. When other celebrities or guest artists appeared at the radio station, he sold them on the joy of learning to love music. He told them how easy it is to learn if one is properly taught. He merely repeated the procedure that had proved profitable in influencing the actor. And that's *know-how.*

That's how the music teacher acquired the *knowledge* to increase his earnings. In addition to teaching music, he sought other means to increase his income—and, because he sought, he found what he was looking for.

Be a Self-Starter

"Seek and you shall find" is a universal truth. It applies to seeking self-inspiration to action, seeking know-how, and seeking knowledge.

In each example given in this chapter, external suggestions started the individuals thinking. The thoughts you think . . . the words you say . . . the things you do—these are self-suggestion. You have the ability to engage in self-suggestion by the thoughts you think, and when you repeat these thoughts and respond to them by action again and again, you establish a habit. By directing your thoughts, you can build and control the habits you wish to acquire and substitute new habits for old.

If, for example, you think of doing a specific good deed, and if you *consciously react by performing* the specific deed each time you think that thought, you soon develop the habit of doing that good deed.

And that's how you consciously develop the inner urge that inspires you to action. It's the *go power* that helps you. You can generate and use it to impel you to worthwhile achievement.

As you read on, you will see that you can intentionally use it to acquire riches, health, and happiness, and to make this a better world in which to live.

The strong drives of inherited emotions, passions, instincts, and other tendencies from our evolutionary past will be explored later. These create inner urges that move us to action—to do the things we should do and often the things we shouldn't do.

There will at times be a conflict between the inner urges that you consciously develop and those that are inherited. But the conflicts can be neutralized by selecting the right thoughts, engaging in proper activities, and choosing the proper environment. Thus we can fulfill the intended purpose of these strong inherited urges, yet be inspired to use them to lead wholesome, happy lives without violating the highest moral standards.

Go power is the inner urge that releases the unlimited force of the subconscious mind of the individual. But we all need the help of others, and the next chapter indicates how you can achieve this through inspiration, know-how, and knowledge.

LITTLE HINGES THAT SWING BIG DOORS

Go power is the mystical motor of your spirit. It is the inner urge that can drive you to success. Its fuel is emotion, desire, or impulse.

To develop *go power,* every night for ten days repeat at least 50 times: *What the mind can conceive and believe, the mind can achieve.*

When *go power* impels you to some good action, consciously react by performing. Each time you do, you add to your ability to start *go-power* at will.

Part III

AN EVENTFUL JOURNEY

Solve each problem as you meet it

Success is achieved by those who try!

Trouble is opportunity in work clothes

Don't be afraid of the unknown

Self-suggestion makes you master of yourself

When the going gets tough . . . the tough get going

8

I SELECTED A GOOD CREW

The *Tuntsa,* a 30-foot ketch, quietly slipped out of Helsinki Harbor, bound for America. Aboard were six men and three women. Only one had ever set foot on a sailing boat before. Each was willing to risk his own life for freedom—freedom from the enveloping force of Communist Russia.

"Tossed and torn by mountainous seas and gale force winds, becalmed in the primordial ooze of the Sargasso Sea, or facing starvation, the crew of the *Tuntsa* was always able to summon the ingenuity and resourcefulness to survive." Teppo Turen, one of the leaders of the expedition, tells the story in his book, *The Tuntsa,* a story both real and symbolic—not only of the sea, but of the human soul.

I had many talks with Teppo about the *Tuntsa* long before he wrote his book, for Teppo Turen is associated with me in business. And as Teppo would tell me his story, I would think: "Here is another instance where the force of an inner urge developed sufficient inspiration to action to prove again the possibility of the improbable."

Teppo and his crew did prove the possibility of the improbable, for they were inspired to risk life itself for freedom. But like many who enter a new venture, they lacked *knowledge* and *know-how.* For knowledge has to be learned, and *know-how* must be acquired through experience.

But when you have a burning desire that drives you to action to reach your goal, you will find the means to gain the *knowledge* and get the experience that will give you *know-how.* Before leaving Helsinki, Teppo Turen did gain the theoretical knowledge of sailing from books and talks with seasoned sailors. And by sailing he learned the know-how to pilot a small boat.

That is how you gain knowledge: You can seek it. You, too, may find it in books and in conversations with other persons. But like the crew of the *Tuntsa,* you get real know-how only by doing.

When the crew left Helsinki in the 30-foot reconditioned potato boat, they knew they would be faced with problems. But fortunately they didn't know how hazardous the journey was to be, any more than you know what problems you will encounter to reach your distant goals. Hunger, thirst, storms, the Sargasso Sea, even shipwreck on a coral reef didn't stop Teppo Turen and the other inspired Finns from reaching their destination. For they, like everyone who achieves success in a great venture, solved each problem as they came to it. They helped themselves. And they were helped through powers known and unknown to them at the time they set out on their voyage. *They kept going,* regardless of the obstacles they met.

HAVE THE COURAGE TO ENTER THE UNKNOWN

That is why many persons succeed—because they start for a specific destination and keep going until they reach it. It's hard to stop them. Also that's why many fail—because they don't get started—they don't go. They don't overcome inertia. They don't begin.

It's a universal law. *It takes more energy to overcome inertia in getting started from a standstill than to continue the momentum of a moving body when it is once in motion.*

It's the fear of the unknown that keeps a person from starting, even though he may have a strong desire. Another may also fear, but he does get started—and once started, he permits nothing to stop him.

Earlier, you read about the self-motivator *do it now!* This is what I term my self-starter. It sparks me to action. Here's how you can learn to use it too:

1. Repeat *Do it now!* to yourself 50 times or more in the morning and evening, and whenever it occurs to you throughout the day, for the next several days. Thus it will be imprinted indelibly in your subconscious.
2. Every time it is desirable for you to do something you may not feel like doing and the self-starter *Do it now!* flashes from your subconscious to your conscious mind—immediately *act!*

When you are faced with fear of the unknown, but have a desire to do the right thing because it is right, say to yourself: *Do it now!* Then immediately get into action. That's what I do. My use of the self-starter *Do it now!* is an acquired habit. It's one technique I employ successfully to neutralize inherited emotions and fear through self-suggestion.

Yet, it was several years after I started to build a sales organization before I began to teach my representatives the techniques I had learned for directing my thoughts and controlling my emotions.

Lay the Proper Foundation

Every member of the *Tuntsa* crew volunteered—and the first salesman I hired volunteered. It happened this way:

One Monday morning, shortly after I started my agency, I was selling door to door in a Chicago office building. I sold a policy to a middle-aged real estate man, who asked, "Where's your office located?"

"29 S. LaSalle Street," I responded.

At noon when I returned to my office to check my mail, there, waiting for me was my customer, the real estate man. He seemed as surprised to find that I, a 20-year-old salesman, was also the manager as I was to have him, a customer, apply for a job.

I had resolved not to hire salesmen in the first year. I knew I could earn a large income by devoting my exclusive efforts to personal sales. I also knew it would take effort, money, and valuable selling time to build a sales organization, and I dared not waste any of these. Since I received all the commission on my personal sales, but only one-third of the gross commission on salesmen's sales, it would take many salesmen to produce net commissions equivalent to what I could earn myself.

Yet I did accept the real estate man as my first salesman. For he was experienced in sales, and he was a man of character—and character is the first thing a sales manager should look for when he interviews a prospective salesman. Moreover, I figured that I had everything to gain and nothing to lose. And I was right, for this salesman remained with me and performed well for many years.

Now the lesson to be learned from this experience didn't occur to me until many years later: You can build an organization by hiring your customers to work for you. But I realized then, as I realize now, something more important: *You must lay the proper foundation for your business before expanding.*

A good salesman may be inspired to go into business for himself and become an owner. Yet he may lack the necessary *know-how* and *knowledge* to operate a business. He is tempted to take one of two routes—one to insolvency and failure, the other to mediocrity—rather than a third short route to success.

Route #1: He lacks working capital. Yet he tries to make a livelihood from the new salesmen he hires. His business and personal expenditures far exceed his income. He goes heavily into debt. He goes broke. All because he dissipates his *personal selling time and effort.* This is the route to insolvency and failure.

Route #2: He has working capital. Yet he is such a star salesman that he devotes himself exclusively to personal selling. He won't invest the time, effort, and money necessary to build a sales organization, so he becomes no better than a salesman with a sales manager's commission. He doesn't go broke, but as a sales manager he is a failure.

This is the route to mediocrity for the owner of a business.

Route #3: Again he lacks working capital. But he guarantees earnings and solvency through personal sales and hires one new salesman at a time, only when he can absorb him. Thus he builds an organization, and when his organization is large enough, he devotes his exclusive efforts to management.

A Hot Dog and A Glass of Milk

A good salesman has confidence in himself. He knows what he can do, and necessity often forces him to do it.

While I was engaged in personal sales, my earnings were what many considered exceedingly high. Yet it seemed there was always a need for money. Payments on the car . . . payments on the furniture . . . payments on life insurance. Perhaps it was because I bought what I wanted, then had to work like blazes to pay for it.

I'd leave home in the morning with very little cash, for I knew I'd have substantial sums by the end of the day. For example, the first time I worked Joliet, Illinois, I arrived at 8:30 in the morning with 10 cents in my pocket. This didn't bother me; on the contrary, it inspired me. I checked into the Woodruff Inn, then walked across the street and had breakfast—a hot dog and a glass of milk. (There's been inflation since.)

Joliet was only 40 miles from my home, yet I took the train instead of driving and stayed at a hotel instead of returning home each night. On the train I'd relax, for I had developed the ability to sleep anywhere at any time under almost any circumstances. So in a railroad coach, I'd just put my elbow on the windowsill, rest my head on my hand, and fall asleep.

But I always did something more before falling asleep: I conditioned my mind; I prayed for guidance and help.

Staying at a hotel instead of returning home each night gave me a minimum of ten hours sleep, for traveling time was saved. With the extra sleep, I'd be in peak condition. When I sold, I deliberately got keyed up and put everything I had into my sales presentation.

GET KEYED UP

Many salesmen have poor days because they are fatigued. Their batteries need recharging. They need rest. But when I called on my prospect, I was rested. Again, before I called on a prospect, I conditioned my mind.

And when I made my sales presentation, my energies were concentrated on one thing only—the job at hand: to make the sale in the shortest possible space of time in a manner that would clearly give the purchaser a concept of what he was buying, and to sow seeds of thought so he would renew this policy year after year on the renewal date with little sales resistance. For I realized:

One way to make a fortune is to sell a necessity that is low in cost and repeats. The fortune is made in the repeat business.

I DETERMINED TO MULTIPLY MYSELF

At Joliet I made my greatest sales record up to that time: an average of 72 policies per day for nine working days. And it was the morning after that eventful day when I sold 122 policies that I resolved to begin to multiply myself—to start building an organization.

At the end of that day, I was happy, but tired. I went to bed earlier than usual, and that night I sold policies in my sleep. The next morning I realized I had reached my peak in personal sales.

At breakfast I reasoned: "If I make 122 sales each day and then sell policies in my sleep, it won't be conducive to a healthy mind. Now is the time to build an organization. Now is the time to multiply myself." And when I completed the Joliet assignment, I fulfilled the promise I made to myself to start to hire salesmen immediately.

When I did, an amazing thing happened: I encountered powers unknown to me. I raised my horizons. For I recognized a principle I could use, and when I did, I saw opportunity and grasped it. What I saw and what I did marked the beginning of a financial empire. It was very simple: I placed a four-line ad for salesmen in the classified ad section of the Chicago Sunday *Tribune.*

I had inspiration to action, but I lacked know-how and knowledge in the skill of hiring. Nonetheless, after much thought I constructed a four-line ad that has required very little change for a period of many years. It got results—at times, fantastic results.

Grasp the Opportunity You Make

"Exceptional Opportunity to Earn. . ." was the lead line. The number of personal calls at my office as a result of the ad was more than satisfactory. But the amazing thing to me was the number of letters I received from applicants outside of Chicago: downstate Illinois, Indiana, Wisconsin, Michigan, and elsewhere. I hadn't realized the power of an advertisement in a metropolitan Sunday newspaper to reach beyond the city limits, but I soon decided to grasp the opportunity I saw—the possibility of expanding beyond the city of Chicago and the state of Illinois.

So I immediately wrote to Harry Gilbert and indicated that I had a prospective salesman in Wisconsin and another in Indiana. "Would it be all right to hire them?" I asked. I felt it unwise to refer to more than two until I got one foot in the door. I sent the Michigan inquiries to my mother in Detroit.

The five anxious days that I waited for a reply seemed mighty long. Before I received an answer, I hired two men for Chicago, wrote to those who had made inquiry from the rest of the state, and engaged in personal sales for four of the five days. I needed immediate income.

On Saturday, the letter from Mr. Gilbert arrived. He was complimentary and encouraging, and he gave me permission to hire the applicants in Wisconsin and Indiana. Mr. Gilbert had no representative in either state for his Special Policy Department. So I wrote to these applicants (it never occurred to me to suggest a personal interview) and they accepted my offer. Then I reasoned: "If Mr. Gilbert would allow me to hire one applicant in each state, he would allow me to hire more."

This was an exceptional opportunity for me, and I decided to take it. In addition to continuing to advertise in the Chicago *Tribune,* I placed ads in the Milwaukee and Indianapolis Sunday papers. Results: more inquiries, more salesmen from these states, and inquiries from other states as well.

Again I wrote to Mr. Gilbert, and it was only a matter of time until I was hiring salesmen in every state where he did not have an agency for his department. For I realized that I had hit upon a success formula, and it paid to get the most out of it.

Ask Advice from the Man Who Can Help You

I moved ahead quickly in building a sales organization through the mail. Yet I continued to sell personally, for I needed the income. My procedure was to answer letters early in the morning, sell until five in the afternoon, then return to my office for an hour or so for any additional office work required. I preferred to work downtown Chicago, for I could then get in additional office time.

Naturally, with the expansion of business it became necessary for me to expand my office facilities. So I gave up my desk space with Mr. Pickering and established my own office. At first I, too, rented desk space to others to reduce overhead expenses. By my agreement with the insurance companies I represented, I owned the business and would pay all expenses except the printing of policies and the payment of claims.

Soon I expanded my advertising to include national magazines, and inquiries came from states where Mr. Gilbert already had established exclusive agencies. So I wrote to him, mentioning these inquiries, and asked his advice.

Harry Gilbert was a generous man, and he was pleased with the volume of business I was producing. He wanted to help me, so he suggested that I write to E.C. Mehrhoff of the Commercial Casualty Insurance Company of Newark, New Jersey, with his recommendation.

Here again I learned an important lesson: When you have a

delicate problem because of the possibility of feelings being affected, go directly to the person involved and ask him for advice in solving the problem. He is the one who can help you. As you read on, you'll see how this principle was used. My self-motivator for such a situation was: *Ask advice from the man who can help you.*

My letter to Mr. Mehrhoff brought the answer I wanted. He gave my agency, Combined Registry Company, exclusive rights in the entire United States to sell a special accident policy of my own design. I named it "The Little Giant" to symbolize a lot of protection for little cost, and ever since then I have used the name for any similar policies. I continued to do business with Mr. Gilbert, and in some states I was running two sales organizations.

More ads. More salesmen. More business. I had to multiply myself again. This time I needed sales managers in each state. The men for these positions were selected from my sales force, and their commissions were increased, so my percentage of profit on each unit sale was reduced—but I earned a larger net income from volume sales. Eventually, my organization was selling several hundred thousand policies a year.

The sales managers were motivated to do their best. The more policies the salesmen under them sold, the more money the sales managers earned. Their overriding commissions were sufficiently high to warrant the investment of their time, effort and money to build an organization in the states under their supervision. Thus my time, effort and money were saved.

It's Never Too Late to Learn

I decided to invest my time and effort to complete my high school education and to prepare for college. It was imperative to have a college degree to get into Harvard Law School, and that's what I was aiming for.

It doesn't take much business experience to realize that it's common sense to continue to gain knowledge—to become educated. I knew it was possible for me to make a fortune without a high school education—many great Americans have. But from studying their biographies I found that they continued to learn after they left school. Besides: *there is more to life than making money.*

I've already said that I had dropped out of high school in Detroit. My mother was on a business trip at the time, and one of my teachers and I had a disagreement concerning his capacity to evaluate my ideas. For some reason, he reported this to the principal, who called me to his office. He endeavored to prove that the time he spent talking to me cost the city of Detroit money—several hundred dollars per minute.

"Money?" I thought to myself. "Why, my earning capacity as a salesman is far greater than my teacher's!" So instead of motivating me to do what he wanted—not argue with the teachers in the future—his logic caused a reverse reaction. I quit school. And if his logic was correct, Detroit saved thousands of dollars, for I never talked to the principal again.

Perhaps at that time, I resented regimented authority, as many high school kids do. Perhaps there were other reasons; there usually are. But I soon entered night school—The Detroit College of Law—and worked days. For I never, at any time, gave up the idea: *Keep learning!*

The economy of the nation was growing rapidly as my national sales organization grew. My business was moving forward swiftly. Now I was in position to go back to school—first night school, then day school at the YMCA. Upon graduating from the Y, I entered Northwestern University in Evanston, where I was living.

My program: a full 18 hour course with classes in the morning; a swim, steam bath, half-hour nap, and lunch at the Hamilton Club shortly after noon; a few hours at the office; then home.

Everything was going along fine. It was quite a life! For then we were in the "boom days."

But after this came the crash and the great depression. People were starving, suffering, jobless, homeless, fear crippled the nation; the wealthy became poor almost overnight.

Yet out of this disaster came individual and national strength, as the negative attitudes of people were changed to positive: enlightenment, courage, appreciation of opportunities, the will to work. And most of all, the people returned to their churches for guidance.

These ideas or concepts will prove inspiring as you read the next chapter: "We Weathered the Storm."

LITTLE HINGES THAT SWING BIG DOORS

Knowledge is knowing about something. *Know-how* is knowing how to do something. *Knowledge* is information. *Know-how* is technique. You need both for the success system that never fails.

Knowledge is gained anywhere and everywhere. It can be acquired from books, people, things, happenings, history, and casual observation. But to be useful it must be organized. You must *know* what you *know.*

Two self-motivators to help you acquire knowledge are: *Ask advice from the man who can help you,* and *It's never too late to learn—so don't stop learning.*

9

WE WEATHERED THE STORM

There was a calm before the storm . . . a storm brought about by the negative attitudes and acts of men; a storm more destructive and enduring than any known natural catastrophe; a storm rightly termed *the Great Depression,* for it symbolized the attitude of the people as well as the state of the economy.

It first struck in October, 1929. Black Thursday the 24th was followed by a disturbing lull, then lightning struck everywhere. Black Tuesday the 29th was the day the stock market crashed. After that, there were more rough seas before the financial hurricane struck with all its fury to reach its apex—the Bank Holiday, March 6, 1933. And then:

There Is Nothing to Fear but Fear Itself

This statement by the President of the United States symbolized the change of attitude from negative to positive on the part of government officials, newspaper editors, radio commentators, the clergy, business leaders, and the people. And with this new positive mental attitude began new life . . . new strength . . . new progress.

The principles to be learned from this experience can be used by you and me to avoid entering a storm area needlessly and to prepare ourselves successfully to weather any storm that does come by developing the right mental attitude.

Prepare to Meet Life's Emergencies

To me, at first, Black Thursday and Black Tuesday were like distant catastrophes I read about in the daily newspapers. I had been building a business and buying a home on credit, and I had no money to invest in stocks. I gambled on my own ability to perform, but not by buying stocks on margin. So it wasn't until 1931 and 1932 that I realized the impact of the market crash on me and my business.

It is true that the papers had been filled with daily stories of tragedy. I had met an exceedingly talented and successful young securities broker at one of my clubs in 1928. When I read the newspaper account of his suicide, I felt pity and compassion for him and the others like him whose answer to this crisis was self-destruction. Pity, because he had not previously prepared himself to meet the emergencies of life with the right mental attitude, and compassion for his mental frailties, fear, hopelessness, and defeat.

This young securities broker had not prepared himself early in life with the strength that comes from a strong moral and religious philosophy. The belief that *God is always a good God* cannot have been a part of his creed. And he must have been ignorant of the power of prayer. You can judge the faith of an individual by what he does at the time of his greatest need, when he must either run, surrender, or fight.

The Aim of Life Is Life Itself

"When a man understands that the aim of life is not material profit, but life itself, he ceases to fix his attention exclusively on the external world," said Alexis Carrel,* the great French scientist who lived through these trying times.

I believe it is desirable for each of us early in life to decide what he would do if life ever seemed to be not worth living. I know I did. My decision: Should my life ever be worth nothing to me, it could at least be worth much to others.

For any mental or physical pain or suffering, regardless of how

**Reflections on Life,* Hawthorn Books, Inc., 1953

severe it might be, can in great part be neutralized by the satisfaction and joy of trying to help others. And that's worth living for.

Perhaps you learned that when you read *Before I Sleep: The Last Days of Dr. Tom Dooley,* written by James Monahan—either in its complete form or as condensed in *The Reader's Digest* or in newspaper syndicated articles.

For Tom Dooley, the young doctor, was tortured with pain from a dreaded disease. He knew his days were numbered. But he was driven by a magnificent obsession to minister to hundreds of thousands of sick people who lived in mud huts in Asia and Africa. He believed *the aim of life is life itself,* and he tried to keep others alive as he himself fought to live to help them.

He tried to make every hour count, for he was pushing against time. By driving himself with almost superhuman effort of will, he was able to multiply the benefits of his work through writings, lectures, and television appearances to raise money for Medico—the organization he established to give medical care to the underprivileged peoples of the world. Large sums are still being received to carry on the work of Tom Dooley.

Tom Dooley, unlike the securities broker, had prepared himself early with a good religious and moral philosophy. His life proved this. He believed that *God is always a good God.* And he was not ignorant of the power of prayer. For it was this power that gave him fortitude to keep living on.

The young broker gave up in despair. He might instead have started a new life devoted to the service of others and lived to become a hero.

Because this is a self-help book, may I suggest that you give some thought to your own religious and moral philosophy. Decide now what you would do if ever your life should seem worthless to you.

For a self-help book can literally save your life. A mother recently wrote:

> I am a housewife with three marvelous children and a fine husband, but because of NMA (a negative mental attitude) I

> was convinced the world would be better off without me, especially my husband and children. I was convinced that I could not control my emotions or thoughts.
>
> I was contemplating suicide. I prayed for help, but it didn't seem to come, until one afternoon I picked up *Success Through A Positive Mental Attitude.*
>
> I have studied it in every available moment ever since. I have adopted PMA (a positive mental attitude) as a way of life, and the changes in myself, my home, and my relations with my husband have been like a miracle. I have read other inspirational books, but yours told me, as no other has ever told me, *how* to actually help myself, and this is what I needed more than any medicine or doctor in the world.
>
> I thank both Mr. Hill and you, Mr. Stone, for writing this book. I thank God for getting it into my hands in time to literally save my life.
>
> *Success Through a Positive Mental Attitude* has motivated me so deeply to change for the better that I am confident that I will never return to my former state. Regular church attendance has also helped me, and this came about as a direct result of reading your book.

Prepare to Fight

A book like *You and Psychiatry* can help you come to the right decision. In it, Dr. William C. Menninger says:

> Most of us have witnessed the differences in the reactions of Personalities to onslaughts from Environment. Some can take the total loss of their homes and fortunes; they adjust to the death of loved ones or maiming handicaps. Others can't. Not many Personalities can still be in there adjusting after a full speed head-on collision with as solid a piece of Environment as a ten-ton truck.

Our failures are expressed in one of two types of reaction—Flight or Attack. If we come up against a situation that is too much for us to take in stride, to accept or manage (and it doesn't knock us out as said truck would), we dodge it or run away from it or we try to kick the stuffing out of it, one way or another.

LEARN FROM THE EXPERIENCES OF OTHERS

In the next chapter, you'll read stories of hardships that made strong men—*men who kicked the stuffing out of adversity one way or another.* But now let me tell just one instance of how I learned from the experiences of others to prepare myself for the future. For as you now realize: a person who succeeds in life develops the habit of relating, assimilating and using the principles he learns from experience—his own and that of others.

As I previously mentioned, I didn't at first realize the impact of the market crash and the economic upheavals that followed. But I saw danger signals that motivated me to action.

On LaSalle Street in 1930, I'd often meet a friend—someone I had admired for his business success in the late twenties. After a friendly chat, and just before shaking hands to say goodbye, he would ask, "By the way, Clem, can you lend me 10 dollars until Tuesday?" I'd lend him the 10 dollars, but the Tuesday he was referring to never seemed to come.

These experiences made me think. For although I had a sales system that never failed me and I had complete confidence in my ability to meet any situation that might arise, I reasoned: "Even the keenest minds in the nation lost fortunes when the market crashed. Who am I not to recognize this? It's time to build cash reserves for an emergency or to be prepared to grasp a great opportunity, should either arise."

I wasn't what you would call the "saving kind." I'd buy what I wanted, then work to pay for it. I'd increase my earnings by increasing sales, and I'd increase my personal sales by increasing my sales knowledge and skill.

Every time I entered the Roanoke Building where I had my

office, I was attracted by a sign in the window of the bank on the first floor, which seemed to verify this philosophy. It read:

A young man can acquire a fortune if he obligates himself, for if he is honest, he will pay off his debts.

I had obligated myself to purchase a home, two cars, and what I termed necessities—and others might term luxuries—on time payments. Besides, I was always trying to expand my business, and the insurance companies I represented had each given me a sizable line of credit.

So I forced myself to save by buying a 20-year endowment policy—the kind of life insurance that had the largest cash value. I bought a big one—big enough to make a loan of $20,000 nine years later when both an emergency and opportunity presented themselves. And I did this notwithstanding the fact that I had debts. I knew I'd pay them in full. For early in my experience I had developed the self-motivator: *A deal's a deal—a promise is a promise!*

To me, this meant that come what may and regardless of the sacrifice necessary, you live up to your deal or promise, whether it's written or verbal. Toward the end of 1931, I began to feel the effects of the Depression. For then I began to realize I had a serious problem—*money.*

I Attacked My Problem

I was still going to school and operating my business. My creditors were hounding me; they all wanted their money at the same time, it seemed. I knew that they would all be paid in full; I believe they knew it, too. But everyone had his own money problems then.

My money problems arose from the fact that, although I had over a thousand licensed agents, they weren't producing a satisfactory volume of business, and my income was unfavorably affected. I was more than $28,000 in debt. When I stopped to think about the matter, I realized that it wasn't how many agents I had that counted, it was how much they sold—it was how much money I made.

"A college education is a wonderful thing," I thought, "but it's more important that I make a livelihood for my family and myself—

and pay off my debts." So once again, I became a school drop-out.

Immediately, I attacked my problem. First I took a look at my assets. By then, I had made arrangements for my agency to represent three more companies, in addition to the two I already had. Thus I was able to appoint additional salesmen in an area where it was desirable to have more than one sales organization.

Fortunately, I did have a large, established renewal business. We were losing policyholders, but I didn't know how many. I didn't realize how serious the situation was until I began to have real personal money problems.

But I did know that opportunities were unlimited. *For sales are contingent upon the attitude of the salesman—not the attitude of the prospect.* The salesman who is inspired and has the proper *know-how* and *knowledge* can influence his prospect to buy. Experience had taught me that.

I had proved it during school vacations, when I would engage in personal sales. One summer, for example, I spent 10 weeks in personal sales in New York State. I had to prove conclusively that *selling was contingent upon the mental attitude of the salesman.* For I had made arrangements with the Commercial Casualty Company to issue a new policy at only a slightly higher net premium cost. My sales managers said it couldn't be sold, and our salesmen didn't sell it. For they had read about the depression, too, and they believed that what they saw and heard applied to them. Like millions of others at the time, they had negative mental attitudes about themselves.

That summer, at Buffalo, Niagara Falls, Rochester, and other cities in western New York, I sold in greater volume than I had ever sold before. I used my sales system that never fails, regardless of territory, boom, or depression. It's just as effective under adverse economic conditions as under favorable. I knew it then, as I know it now.

So when I returned to Chicago, I wrote each of my sales representatives and urged them to sell the new policy. Because they had confidence in me, they were motivated to try. Because they tried, they found that the new policy was just as easy to sell as the older one. I had inspired them.

What I Didn't Know

Although I had a sales system that never fails, my salesmen were not applying it fully. They hadn't learned to; they hadn't been taught. Now I began to realize that, as a sales manager, I lacked two of the ingredients to a *success system that never fails* as it applied to training, supervising, and retaining sales representatives. These were *know-how* and *activity knowledge.*

When I look back, I am amazed at how little I knew about proper communications, sales training, and business administration. Perhaps it was because in the boom days, anyone could sell anything. All he needed to do was see people and tell them what he had.

Had I known then what I know now, sales production records would have indicated exactly how the business stood at any particular time—where my selling organization was headed. Salesmen and sales managers would have been properly trained. I would have had *a success system that never fails* for sales management. But I didn't. For in the boom days:

- I didn't even bother to see my salesmen and sales managers. I didn't think of it.
- Representatives received only printed sales instructions in the form of a four-page folder, which consisted primarily of an organized sales talk, a few sales suggestions, and some self-motivators. They were urged to memorize the sales talk, word for word.
- No sales meetings or conventions were held. It never occurred to me.
- No specific instructions on management were given to the sales managers. They knew how to sell new policies, because each was promoted from the sales force.
- The only records I kept were the names of policyholders, a simplified cash bookkeeping system and a list of the agents' names and addresses—no sales production records of any kind.

Like many men who start a one-man-business, I learned from experience. But had I known then what I know now, I would have employed modern techniques in sales training, communication, and business administration. This knowledge can be acquired at school or from books.

Necessity Motivated Me to Action

When I dropped out of school, I got into action—first mental, then physical.

All personal achievement starts within the mind of the individual.

I knew what my problems were. *And knowing your problem is the first step in finding the solution.* To solve my problems, all I had to do was:

1. Make as large an income through personal sales as possible.
2. Continue to hire additional salesmen.
3. *Train* new salesmen, and those I already had, to do as well or better than I.
4. Develop a sales-production record system whereby I would know exactly how much business was in force in every city, town, and village throughout the nation.

But before I describe the action I took, let me give you a feel of the necessity that motivated me. I had been slow in paying my bills and my creditors were hounding me. But there was one obligation I always met on time: the payroll each Saturday.

Did you ever pawn a watch? I did, on two occasions—to get enough additional money to meet the payroll in full. And what about paying the office rent?

When the lights went off in my office, I knew the reason why. I'd telephone the manager of the building, who would ask, "When are you going to pay your back rent?" Five minutes after I gave my answer, the lights would come on again. This happened to me on many occasions.

Remember, I was putting every dollar possible into the payment of my debts. It's tough to pay your current bills while paying your old obligations, and at the same time, save a few dollars for the future. (But it's good for you.)

So necessity motivated me to make each selling hour count—and I did. The hours that were formerly spent attending classes were now devoted to selling time. I'll tell you later about some of my experiences, for they'll prove the power of inspiration to action. And the principles can be applied by anyone.

Hiring additional salesmen was no problem, for I had been hiring right along, using the same four-line ad that got results.

Trial and Success

Here again, I found what was for me a system that never fails to hire salesmen through the mail. Through *trial and success* I had developed a two-page form letter and two circulars to accompany it that got such fantastic results that they were subsequently never changed, except for a few minor details.

The letter and the circulars made the promises in our ad believable, desirable, and attainable—the three ingredients necessary to motivation. They urged the reader to action.

They contained such powerful self-motivators as these:

Success is achieved by those who try.

If there is nothing to lose by trying and a great deal to gain if successful, by all means try!

Do it now!

The letter pointed out disadvantages as well as advantages. For example, it indicated the necessity for the applicant's making a deposit in advance for his state license fee and the supplies that would be issued to him. I mention these details because:

- You may have wondered how I could build a national organization without devoting a great deal of my personal time to the effort. I used the form-letter method.
- You may see, now, how I was able to build with relatively little working capital. By having the representative make a deposit in advance for supplies and their license fees, I was

able to use their deposits as working capital. I guaranteed a refund on demand.

- In addition, you'll see how this letter and literature were useful in hiring by personal interview, for they saved my interviewing time by giving me the complete story.

Character–Attitude–Willingness to Learn

Often during the Depression years, as many as 200 applicants would call at my office on a Monday morning for a personal interview in response to the ad in the Chicago Sunday *Tribune*. A line would start outside my office door in the Roanoke Building and extend around the entire seventh-floor hallway.

Experts may scoff, but I knew then—as I know now—that I had the ability to evaluate an individual rather accurately within a few minutes. For my selling experience made me sensitive to another person's reactions and enabled me to interpret them correctly.

I developed a technique that enabled me to move rapidly—to select those I wished to hire and to eliminate those I thought would not qualify without making them lose face. Here's what I did:

1. Everyone was given the same literature that was sent to an applicant who applied through the mail. I didn't bother to take names and addresses of any applicant on the first interview.
2. "Is he a man of character? Is his attitude positive or negative? Is he willing to learn?" These were questions I asked myself.
3. If I didn't believe an applicant qualified, I tried to be as courteous and thoughtful of his feelings as possible. I'd say, "In fairness: I plan to interview everyone. Here's the literature that explains the entire plan. If you're interested, return for a second interview." I knew that few would return, because of the requirement of a cash deposit, but the applicant did save face.
4. Those men I wanted, I got. My procedure was exactly the same as with the applicants I wanted to eliminate, with this

> exception: I'd say, "Read the literature—and keep in mind that I'll prove to you by actual demonstration how easy it is for you to earn a large income. If the plan appeals to you, we'll get you licensed immediately. I'll do all the selling for a full day and turn the commissions over to you." Then I'd take a minute or two to tell him what large commissions I had made on a salesman's basis the previous week.
>
> When an applicant was broke and a sales manager offered to do the work and turn the commissions over to him, he was willing to see what it was all about. Then, when he received $30 to $50 in cash at the end of the first day, the opportunities were apparent. (In those days, a dollar was a lot of money!)

Attitude Made Them Has-Beens

I had pity and compassion for the *has-beens.* These were men who had made from $15,000 to $30,000 a year in the boom days. But they became *has-beens,* either because they weren't willing to start at the bottom and climb back up, or because their attitudes were so negative that any job they might take would result in failure. Their futures were behind them—unless their employers knew the art of inspiration to action.

I tell these experiences because I made a great discovery. I realized that I could train the salesmen I hired by taking them out to sell and demonstrating my sales system to them. In doing this, I began to get the knowledge to develop the know-how in perfecting *a success system that never fails* for training salesmen—something that I didn't have before. The stories you'll read in the next chapter will indicate how this system was finally perfected.

Realizing that my sales representatives needed to receive training, I began to send out a daily one-page sales bulletin. Each contained a successful sales rebuttal or a suggestion that I had personally found effective. You see, I was selling—and I was in selling trim.

In the bulletins, I told the salesmen what to say and how to say it. Thus, for example, these salesman would be instructed how to make the sale to a prospect who said "I don't have the money," even if it were necessary for the prospect to borrow the premium from his boss or a neighbor.

In addition, each release contained an idea or self-motivator to inspire the salesmen to action, such as: *With every disadvantage, there is always a greater advantage.* Writing this material helped me crystallize my thinking on paper. It was a step toward discovering my *success system that never fails* in training others.

My problems were small in comparison to those of others who, during the Depression, maintained a negative mental attitude. But I did have problems—telephone calls, letters, and interviews from my creditors became quite irritating. So one day, I let my creditors know that they were going to get 100 cents on the dollar plus 6 percent interest from the date of the obligation. They would receive payments in proportion to my earnings. Although this was a statement of my definite decision rather than a request for permission, no one complained. In due course, all were paid in full.

In the next chapter, you'll read story after story telling how hardships made strong men . . .how you can build when everything around you is falling . . .how you can turn disadvantages into advantages.

LITTLE HINGES THAT SWING BIG DOORS

All personal achievement starts in the mind of the individual. *Your* personal achievement starts in *your* mind. The first step is to know exactly what your problem, goal or desire is. If you're not clear about this, then write it down, and rewrite it until the words express precisely what you are after.

Every disadvantage has an equivalent advantage—if you'll take the trouble to find it. Learn how to do that and you'll *kick the stuffing out of adversity* every time.

10

IT'S EASY IF YOU KNOW HOW

The Depression was a blessing in disguise for those who developed the right mental attitude. For necessity makes or breaks a man.

Necessity made Leo Fox. I can picture the first time I met him. He made an indelible impression upon me. Leo had answered my ad. He had a winning smile then, and he has a winning smile now. He was so enthusiastic that I hired him on the spot.

Leo had a job, but he wasn't making money. Although his problems were serious, he reflected health, happiness, enthusiasm, and the appearance of success. Yet when he first started working for me, he was so broke that he, his wife, and two children lived in an inexpensive hotel on the near north side of Chicago. They couldn't afford furniture or pay rent in advance on a furnished apartment. In fact, he was behind in his hotel rent.

Mrs. Fox didn't dare to leave the hotel room with the children when Leo was away, for when the family left the room, the manager would lock them out until a few dollars were paid on back rent. Yet Leo could smile enthusiastically when I interviewed him that morning. I was still going to Northwestern University and hadn't started the practice of personally working with salesmen on the first day. But I did train Leo later.

After a few months, Leo Fox informed me that the earnings he made the first day went on his hotel account, and he had to get up early the next morning to earn enough commissions to get food for the family's breakfast.

Leo had a willingness to work, and it wasn't long until he had his urgent bills paid. After four months, he was in a position to make a down payment on a car. Within two years, his success warranted my giving him the opportunity to become our Pennsylvania sales manager.

ENTHUSIASM ATTRACTS

Leo had been working for me just a few weeks when something surprising happened. A salesman from his old organization came up to see me. He mentioned that he had met Leo on the street, and Leo had appeared so happy and prosperous that he wondered if I had another opening. Of course, I did.

Within a period of two months, I hired five additional salesmen from Leo's old organization. They, too, had met him on the street and asked where he was working, and they, too, applied.

Leo Fox is a man I hold in high esteem. He had a personal problem that has ruined many men: He was an alcoholic. That's why, as Leo told me, he was "kicked out of the house" by his father, John Fox, owner and president of the First National Casualty Company at Fond du Lac, Wisconsin. About a year after, he became associated with me, Leo told me his problem and said: "I'm going to the Keeley Institute at Dwight, Illinois. And I'm going to win this battle with myself." He did go to Dwight—and he did win his battle.

At a social gathering, or at a convention, if someone asks, "Will you join me in a drink?" Leo is enthusiastic. "I'll be glad to," he replies. And when the orders are taken, he makes no apologies. He's proud to say, "Make mine a cup of hot coffee." He hasn't drunk an alcoholic beverage since the day he entered the Keeley Institute.

Leo Fox and his family drove to Fond du Lac to see his father and mother before he was to leave for Pennsylvania to become a sales manager for me. When his father saw what Leo had done to improve himself, he said: "If you're good enough to be a sales manager for Mr. Stone in Pennsylvania, then you're man enough to become president of the First National."

Leo accepted a job with his father, and eventually he did become president. Later it was through Leo Fox that I had the opportunity to purchase the First National Casualty Company. Today Leo is a wealthy man and successful in his chosen work. His story has been an inspiration to the many men who have heard it from me.

I Had a Problem

But now I'll tell you how I made progress in developing my system that never fails me in training salesmen. Also, I shall reveal how the self-motivator, *Turn every disadvantage into a greater advantage,* was used.

After I left Northwestern, I began to devote most of my time to personal sales and training salesmen *in the field.* The term "in the field" means actually calling on prospects or customers. It's "doing," as contrasted to mere theory. When I sold with a salesman, he could see that if he sold exactly the way I did, he, too, would make a large income. But I soon discovered that this wasn't good enough.

The trainee was often carried away by the thrill of the game and didn't observe the specific principles he needed to apply. It's like reading the stories in a self-help book: Some individuals are so interested in the narrative that they completely miss the principles to be applied. So I concluded: Salesmen are inspired to action by the necessity of the times. But they don't learn without being taught, and no one has taught them how to acquire knowledge through observation. Realizing this I began to develop an effective teaching method.

First the salesmen were motivated to study the sales talk and rebuttal arguments word for word. I told them of the large daily incomes that could be earned if they knew what to say and how to say it; why they would be happy in their work if they knew the theory; and how they could save time when they used an organized sales presentation. Then, when the salesman had learned what he should know, I would take him in the field with me for one full day. He could then more clearly understand what was said and done.

A Blueprint for Success

When a salesman worked with me, I gained knowledge and know-how in training. And it wasn't long until I developed a blueprint for success for training new or experienced representatives. And here it is:

1. I'd get keyed up, move fast, and work a full day. My aim would be to make that day the best I ever had. The trainee was not to disturb me in conversation or interrupt the sale. He was to keep close to me, show interest in what I was doing, and move as fast as I did.
2. We'd make our first call at nine in the morning, and I would sell until 11:30.
3. The representative would sell for half an hour.
4. On every interview that he made, I would take notes of any specific errors.
5. At noon, I instructed the salesman specifically what to write down as I discussed the morning's work. First, I would tell him some of the good things he did. Then I'd give him the specific suggestions that would help him. The points that would make or break a sale were emphasized, and the minor points were just mentioned.
6. After lunch, I would start selling again and continue until 4:30.
7. The salesman would then sell until quitting time.
8. Once again, I would take notes during each sales presentation he made.

9. We would then repeat the process in paragraph 5.
10. That evening after dinner, the salesman would give a sales talk at a sales meeting, if a group of us were selling in the same general area outside of Chicago. (If we were selling in Chicago, a sales meeting would not be held.)
11. Everyone attending the meeting was instructed to look for the good points and for whatever might make or break the sale. Any salesman who was unable to detect the imperfections in the presentation would probably have exactly the same faults as the salesman who gave the presentation.
12. After the representative gave his sales talk, the procedure was as follows:
    - He was given first opportunity to comment on how he could have made a more perfect talk.
    - Every person was then called on in turn to give his comments. But the trainee would write down only those suggestions I instructed him to.
    - Finally, I'd give a review of the principles that were enumerated and point out any additional principles that might not have been mentioned.
    - Because inspiration to action is the most important ingredient to success, I would try to inspire each of the representatives—particularly the trainee with whom I had worked that day.

After I had worked one full day with a salesman and followed the above procedure, the next steps were as follows:

- He would work by himself all the next day.
- He would give a sales presentation that evening at a sales meeting, if one were held.
- We'd repeat the procedure of the previous evening as outlined in paragraph 12. This was a check on what he had learned from the night before. It indicated what habits, or know-how, he was acquiring.

- The next morning I'd go with the salesman. He would sell for half an hour. If desirable, I would make a call or two and show him how to handle a particular situation, then have him try another sale or two. While he was selling, I'd again take notes.
- I would then give him a few suggestions and leave him on his own until we met that evening.
- If the representative was not following suggestions previously given and needed to study the theory, he was encouraged to spend the entire day studying. This happened very seldom, for during the Depression men were motivated by the need for money to try to learn anything that would help them.
- As soon as I returned to my office, I would dictate a letter to each salesman with whom I had worked. In this letter, I endeavored:
    - to point out something good about the improvement he had made;
    - to inspire him with other comments;
    - to list each and every one of the important, specific suggestions that he had been requested to write down for himself.

This program became a true blueprint for success in training my sales representatives. The principles, as far as they are applicable, can be related, assimilated, and used by anyone to develop a success system for training others.

Again, I repeat: At that time I needed money, and I needed it badly, for I was desperately trying to get out of debt. The program didn't require a great deal of time to train any one representative, but it was thorough. And these men were motivated by their need for money to try to do their best; they didn't need me as a permanent crutch to lean on. For when they had the knowledge and know-how, they would move on their own power. It wasn't long until I had enough well-trained salesmen for the state of Illinois.

Some of these were encouraged to go to other states.

I was faced with another serious problem—one that was more important to me than making money. It concerned the health of my son.

To Succeed—Select Your Environment

Our son, Clem, Jr., was born June 12, 1929. During the first two-and-a-half years of his life, it seemed that he was always suffering from colds, hay fever, and asthma. Throughout the winter months, he was constantly ill. The doctors didn't seem to be able to do much for him.

Now one of the basic principles of self-help, which became a part of my philosophy when I first started exploring the functioning of the human mind at Senn High, is this:

> *Because man is a product of his environment, he should purposely choose that which develops him best towards his objectives.*

And this I endeavored to do.

Almost anything can be found in a book. While I was still going to Northwestern, I read that certain areas in the United States were out of the ragweed pollen zone—states such as Oregon, Washington, Colorado, and northern Michigan. So I purchased a membership in the North Woods Club at Ishpeming, Michigan.

It had 43,000 acres of land—private lakes and resort facilities. It wasn't my intent to go there until Clem was old enough to enjoy it. I was just preparing for his future.

Clem, Jr., always seemed healthy in the summer, except when the ragweed pollen count was high in September. It was October, 1931, when I received another letter from home stating that Clem was ill. I'll never forget it. I was at Pontiac, Illinois, on a selling trip. Then and there I decided to get into action—to select an environment that would build up his health immediately. I said to myself:

"If Clem feels best in the summer, why not take him to a warm climate? Why not keep him out of the ragweed pollen zone when the pollen count is high? Why not follow the sun? Then, when he is well, we can return home."

So beginning in November, 1931, Mrs. Stone, Clem, and I drove from state to state. We followed the sun for a year and a half—south in the winter, north in the summer. Clem gained weight and grew strong and healthy.

We stayed at the best resort hotels. And because I needed the money, I sold the management of these hotels on giving me their best commercial rate.

Turn a Disadvantage into an Advantage

I would obtain a license in each state so I could personally sell there. It was my thought that the renewal assignments could be given to a salesman I had or would appoint. I personally trained each salesman who remained with my organization. My training program was exactly the same as that outlined in "A Blueprint for Success."

At that time, the mills were closed in New England. The mines were closed in Pennsylvania, Arizona, and elsewhere. The price of cotton and peanuts in Virginia and other southern states was so low that the crops were turned over to enrich the soil—it didn't pay to bring them to market. Oil in Texas was selling at 60 cents a barrel. Nevertheless, the salesmen I trained could immediately earn from $20 to $50 a day.

For necessity gave them *inspiration to action* . . . experience gave them *know-how* . . . and I taught them the necessary *knowledge.* These are the three ingredients in every *success system that never fails.*

During the year and a half of travel, my sales force was reduced to 135 well-trained representatives, for I had lost many before I had the opportunity to train them personally. But these 135 salesmen produced a greater volume of business in the Depression years than the more than 1,000 untrained representatives who had worked for me during the boom days.

So in seeking and finding health for my son by selecting the environment that was conducive to his good health, several disadvantages were turned into advantages: I built a solid foundation for continuous expansion of my business and gained the missing knowledge and know-how to train salesmen successfully. And I made a most amazing discovery.

The Amazing Discovery

When I finally reviewed the letters I had sent each representative, outlining the principles he needed to succeed, I was amazed. For I discovered that the number of necessary corrections was relatively small. What applied to one would apply to several.

On the basis of this discovery, I wrote a series of training manuals from which a representative could learn the principles we had to teach him. Then, with proper field training, he could begin to develop a large income.

As he began to read the first page of Manual #1, he'd begin where inspiration to action can always be found—with thoughts of God. For this is what he read:

> Success in all fields of endeavor has been assisted by the employment of prayer. Regardless of one's beliefs, prayer from a psychological viewpoint is beneficial in crystallizing one's ideas towards an objective, and develops a stimulating internal force. To thank the Divine Power at the end of a good day has never harmed anyone—to ask the Divine Power for assistance toward success has helped many . . .

. . . *If You Want to Get Results, Try a Prayer!*

The Sales Log

When the Depression hit, I had no indicator of exactly what was happening to my business. But when I did awaken to this fact, I had Rand McNally install special Kardex systems. These were designed to give monthly and annual information on sales production by states, cities, sales managers, and salesmen. They were designed by experts who had the necessary *knowledge* and *know-*

how from experience. Colored tabs were used to indicate the last date we heard from a representative and the day we should write to him.

Under these systems, a "sales log" was finally evolved. When properly used, it would indicate past performance, immediate position, the direction we were headed, and danger areas. But I didn't need a system to see how hardships made men strong, or why the Depression was a blessing in disguise for those who met it with the right mental attitude.

In the next chapter, you'll see how those with a negative mental attitude were taught to motivate themselves to develop the right mental attitude.

LITTLE HINGES THAT SWING BIG DOORS

You are a product of your environment. So choose the environment that will best develop you toward your objective. Analyze your life in terms of its environment. Are the things around you helping you toward success—or are they holding you back?

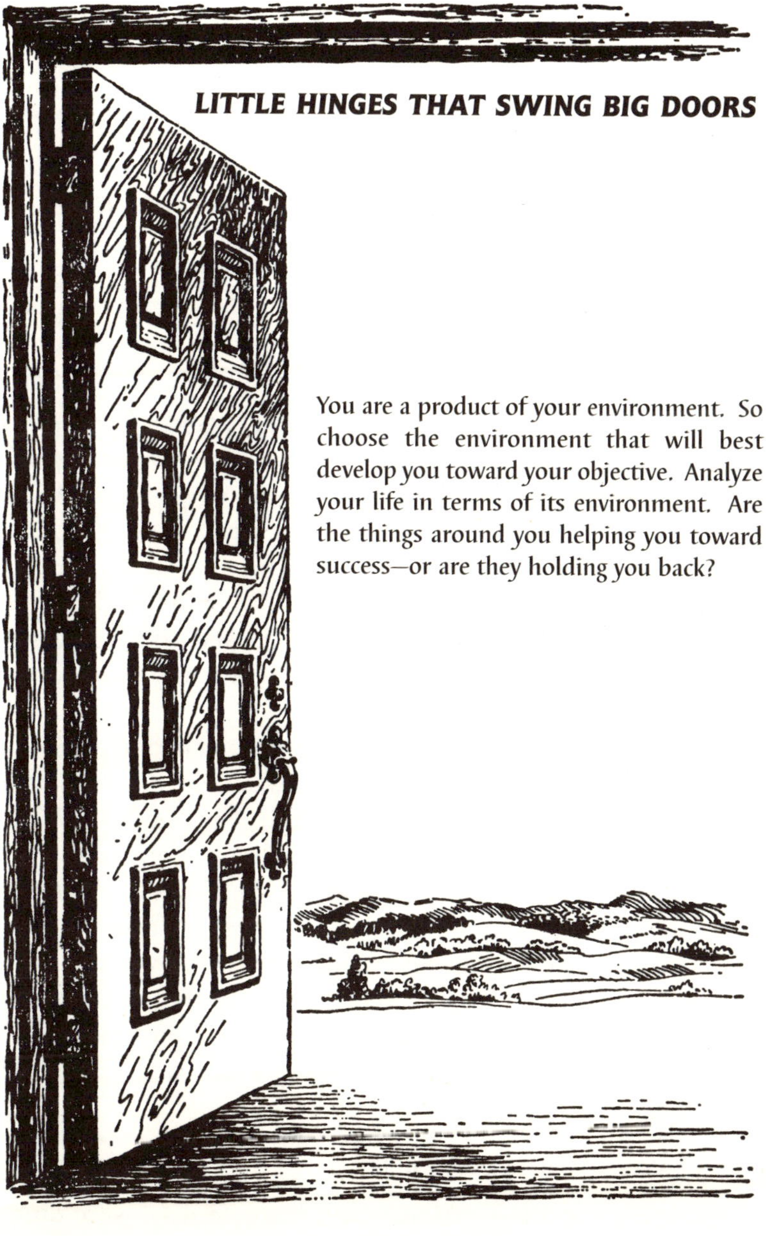

11

MYSTERIOUS SOURCES OF POWER

"Please, God—let me be rescued . . . Please, God—let me be rescued . . . !" Over and over again, Bill Toles kept repeating, with humility, sincerity, and expectancy: *"Please, God—let me be rescued . . . Please, God—let me be rescued . . . !"*

William Toles, a Navy seaman, had been washed overboard from his carrier at four in the morning. When he landed in the water, he followed naval instructions: He kicked off his dungarees and made an improvised life jacket of them, just as he had done so often in practice.

Hour after hour passed; apparently, no one had seen him fall overboard. At three that afternoon, he was sighted by sailors on the *Executor,* an American freighter. And when he was brought aboard, the first thing he did was to give prayers of thanks.

This story is told in the great self-help book, *TNT, The Power Within You.* I have used it many times in speeches, and I have sent the book to inspire sales representatives under my supervision. Why? Because the captain of the *Executor* had changed his course and picked up Bill Toles 200 miles off his usual route—and to this day, he doesn't know why he changed his course.

Her Prayers Were Answered

Recently, Dr. Joseph Maddy and his wife, Fay, were dinner

guests at our home. I told them the story of Bill Toles, as author Harold Sherman told it to me shortly after *TNT* was published.

Fay said: "That's interesting, because we had a similar experience. Up at Interlochen, we have a neighbor across the lake whom everyone calls Sailor. A few winters ago, Joe and I had our trailer at Marathon, Florida, and Joe met Sailor while shopping in town one day. Sailor told Joe about the good luck he was having fishing.

"The next morning, Joe and Sailor went out in separate small motorboats. They both chose to ignore the warning flags, and in the afternoon, a rough sea developed.

"Sailor came in at four o'clock. So did the regular fishing boats. When Joe didn't return, I began to worry. And I began to pray."

"What happened?" I asked Joe.

He replied: "Well, the storm came up in a hurry. The waves were so high and the boat so small that a wave knocked me overboard. I went down once. I went down again. But this time when I came up my arms were extended, and my hand grabbed the side of the boat, and I climbed in.

"The boat had made a complete circle, for when I looked around the first time on coming up, I couldn't even see it."

Then Fay said: "As nearly as Joe and I can figure out, this happened shortly after four . . . during the time I was praying."

The stories of Bill Toles and Dr. Joseph Maddy are mentioned because I, too, believe in the power of prayer. It plays a very important part in my *success system that never fails.*

The power of prayer is mysterious. So are all natural and psychic phenomena, until man becomes enlightened enough to understand them.

But whether or not we understand, truth will be truth. For each effect there is a cause, and when we know a given act brings a given result, we can use the principle that is applicable, even though we don't know why it works.

The Man with the Radar Mind

Many writers in the self-help field are searching for the truth as it applies to powers known and unknown that affect, or can be affected by, the human mind. That's why I made it a point to meet Peter Hurkos, the man with the radar mind. I have visited in his home and met his wife, Maria, and their lovely little daughter, Carolina, and we have become good friends.

In the course of our first visit, Peter Hurkos asked Mrs. Stone to write down a name on a piece of paper and hand it to him. She did.

Without looking at what was written, Peter crumpled the paper in his right hand. Then he amazed us by telling us many experiences that had occurred years ago. Each was 100 percent correct. And he described the person whose name was written on the piece of paper, and again amazed us with his accuracy.

Another time, when Peter was in my office in Chicago, I made a long-distance call to a friend connected with the movie industry in Hollywood. Peter merely held the telephone wire, and when the conversation was completed, he described the physical appearance of the man with whom I was talking and some of his characteristics. On another occasion, he shook hands with Lou Fink of my public relations department and told Lou things that only Lou himself knew. When he visited the Robert R. McCormick Chicago Boys Club, he again amazed me, as well as the boys, with the accuracy of his description of specific problems and happenings in their lives.

Before my first meeting with Peter Hurkos, I had made it a point to read his book *Psychic, The Story of Peter Hurkos,* as well as Norma Lee Browning's articles in the Chicago *Tribune* and her spine-chilling report of her first meeting with him.

Norma Lee later told me: "He scored nearly 100 percent on the tests I put him through."

Perhaps you have read reports of his accurate prediction of baseball scores and his crime-solving feats. In Europe, he is known as the "telepathic detective," for he is credited with solving many crimes—including 27 murders in 17 countries. His power of psychometry—touching an object and telling the experiences of those who own the object—is most baffling.

Peter's chief aim in life is to discover the extent of his psychic powers and to learn how to use them for the good of mankind.

Hidden Channels of the Mind

The man who has perhaps done most in the field of parapsychology is Dr. Joseph Banks Rhine of Duke University. More than 34 years of his life have been spent at Duke exploring the powers of extrasensory perception scientifically and endeavoring to prove their validity.

I have met Dr. Rhine on many occasions, and in our discussions I have become more and more convinced of the possibility that the world is on the brink of a breakthrough into discoveries of psychic phenomena more awesome than the discoveries of technology in the past decade.

Dr. Rhine's books, *New World of the Mind, The Reach of the Mind,* and *Parapsychology,* co-authored with J.C. Pratt, are authoritative. Now his wife, Louisa E. Rhine, who has been engaged in research with him for many years, has given us *Hidden Channels of the Mind,* an easy-to-read book that tells many interesting stories of spontaneous experiences—the kind you may have but not recognize because you may think them only coincidence. They may be in the realm of telepathy (thought transference), clairvoyance (the power of discerning objects not present to the senses), postcognition (seeing into the past), precognition (seeing into the future).

The reason psychic phenomena are mentioned here is that it is wholesome to realize that there are unknown powers. For when you realize the possibility of even that which seems improbable, you are taking the approach of a scientist. You broaden your horizons.

Forecasting

It isn't necessary to study psychic phenomena to lead a happy, healthy, successful life, regardless of how thrilling and exciting such a study may be or the impact that unknown forces may have upon you.

But it is desirable to *see into the future as best you can, with the help of scientific knowledge.* For then you can more intelligently make decisions—particularly those affecting a business or tangible wealth. *And the understanding of cycles and trends is very important in the science of forecasting.*

I first gained an understanding of *cycles* and *trends* when Paul Raymond, vice-president in charge of loans at the American National Bank and Trust Company of Chicago sent me the book *Cycles,* co-authored by Edward R. Dewey and Edwin F. Dakin.

I have used the principles set forth in this book so effectively that I wish to share them with you. For example, when I see my business leveling off, I use a principle learned from *Cycles:* Start a new trend with new life, new blood, new ideas, new activities.

Today I am chairman of the board of directors for the Foundation for the Study of Cycles, and Edward R. Dewey, who created the foundation, is the executive director.

Because the study of *cycles* and *trends* is so important and is so little understood, I asked Mr. Dewey to write a letter explaining them in simple terms. (He also wrote a letter on *leading indicators,* about which you will read in Chapter 19.) Here is what he has to say on the fascinating subject of cycles:

Cycles

> If you will observe closely, you will notice that many events tend to recur in cycles at reasonably regular time intervals.
>
> There is a tendency for cyclic patterns, once established, to continue. Thus, cycles can be a forecasting tool of considerable value.
>
> For example, you know about the 12-month cycle of the

seasons. If it is now summer, you know that six months from now it will be cold and blustery. If now winter, you can predict half a year ahead to tennis and swimming. When you do this, you are making use of knowledge of cycles.

Of course, everyone knows the cycle of the seasons. It is not so well known that there are other cycles, too.

Every hunter knows that some years there is plenty of game; other years it is scarce. What the hunter for the most part does *not* know is that the intervals between years are often quite regular—and hence predictable. But the Hudson's Bay Company knows this fact and uses this knowledge to predict the kill, years in advance, and to prepare for it.

Every fisherman knows that there is variation in the number of fish from season to season. This knowledge can be (and has been) refined to reach a determination of exact wave lengths and permit very accurate forecasting of fish abundance.

Volcanologists use knowledge of this sort to predict eruption of volcanoes; seismologists use cycle knowledge to predict—in a very general way—the coming of earthquakes; and so on and on, throughout the whole range of science.

Even economists are learning that some of the ups and downs of human affairs come at such uniform time intervals that the regularity cannot easily be the result of chance. This fact leads to better foreknowledge.

The determination of these cycles is often quite simple. Mere inspection of a chart of the figures in which you are interested will often reveal the dominant wave pattern. However, it takes skill to distinguish cycles that are "real" from mere accidental fluctuations.

One thing you can do by yourself is to determine your own emotional cycle, or the cycle of your wife, husband, boss, or employee.

Make a grid like the one shown on top of page 126.

		MONTH										
		1	2	3	4	5	6	7	8	9	10	Set up graph for 30 days
Elated	+3											
Happy	+2											
Pleasant Feeling	+1											
Neutral	0											
Unpleasant Feeling	-1											
Disgusted; Sad	-2											
Worried; Depressed	-3											

Each evening, grade your mood for the day and place a dot in the proper box. Connect the dots by straight lines.

Soon, a pattern will emerge. For men the cycle will probably be from two to nine weeks. This is your natural rhythm, and in most cases it will continue. Use your knowledge to forecast your moods and thus protect yourself against undue optimism or undue pessimism.

Most women have a 14-day cycle of amorousness that can be detected and timed in the same way. (Every second wave tends to be more intense.) Women's emotions also seem to conform to a 29 1/2-day cycle that varies with the phases of the moon (cresting in the third quarter).

Cycle knowledge can be of great benefit to mankind. It will help us to change what can be changed, and to conform to what cannot be changed.

Growth Trends

The essential thing for you to know about growth is this: In the long run, everything in the universe grows at a slower *rate* as it gets older.

A baby doubles its weight in about six months. If it kept on at this rate, it would shortly weigh several tons. Trees, like human beings, grow more and more slowly and finally stop growing altogether. Trees do *not* grow to reach the sky. Neither do businesses, nor nations, *unless something new is added.*

Growth is usually figured in *actual* numbers. Sales were $100,000 two years ago, $200,000 last year (growth of $100,000), $300,000 this year (growth of another $100,000), and so on. This seems good.

Rate of growth is figured in *percentages*. If sales were $100,000 two years ago and $200,000 last year, the *rate* of growth was 100 percent. If sales totaled $300,000 this year, the *rate* of growth has dropped 50 percent! What a drop! If the *rate* of growth continues to drop at this rate, there is trouble ahead.

Always figure growth in *percentages!*

This matter is so important to those who are responsible for the growth of a business that I want to stress the point. Just as a mother keeps a weight chart for her baby, let us construct a sales chart for an imaginary business.

		Annual Sales	Five-Year Growth
1920	Company founded.	$ 20,000	———
1925	Five years after founding.	38,000	$ 18,000
1930	Ten years after founding	68,000	30,000
1935	Fifteen years after founding.	116,000	48,000
1940	Twenty years after founding	186,000	70,000
1945	Twenty-five years after founding . . .	279,000	93,000
1950	Thirty years after founding	391,000	112,000
1955	Thirty-five years after founding. . . .	508,000	117,000
1960	Forty years after founding.	609,000	101,000

These figures are charted as the solid line in Fig. 1.

Offhand, this looks like a business that has been expanding rapidly, with a satisfactory forward thrust every five years.

Let us project the growth trend as an uninformed person might do it (the broken line in Fig. 1).

Let us now look at these figures from the standpoint of *rate* of growth. We see that there has been a steady decline in the rate of growth, as shown in the following table:

Figure 1

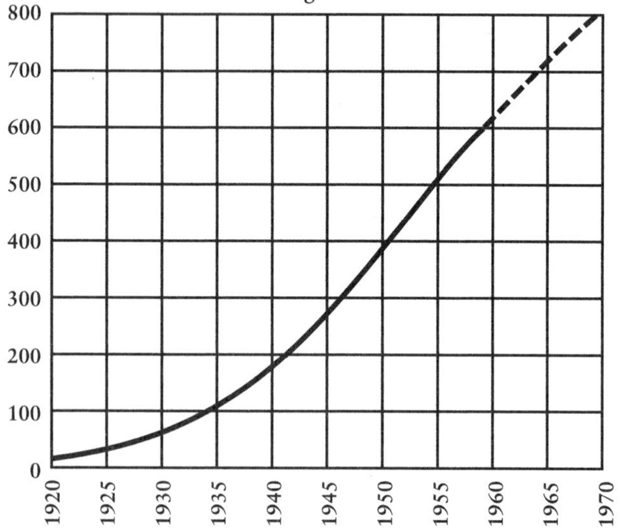

<u>Rate of Growth</u>

1920-1925, 90% of actual sales in 1920
1925-1930, 80% of actual sales in 1925
1930-1935, 70% of actual sales in 1930
1935-1940, 60% of actual sales in 1935
1940-1945, 50% of actual sales in 1940
1945-1950, 40% of actual sales in 1945
1950-1955, 30% of actual sales in 1950
1955-1960, 20% of actual sales in 1955

It is obvious from the table that during each five-year period the rate of growth of this hypothetical business has decreased 10 percent and that, if these tendencies continue, the rate of growth in the future will be:

1960-1965, 10% of actual sales in 1960
1965-1970, 0% of actual sales in 1965

Knowing these facts about rate of growth, the probable sales figures for 1965 and 1970 can be projected more accurately. We have assumed that sales in 1965 would be 10 percent greater than in 1960. The table shows that sales in 1960 were $609,000. Adding 10 percent gives $669,900, projected sales for 1965. Assuming that 1970 sales will show no growth over 1965 gives a sales total to $669,900, for this year also. The projected figures are shown by a broken line in Fig. 2.

Figure 2

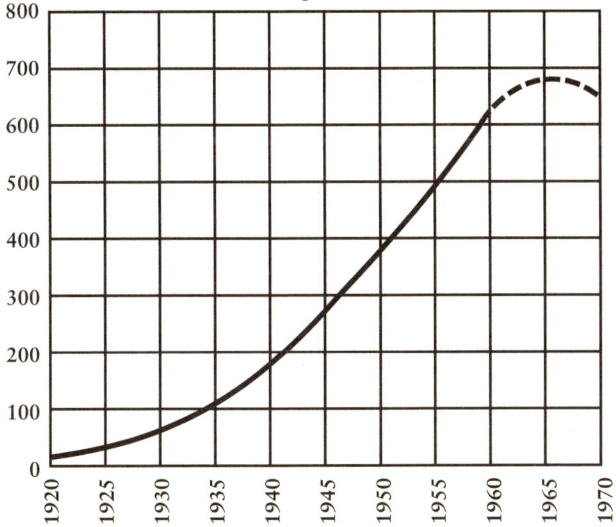

In other words, we see that by 1970 the momentum will cease entirely. By then the organization will become another of the many that follow a groove in a mature and conservative way—probably entering into a moderate decline until either aggressive competition shoves it aside entirely or "new blood" comes into the picture to give the aging institution a new start.

Projections of this sort, based on rate of growth pattern and showing the approach to what we may call "maturity," are important tools for all students of practical economics.

In our hypothetical picture, the design is that of a very regularly declining rate of growth—a regularity that is hardly typical of any institutions in real life. But it is useful for illustrating a fact that both businessmen and investors usually overlook: The rate of growth in an organism is a sound index to its vitality.

So far what I have said is negative. Granted that this is the natural state of affairs, the positive point of view refuses to accept these natural tendencies. It does something about the situation.

The essence of changing natural growth trends is to introduce something new that will cause a rebirth of the growth trend.

Seventy years ago, for example, the carriage industry was reaching a state of maturity. Someone had the idea of mechanical propulsion, and look where the carriage industry is today! Dozens of other examples could be given.

In summary: It is natural for the rate of growth of anything to decline, but with enough imagination and diligence, new growth trends can be substituted for old.

Free Yourself from Bondage

If you are the type of person who allows external conditions to control your destiny, free yourself from bondage!

For *bondage* is a state of being bound to a state of complete subjection to the will of another; as used here, *subjection to external influences and internal negative thoughts and attitudes.*

The more I search to discover the powers of the human mind and how to use them, the more I am convinced that *success or failure is primarily the result of the attitude of the individual.*

The attitude of the individual is the result of a motive, and a *motive* is the *inner urge* that incites him to action. The term "inspiration," when used in *inspiration to action,* is the inner urge that incites him to actions that are good. And this develops a positive mental attitude.

But a motive may be bad. And when it is bad, this inner urge develops a negative mental attitude.

When there is a conflict between an inner urge to live up to the moral law, which is good, and strong, inherited instincts, emotions, and feelings (which are also good when properly directed and controlled), you have a problem.

But what is good or bad?

And what do you do when one virtue is in conflict with another?

How can you develop a positive mental attitude?

The title of Samuel Butler's novel, *The Way of All Flesh,* is so earthy and symbolic that I have used it for the next chapter, where you will read stories of many individuals who were faced with the necessity of answering these questions that everyone encounters. Some experienced success in the internal struggle, and others failed . . . all because their attitudes were positive or negative—good or bad.

The purpose of Chapter 12 is to help you to help yourself to meet these internal struggles intelligently and successfully.

LITTLE HINGES THAT SWING BIG DOORS

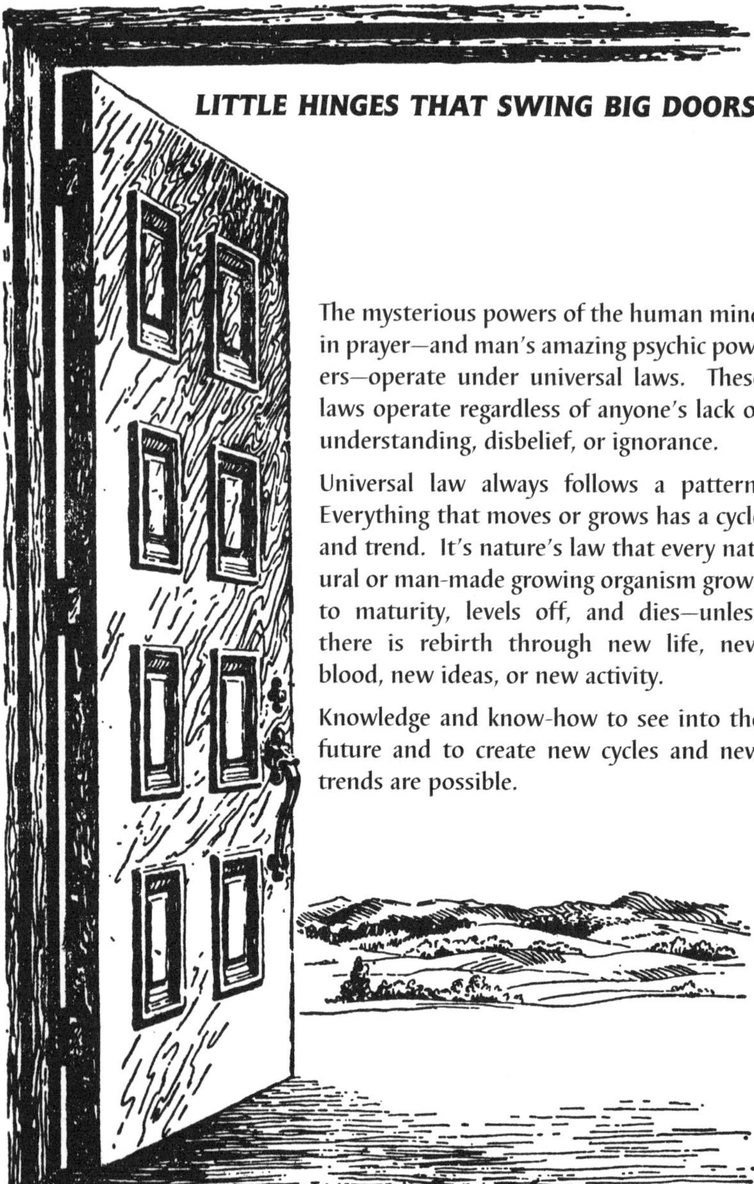

The mysterious powers of the human mind in prayer—and man's amazing psychic powers—operate under universal laws. These laws operate regardless of anyone's lack of understanding, disbelief, or ignorance.

Universal law always follows a pattern. Everything that moves or grows has a cycle and trend. It's nature's law that every natural or man-made growing organism grows to maturity, levels off, and dies—unless there is rebirth through new life, new blood, new ideas, or new activity.

Knowledge and know-how to see into the future and to create new cycles and new trends are possible.

12

THE WAY OF ALL FLESH

See him at his best, see him at his worst, and you see man and the way of all flesh: part animal, part sinner; part saint, part divine. In my search for the success system that never fails, I soon came to realize that morality, too, plays a part in all successful, sustained achievement. Unless man learns to control the sinner, the animal in himself, he can never release his full power for accomplishment.

In time, I came to recognize four basic causes for failure among salesmen; they apply equally, of course, to the pursuit of success in any line of endeavor. They are: illicit sex, alcohol, deception, and stealing. Through trial and error—trial and success—I gained the necessary know-how to combat these destroyers of men among my sales force. When you relate, assimilate, and use the principles in this chapter, you will find it easier to bring out the good—yes, even the saintliness—of your own nature. When you do, you will find that goodness gives you a power you never dreamed of.

The Good That I Would . . . I Do Not, The Evil That I Would Not . . . That I Do

The reason that you don't do the right thing when you should is that you haven't established the right habits. So we'll talk a little about habits, and how to establish the right ones.

When you do the wrong thing, knowing it is wrong, you do so because you haven't developed the habit of effectively controlling or neutralizing strong inner urges that tempt you, or because you have established the wrong habits and don't know how to eliminate them effectively. It's important to recognize the truth: *You always do what you want to do.*

This is true with every act. You may say that you had to do something, or that you were forced to, but actually, whatever you do, you do by choice. Only you have the power to choose for yourself. So one of the secrets to be learned is how to develop the "I want to!" at will.

"But what about hereditary tendencies?" you may ask.

Here's a story of how a young man effectively protected himself against great possible harm.

At a cocktail party preceding a Chicago Sales Executive Club meeting not so long ago, Bob was asked by a friend: "Do you want a Scotch or a bourbon?"

He smiled as he replied: "I don't want either. I don't drink." After a few seconds' hesitation, Bob asked, "Would you like to know why?"

The friend said he would, and Bob continued: "You know my father. Everyone knows him by reputation. He's been called a genius in his field of work. He is one of the finest men who ever lived. Yet my mother, who worships him, has suffered unbelievable agony because Dad is an alcoholic.

"Dad's income in some years has been as high as $50,000. Yet our family has often experienced financial need. But what was even worse . . . my mother would be tortured with humiliation, agony, and fear." He hesitated for a moment and then continued: "I love my mother. I love my father too. I don't blame him. But as a boy, I resolved that if a person as wonderful and smart as my father could bring such misery into his home because of his drinking habits, I would never drink. Why should I, his son, take a chance that I haven't inherited a tendency to be an alcoholic, too? If I did inherit such a tendency, it couldn't harm me if I never took *my first drink.* And I never have. I'm sure you understand."

Is there anything you can do about heredity?

Yes. You can control hereditary tendencies. You can develop those that are desirable and neutralize those that are undesirable. For you have the power to choose. Don't make the first step in the wrong direction. Don't deliberately begin a habit if the tendency toward that habit has proved to be harmful in your family. Like Bob, don't take a chance. Learn to say, "No."

William James, America's great psychologist, wrote: "As we become drunkards by so many separate drinks, so we become saints and authorities and experts by so many separate acts and hours of work." And he emphasized an important principle for breaking any habit:

Break off abruptly. Let everyone know about it. *And never let an exception occur.*

When you are tempted by your friends to commit a wrong act for the first time, or to engage again in wrong or harmful acts, develop the courage to say "no." Here's a story to illustrate.

I was riding in a taxicab from Idlewild Airport to New York City. The driver seemed to have definite ideas about anything and everything. I said nothing until he remarked:

"Here's the neighborhood where I was born and raised. I'll never forget the night I was called a *sissy* because I refused to go along with the gang and rob Tony's grocery store across the street there.

"That night as I ran home, I knew I was traveling with the wrong crowd. It's funny how some kids don't have the guts to say 'no' when they're tempted by their buddies."

"But it isn't funny," I said. "It's a tragedy. For that's how most kids go wrong. They travel with the wrong crowd. And they don't have the guts to say 'no' when they are tempted."

Suggestion Tempts . . . Self-Suggestion Repels Evil

Then I continued: "Did you know that a million and a half teenagers enter penal institutions for car thefts and other crimes each year?"

We had arrived at my hotel, so I could not go on to explain how these personal tragedies could, in many instances, be avoided if the parents learned how to employ suggestion effectively. For then they could teach their sons and daughters to use the power of self-suggestion to do good and avoid evil.

You've observed from your own experiences that every time you're in a new environment, or before you do something you have never done before, there is an awareness or fear that makes you hesitate. This is especially true when you are first tempted to do wrong. Perhaps the fear is strong enough to prevent you from undesirable action. This is nature's way of protecting you against unknown danger.

That's why we know for a certainty that no one commits a serious wrongful deed without stopping to think, unless he has established a habit by previous actions of a minor nature. It just doesn't happen.

Nor does a person act except in response to *suggestion, self-suggestion,* and *autosuggestion.* These will be understood as you continue to read, but here, in brief, are simple definitions:

Suggestion is anything you see, hear, feel, taste, or smell. It comes from the outside. For example, a child learns to walk because he sees his parents walk. He learns to talk because he hears others talk. He gets ideas from books when he knows how to read.

Self-suggestion is the suggestion you purposely give to yourself. It can take the form of thinking, seeing, hearing, feeling, tasting, and smelling through the power of your imagination. You can picture word symbols, or you can say the words to yourself or aloud, or you can write them down. That's what you do when you try to learn self-motivators. Thus, when you purposely make a statement to yourself or think a thought to affect your subconscious mind, it's self-suggestion.

The following statements can become self-motivators if you attach meaning to them and develop the habit of reacting to them:

Have the courage to say "no!"
Have the courage to face the truth.
Do the right thing because it is right.
Do it now!

Autosuggestion, as the name implies, is automatic. It is a suggestion from the subconscious mind that flashes to the conscious in the form of an image of seeing, hearing, feeling, tasting, smelling, or word symbols. It may also be a thought.

John enters high school as a freshman. He wants to make friends, and he does. Some of the boys half jokingly and half seriously suggest that they go to the junk yard that night and pick up some hub caps. That's suggestion. John's conscience will bother him unless he has developed the habit of stealing. Now, if John's parents have taught him the use of self-suggestion through a self-motivator such as *Thou shalt not steal,* or *Have the courage to say "no,"* then the word symbols or thoughts "Thou shalt not steal" and "Have the courage to say 'no'" will flash from his subconscious mind to his conscious mind. That's autosuggestion.

In the process of teaching, the parents may suggest to John that he repeat *Thou shalt not steal* and *Have the courage to say "no"* several times each morning and each evening, every day, for a period of one week. As John voluntarily repeats these affirmations to himself, with the desire to impress his subconscious mind for help in time of need, he is using self-suggestion. His subconscious mind is affected, and it will flash back the motivators when he is faced with an emergency with which these thoughts are associated. This is autosuggestion. Then he, like the cab driver, will have the courage to say "no." He may even use his influence to motivate his companions to do the right thing because it is right.

TOGETHERNESS

Let us say that John has an attractive sister, May. As with every other adolescent girl, the inherent instinct of sex to fulfill her mission in life is an ever-present inner urge. But again, nature protects her with its safeguards—the feeling of fear and awareness of danger, to make her hesitate and think. May, like her brother John, wants to make friends, and she does. But she gets in with the wrong crowd. And some boy friend, jokingly and then seriously, makes suggestions—the wrong suggestions. The more persistent and repetitious these suggestions are, the more impact they have on her subconscious mind.

But if May's parents have taught her how to use self-suggestion so she will do the right thing, at the right time, May will face her problems intelligently—and do the right thing.

If John and May had parents who understood the use of the power of suggestion, self-suggestion, and autosuggestion, May wouldn't have become a member of the wrong crowd in the first place. For the teenager who is properly trained knows that he or she is affected by environment. Suggestion comes from environment. And in this instance, close friends and companions are one of the strongest environmental influences.

Perhaps you've read this oft-quoted verse:

Vice is a monster of such awful mien
That to be hated needs but to be seen;
Yet seen too oft, familiar with its face,
We first endure, then pity, then embrace.

Again, if the parents of John and May were the kind of persons who would take the time to fulfill their mission in life as parents by talking to their children concerning life's important problems, then through suggestion, John and May would learn to develop for themselves high, inviolable standards of conduct. Each would learn how to select friends of character . . . how to discriminate in choosing permanent ties . . . how to help their friends to meet life courageously.

We can assume that if the parents regularly took the time to discuss these matters, the feeling of empathy between John, May, and their parents would be such that John and May would have the desire to accept and act on the advice of their parents.

When parents don't take time each day to develop togetherness with their children, the suggestions they give, when they do make them, often cause a reverse action. Then the boy or girl will consciously or subconsciously do exactly the opposite of that which the parents desire. And instead of neutralizing, resisting, and repelling undesirable external influences in time of temptation, they yield to and embrace temptation—some psychologists say—just to spite the parents.

If you would like to learn how to develop *togetherness,* to understand yourself, to understand your children and life's important problems, read *You and Psychiatry.**

The principles I used in dealing with the problems of my salesmen can be used as effectively by you, for like all universal principles, they are relatively simple.

- I used suggestion to develop within the individual the desire to do the right thing because it was right.
- I taught him how he himself could use self-suggestion to strengthen the desire to do the right thing because it was right.
- I changed the environment of the individual as often as necessary to get him to make each step upward toward his desired objectives.
- I gave him the knowledge of how he could select the environment that was wholesome and good for him.

The stories you have read have indicated the use of some of these principles. And the experiences you will read in future chapters will, in many instances, employ them all.

But at this time, you should be in a position to use the principles of suggestion, self-suggestion, and autosuggestion, and to understand the importance of selecting the environment that will help you reach your desired objectives.

For example, you can:

- Use the self-motivators mentioned in this book.
- Develop your own self-motivators.
- Influence others through suggestion.
- Continue to read this book, and other self-help books that are recommended herein.

**You and Psychiatry,* Menninger and Leaf, Scribner's, New York, 1948.

But now let's talk about deception . . . the most common of the four basic causes of failure: *sex, alcohol, deception,* and *stealing.*

Deception makes traitors out of heroes. The adult who hasn't established high, inviolable standards of moral conduct as a guide for himself hasn't grown up. Like the child, he, too, is self-centered. He, too, is all that he cares about. But unlike the child, psychiatrists tell us he doesn't have a healthy mind. He's immature. Because he hasn't grown up, he hasn't learned to have the courage to face the truth. So small acts of deception grow into bigger acts of deception, and then into heinous crimes.

For like Benedict Arnold in the Revolutionary War, a hero may become a traitor if he doesn't grow up emotionally and always despise deception.

The Traitor

Benedict Arnold's daring attack at Fort Ticonderoga proved him to be one of our most enterprising and successful generals during the Revolution. Arnold, I have always thought, possessed many of the outstanding characteristics of a successful sales manager. But he also had the faults that cause many gifted men to fail in life. He was a man of great capacities, many interests, and great stamina. He possessed initiative and a terrific amount of drive. But like some sales managers, Benedict Arnold was exceedingly selfish. And often, when his personal interests were involved, *his actions were based on emotion* rather than reason. In this respect, he hadn't grown up.

Because he was a fighting general, he was esteemed by his men. But members of Congress and higher Army officers who associated with him found him quite a problem. His arrogance, unreasonable demands, impatience, and stubbornness made him as difficult to get along with as a sales manager with the same characteristics.

Just like the emotional type of sales manager who is criticized and disciplined by demotion, Benedict Arnold felt deeply hurt and insulted when, in 1777, he was deprived of his command. Nonetheless, when the British attacked on October 7, Arnold rallied the Revolutionary forces without any vested authority. His leadership, enthusiasm, and fighting ability once again brought victory, and Congress showed its appreciation by making him a major general.

A woman is often the greatest influencing factor in determining a man's eventual success or failure. It was in 1779 that Benedict Arnold married the 18-year-old daughter of a Tory. It is significant that in the spring of that year *he first offered his services to the enemy.* In May of 1780, Arnold asked for command of West Point. He got it. And he immediately informed the British that he would turn the fort over to them for 20,000 pounds sterling, for he had planned it that way.

His motives for treason were personal, not political—just like disloyalty on the part of a sales manager toward his company is personal, not a matter of principle. Arnold, like a sales manager who betrays his employer, rationalized his actions. He, like any disloyal person, acted on a negative self-motivator, *What's in it for me?*

Arm Yourself Now to Resist Later

But you can arm yourself now to resist temptation later. Make it a habit to react immediately, when tempted, to two positive self-motivators:

> *Count your blessings!*
> *Do unto others as you would have others do unto you.*

The power of self-motivators will be evident to you when you are next tempted, if you react to them.

Now you are ready for the next chapter: "How to Get from Where You Are to Where You Want to Be."

LITTLE HINGES THAT SWING BIG DOORS

High moral and ethical standards play a part in successful achievement. This is especially true in the areas of sex, alcohol, deception, and stealing. These four things have wrecked more success-bound careers than any other cause.

The keys to the habit of doing only what's right can be found, to a large degree, in *self-suggestion.* Through self-suggestion, you bring into play the powers of the subconscious and the imagination.

Here are three self-motivators for good. Repeat them a number of times daily:

> Have the courage to say "no!"
> Have the courage to face the truth.
> Do the right thing because it is right.

13

HOW TO GET FROM WHERE YOU ARE TO WHERE YOU WANT TO BE

"I want your best commercial rate," I said. I looked the assistant manager squarely in the eyes.

He hesitated for about 30 seconds, looked at the registration card I had just filled out, smiled, leaned over and whispered in a paternal manner: "We like our Arkansas boys. It's the people from Chicago we take for a ride."

I laughed. And he thought he understood why. But he didn't because he didn't know I was from Chicago.

"You and your family will be here for two weeks? I'll let you have the finest accommodations we have for $5 a night. Will that be all right?"

This happened back in '32 when we were following the sun. I had obtained an Arkansas state license. While working there my official mailing address was in Little Rock. So when I registered in Hot Springs' finest resort hotel, I gave my local address, as was my custom. Arkansas, as you will later see, was very kind to me. Many of our best sales managers came from there.

While at the Arlington Hotel, I took advantage of my environment. First, I would sell during regular working hours, with one exception: I would take an extra hour off at noon. The bathhouses closed officially at noon for two hours. But the manager of the bathhouse I liked best and his employees became policyholders of mine, and because they liked me, I became an exception to the closing rule. I'd get in the bathhouse about five minutes before twelve. I'd be the only customer there. This gave me an opportunity to relax and receive the health benefits of the warm waters of Hot Springs. Then I'd figuratively start a new selling day at two in the afternoon.

I had made it a practice to try to get some physical exercise every day, such as tennis in the summer and ice skating in the winter, and when I was at a health resort, I'd take advantage of its facilities. I was convinced that to have a healthy mind, one should try to develop a healthy body.

If You Want a Job, Go After It

Each year in March, I would return to Hot Springs and increase the business. In 1935, just before the renewals came due on the policies I had sold and renewed there the previous year, I received a letter from D. A. Cooke, who was seeking a connection as a sales manager. He especially made inquiry as to who would handle the established business. It wasn't difficult to get him to represent me, for it was he who went after the job and got it. I had no one else there at the time.

D. A. Cooke, like so many natives of Arkansas, was a gentleman in the true sense. Because of my experiences with them, I've often thought that there must be something in the Arkansas soil that develops fine people. Take W. W. Sutherland, for example.

Bill is one of the finest persons of character I have ever met. It was he who proved to me that I could operate a company 800 miles away from home when I had the right man protecting my interests. It is he to whom the real credit for building the Combined American Insurance Company in Dallas belongs. Every time Bill made a decision, it was the right decision—for he is an honest man with good common sense.

The day I worked with D. A. Cooke, we drove from Hot Springs to Malvern. But try as I would, I made only a few sales. In my entire experience in working with representatives, I doubt if I have had as many as 14 poor days, but this was one of them.

Every time I did have a poor day, I subsequently conditioned my mind and made outstanding records the next day, except the time I introduced a new policy in Seattle, Washington. Then it took me three days to get in selling trim, but then with the salesmen I trained I made outstanding records. It was sale after sale, day after day.

As was my custom when I had a poor day, I didn't blame conditions, the people, or the service. I knew the fault lay with myself. And I told this to Mr. Cooke that evening. He said: "I understand. But it really doesn't make any difference, for I can see how your system would work."

If I had known then what I know now, I would have worked with Mr. Cooke the next day. But it hadn't occurred to me that I would have a poor day; therefore, I had previously arranged a heavy traveling schedule. Because this experience was unexpected, it didn't occur to me then to readjust my schedule. So I moved on to the next representative I was to train in another state, and when I worked with him, I was motivated by inspirational dissatisfaction to do an outstanding job because of the poor sales results I had with Mr. Cooke.

Although I had a national business, there were very few representatives in some states because of my practice of training personally those that I did have. This took time; I'd cover the eastern and southern states once a year and the western states every two years on several quick trips in which every day had to get results. Remember, my sales force had been reduced, and as I rebuilt it, I wanted the representatives to be properly trained.

My program was to meet a salesman at night, try to cover all matters of importance at that time, work with him the next day until about three in the afternoon, then drive on to my next stop.

But Mr. Cooke never became an outstanding salesman, and in a sense that was good, for it forced him to become a sales manager. And he became an outstanding sales manager, partly because he attracted one outstanding salesman—Johnie Simmons. Johnie, as you will see, had the qualifications that Mr. Cooke lacked. And this taught me another principle:

If you lack experience or a particular talent or skill and you don't want to pay the price to acquire it, then hire someone who has it to do the job for you.

Mr. Cooke proved to be a good sales administrator. He had the knack of selling the salesmen he wanted to represent us. His system was very simple: He didn't know what better to say, so he told them the story of W. Clement Stone as he knew it. And again I learned a principle: In interviewing salesmen, appeal to their imagination, appeal to their emotions, *by telling the stories of other men* in the organization who are a success in your work. When I later used this technique, I learned to use it skillfully.

It Pays to Study, Learn and Use a Success System

D. A. Cooke used this technique in his talks with Johnie Simmons, whose office was next door to his. It was so effective that to this day Johnie thinks he was the one who applied for the job. But Mr. Cooke's idea was if you want a man—go after him. And he went after Johnie Simmons and hired him. When Johnie retired, he was a millionaire.

He Wove an Endless Chain

As a sales manager, Johnie Simmons started to weave an endless chain for attracting quality representatives. He never advertised—that cost money. But he always seemed to have a waiting list of policyholders and friends who wanted to work for us. He saw to that. And he trained the representatives he hired to develop the same skill, so that they were glad to help Johnie.

Many followed Johnie's example and advice when he said: "If you're happy in your work . . . if you're doing well . . . if you see a real future, then share your opportunity with your relatives and friends. Give them the same opportunity you have to earn large incomes and to acquire wealth some day."

Brothers, sisters, fathers, sons, in-laws—they were all attracted by those who followed Johnie's advice. The chain that Johnie began to weave finally reached into Arkansas, Tennessee, Louisiana, Texas, Mississippi, Alabama, New Mexico, Arizona, and North Carolina. The salesmen he hired and trained became sales managers for me in several other states.

One Good Man Attracts Another

Now it occurs to very few salesmen or sales managers who are successful to share their good fortune with their blood relatives and in-laws by encouraging them to do what they themselves are doing. When I saw the value of this endless chain system, I encouraged our other representatives to share their good fortune with their relatives, and many of them did. It seems that this system attracts men and women of real quality—and it is an inexpensive way to hire.

Several books could be filled with exciting stories of the sales representatives who helped me build my business. You'll read some of these stories here. But now it's best that I tell about some of the additional missing parts of what I term my "treasure map."

It wasn't long before I realized that as the organization grew, my training in the field should be with sales managers, star salesmen on their way to promotion, and those representatives whom, for some reason, the managers couldn't motivate. As long as the managers could train in the field, I could help more individuals through sales meetings, where I could teach them knowledge and inspire them to action.

It was my good fortune to discover methods for motivating sales managers to become builders of miracle men and helping individuals develop inspiration to action. I decided that, much as I loved selling, I owed it to the organization to devote my entire time to sales management and training.

And it was in 1937 that I was given the strangest book ever written.

The Strangest Book Ever Written

Morris Pickus, a well-known sales executive and sales counselor, was at that time selling a book to sales organizations. When he endeavored to get me to purchase this book for my sales force, I turned him down, for as I paged through it I knew for a certainty it was something I didn't want. It was a book on phrenology—the study of bumps on your head, the shape of your nose, etc. I didn't want it because under my system it doesn't make any difference how many bumps you have on your head or how long or short your nose is—you can be sold. For selling is contingent upon how the salesman thinks. If a salesman thought a long-nosed individual was easy to sell, he would sell him—not because the person had a long nose, but because the salesman thought he could sell him.

When Morris Pickus lost the sale, he did something that changed the course of my life. He gave me another book, *Think and Grow Rich,* in which he had inscribed a personal note of inspiration. When I read *Think and Grow Rich,* its philosophy coincided with my own in so many respects that I, too, started the habit of helping others by giving them inspirational self-help books. The one principle that particularly helped me was Napoleon Hill's mastermind principle—two or more persons working together in harmony toward a common goal. It made me realize that I could employ others to do much of the work that I was doing, and thus I would have more time for additional activities.

But I seem always to have had a horror of being obligated to anyone, so after I had read the book, I telephoned Morris, thanked him, and purchased one of his books for myself. And while I have tried to show my appreciation from time to time in other ways, I shall never be able to repay him for the help I received from the book he gave me.

Think and Grow Rich

For I did think—and grow rich. And my sales representatives who were willing to relate, assimilate, and use the principles—they, too thought and grew rich. Each of them received the book from me. Things began to happen—big things. Remember, in 1937 we were coming out of the Depression. The very title of the book had appeal. Its contents were electrifying and motivating to readers who were searching for financial wealth and business success. Whenever I made a speech, I would try to share this new working tool with my audience by giving a few copies of *Think and Grow Rich* as door prizes.

The giving of self-help books became a habit. Now I make it a practice to send three or four inspirational books each year to all sales representatives, office personnel, and shareholders of the companies I manage. I also send inspirational record albums and the magazines *Guideposts* and *SUCCESS unlimited.*

In *The Success System That Never Fails* you read stories indicating how this literature has changed lives of many persons for the better. But to me it is truly amazing that, although America has been fortunate enough to develop a group of authors who have the power to motivate the reader through self-help books, so few persons take advantage of them.

Beginning with the distribution of *Think and Grow Rich* in 1937, my sales managers began to be builders of miracle salesmen, and our salesmen began to make such phenomenal sales records that the results achieved seemed unbelievable to those who haven't learned the art of motivation. Within two years after I received *Think and Grow Rich,* I again had over a thousand licensed representatives. My bills were paid. I had a savings account and other equities, including a winter home—a modern duplex at Surfside, Florida. I bought the duplex because the rent from one apartment paid for the entire property.

Although there is no real way to prove it, I believe that *Think and Grow Rich* has inspired more persons to business and financial success than any book written by a living author. Here's the story of one such person.

A Chunk of Coal . . . and Something More

I was holding a sales meeting at Salt Lake City in the Utah Hotel. It was scheduled for 10 A.M. I had arrived about eight that morning, so after breakfast I walked down the main street for some exercise. And as I returned to the hotel, I noticed a four-foot cube of coal in a large window. In front of the chunk of coal were two books: *Think and Grow Rich* and *The Richest Man in Babylon.* It didn't seem strange to see the coal there, for the sign outside read *Martin Coal Company*, but it did seem odd that the two books were in front of it. Since I had some time before the meeting, I walked into the store and asked for the owner. I told Mr. Martin stories of how *Think and Grow Rich* had changed the lives of so many people for the better. Then I said:

"Now, the reason I am here is to inquire why you put the two books in front of the chunk of coal."

Mr. Martin didn't hesitate long, but he was serious when he said:

"What I am going to tell you now is something that I would never tell a stranger. But I have a feeling that you and I have something in common. I don't feel towards you as I might toward a stranger."

"Thank you," I answered.

"My partner and I had two businesses—a gravel business and a coal business. Each business was so far in the red that we hoped we could sell one to save the other. We tried and found that we couldn't. Fortunately I ran across *Think and Grow Rich.*"

Then he hesitated before continuing: "Now this is the thing I wouldn't dare tell to a stranger: Within a few years after studying *Think and Grow Rich* my partner and I got both businesses out of the red. It's a coincidence that you should come in today. For it was only a few days ago that we paid off all of our bills, including our entire inventory. Now let me show you something . . ." and he opened his checkbook and said with pride, as he pointed to a figure:

"We have cash, above all known liabilities, of $186,000. I used to lend *Think and Grow Rich* to my friends. But they didn't always return it. So I felt that I could render a service to my fellowmen by advertising the book in the window. And if anyone wants it, I'll let them have it at my cost.

"And the other book, *The Richest Man in Babylon,* is a book I'd recommend to you if you haven't read it. For it tells how anyone, even on a salary, can acquire wealth if he follows its principles."

The Treasure Map Is Complete

By the year 1939 all the parts of the treasure map had been found by me:

1. Inspiration to action at will . . .
2. Know-how to acquire wealth and success . . .
3. Knowledge of how to build a successful and profitable business . . .
4. And something more . . . a living philosophy.

I knew I had brought together all the elements of my system for I was put to a severe test in 1939, and I met the test successfully. I realized then, as I realize now, that to succeed in life you need to seek more than a definite major objective . . . with singleness of purpose. To succeed: You must first seek the essence of many things. And these are the finer things of life. Now the essence of anything is abstract. It is never found. It is never reached. Yet if you search for the essence of perfection, you become more perfect. Search for the essence of success and you become more successful. Search for the essence of achievement and you achieve more.

But in searching for the essence of anything, you also strive for specific major objectives, with singleness of purpose. And thus with each successful step forward you get closer and closer to the essence of that which you seek. And when you seek tangible riches and success as you search for the true riches of life, you will find them if this be your desire. The essence of success in any man's life depends on his living philosophy.

A Living Philosophy

The essence of a living philosophy is that it must be alive. To be alive, it must be lived. To be *lived, you* must act! Actions, not mere words, determine the validity of a man's living philosophy.

For: *Faith without works is dead.*

Whether he recognizes it or not, everyone has a philosophy. You become what you think. My living philosophy is this:

First, God is always a good God.

Second, truth will always be truth, regardless of lack of understanding, disbelief, or ignorance.

Third, man is the product of his heredity, environment, physical body, conscious and subconscious mind, experience, and particular position and direction in time and space . . . and something more, including powers known and unknown. He has the power to affect, use, control, or harmonize with all of them.

Fourth, man was created in the image of God, and he has the God-given ability to direct his thoughts, control his emotions, and ordain his destiny.

Fifth, Christianity is a dynamic, living, growing experience. Its universal principles are simple and enduring. For example, the Golden Rule, do unto others as you would have others do unto you, is simple in its concepts and enduring and universal in its application. But it must be applied to become alive.

Sixth, I believe in prayer and the miraculous power of prayer.

Now, what does this philosophy mean to me? It wouldn't mean a thing unless I lived it. To live it I must apply it. Therefore, I shall give you an illustration of how I applied it in a time of need; then it may be more meaningful to you.

In 1939, I owned an insurance agency that represented a large eastern accident and health insurance company. Over a thousand full-time licensed agents were operating under my supervision in every state in the United States. My contract was verbal, and it provided for exclusive distribution of a specified series of accident policies. Under this working agreement, I owned the business, the company printed the policies and paid the claims, and I assumed all other expenses.

It was spring. My family and I were vacationing in Florida when I received a letter from one of the top executive officers of the company. It stated briefly that my services would be terminated at the end of two weeks; my license to represent the company, and the licenses of all my representatives, would be canceled on that date; no policies could be sold or renewed after that date; and the president of the company was leaving on a trip and couldn't be reached for two months.

I was faced with a serious problem. The type of contract I had just wasn't being made any more. Making a new connection for a national operation such as mine within two weeks was an improbability, and the families of the thousand representatives who worked for me would also have a problem if I didn't find a solution.

Now what do *you* do when *you* have a serious personal problem—a physical, mental, moral, spiritual, family, social, or business problem?

What do *you* do when the walls cave in?

What do *you* do when there is no place to turn?

That's the time *your* faith is tested. For faith is mere daydreaming unless applied. True faith is applied continuously, but it is tested at the time of your greatest need.

Now what would *you* have done if you had been faced with my problem? Here's what I did:

I told no one, but cloistered myself in my bedroom for 45 minutes. I reasoned: God is always a good God; right is right; and with every disadvantage there is a greater advantage, if one seeks and finds it. Then I knelt down and thanked God for my blessings; a healthy body, a healthy mind, a wonderful wife and three wonderful children, the privilege of living in this great land of freedom—this land of unlimited opportunity—and the joy of being alive. I prayed for guidance. I prayed for help. And I *believed* that I would receive them.

And I got into positive mental action!

On arising, I began to think, and I made four resolutions:

1. I wouldn't be fired.
2. I would organize my own accident and health company and

by 1956 would have the largest in the United States.

3. I would reach another specific objective by 1956. (This was of such magnitude and so personal that it would be improper to mention it here.)
4. I would contact the president of the company, regardless of what part of the world he might be in.

Then I got into physical action. I left the house and drove to the nearest public telephone booth to try to talk to the company president, for I didn't want my family to know the emergency with which I was faced. I succeeded because I tried. The president was a kindly, understanding man of principle. He gave me permission to continue operations upon my agreement to withdraw from the state of Texas, where the general agents of the company were having some competitive difficulties with my representatives. We were to meet at the home office in 90 days.

We did meet in 90 days. I am still licensed for that company, and I continue to give it business.

When 1956 came, the company I organized in 1939 was not the largest accident and health company in the United States, but it was the largest of its kind: the world's largest stock company writing accident and health insurance exclusively. My specific personal objective had also been achieved.

Now, what do *you* do when you have a serious personal problem—a physical, mental, moral, spiritual, family, social, or business problem? Your philosophy will determine your answer.

Remember: The essence of a living philosophy is that it must be alive. To be alive, it must be lived. To be lived, *you* must act! Actions, not mere words, determine the validity of a man's living philosophy.

LITTLE HINGES THAT SWING BIG DOORS

The book you are now reading is a self-help book. By itself, if you learn its lessons, it can start you on the road to a better life. But there are hundreds of self-help books available in America—books that have grown out of the experience and wisdom of their authors. Take advantage of them, for the more information and techniques with which you arm yourself, the quicker and surer will success come your way.

Part IV

WEALTH . . . AND THE TRUE RICHES OF LIFE

A nation's wealth is created by its people

You've got a problem? That's good!

Intelligence is a way of acting

Think first, and the job is half done

When you share, the remainder multiplies and grows

14

WEALTH AND OPPORTUNITY

"How does one acquire wealth?"

This question was asked me most often on my last lecture tour through Australia and New Zealand. It was asked because *Success Through a Positive Mental Attitude* had just been published in Australia, and the jacket of the book referred to me as ". . . the man who built $100 into a $35,000,000 personal fortune."

The Success System That Never Fails tells how I acquired financial wealth for myself and family. Its purpose is to share with you the principles I have learned. But before you determine how you can make a million dollars—if you want a million dollars in the first place—let's first consider how *modern wealth* is acquired.

Opportunity for the acquisition of wealth is as plentiful as the air we breathe—provided we breathe it in a land of freedom. Because a self-help book like *The Success System That Never Fails* endeavors to get you to think about yourself and all outside influences that affect you, or that you can affect, it is desirable to think of government. How does it affect you? What can you do to affect it?

Our Great Inheritance

Washington, Franklin, Jefferson, and all the founders of our nation were dedicated men. They were inspired to establish a government for the greatest good of the greatest number—"a government of the people, by the people, for the people," as Abraham Lincoln so aptly expressed it.

And with the Constitution and the motto *In God We Trust* began a tradition and philosophy of government in America that encouraged integrity, rewarded initiative, and fostered prosperity for the nation and its people. For the nation prospered as its people created wealth.

Wealth is created through the positive mental attitude, education, labor, knowledge, know-how, and moral character of people, under a government that guarantees freedom of private enterprise and respects and protects the life and property rights of each individual. The important ingredients for its acquisition are thought, labor, raw materials, good credit, and fair taxes. Money, or the medium of exchange, must have a recognized and acceptable value.

All these things are important. All are good. All are traditional in America. They have made her rich. The government of the United States of America, through the *enforcement* of its Constitution, creates a favorable climate for the acquisition of wealth by you and everyone who seeks it through the use of *the success system that never fails: inspiration to action, know-how, and activity knowledge.*

In many countries, the climate is unfavorable for the acquisition of wealth by the masses because different philosophies are traditional with them. Neither these countries nor their people will acquire great wealth until they abandon outmoded economic theories regarding wealth and credit and adopt the right mental attitude toward the acquisition of wealth.

How Wealth is Made

You have often heard it said that the monetary value of a needle is more than a thousand times the value of the raw material from which it is formed. Similarly, the value of the raw materials in a 60-story office building, a large ship, or a modern computer is trivial in comparison with the final cost of the finished product. The real costs are paid in wages for the *thought and labor* that convert the raw materials into usable products. The wealth represented by the building may fluctuate, but the market value will be there as long as the structure is in existence. And so it is with the computer or ship, as long as they can be used.

In our day, *thought and labor* make additional wealth, represented by such intangible property as stocks, bonds, and contracts. Intangible property can often create greater riches for the individual than can property. The market value of the stock in a successful corporation, for example, is more than the market value of its tangible assets. The investor considers the earnings, established business, the trend for the industry, future earnings, and the greatest asset of all: good management. Thus, the market value is based on the future, as well as the present.

America has millions of persons with good jobs that bring large incomes; hundreds of thousands who are wealthy; and tens of thousands who are millionaires. They are wealthy and millionaires not because of the liquidating value of the companies they may own, but in most instances because of the market value of the securities they hold—securities they were able to purchase by *saving money from the incomes they earned.*

Again, thought, labor, and raw materials make jobs and create wealth. And its acquisition requires a good business and consumer credit system.

In this country, any person of good character has the opportunity to establish and maintain credit. You can convert your creative thinking, artistic talent, knowledge, know-how, personality, and physical energy into great wealth if you have the right mental attitude.

You can enjoy the use of an automobile, furniture, or a home—you can establish a business or acquire and equip a farm while you are paying for them under our credit system. But if you are to maintain credit, you must live up to your obligations and meet your payments on time.

And when you purchase, you and other consumers like you create jobs for other Americans who, in turn, purchase necessities and luxuries on credit.

When you have made payment in full for your home or whatever else you have purchased through credit, you possess tangible wealth to the extent of its market value. And the market value of a business or investment purchased or made with borrowed money may be many times the purchase price by the time it is fully paid for.

While you are acquiring wealth on borrowed money, you increase the wealth of the nation. *For the wealth of a nation depends upon the wealth of its people.* And the wealth of the people depends on steady income from jobs.

The National Sales Marketing Executives Club, Inc. tells us that one salesman will keep 32 other persons employed. When you buy an automobile, for example, the car salesman and the employees of the manufacturer receive income. So do the suppliers of the manufacturing company and their employees—and the owners and employees of the companies that supply the suppliers.

Each of these persons pays taxes, direct and indirect. In turn, the government pays its employees, and they make purchases. Thus, additional persons are kept working and become consumers, and they, too, buy on credit. They, too, pay taxes.

Shareholders also pay taxes on their profits, and their wealth increases through increased market values of the shares as the company prospers.

Taxes are Good

A fair tax on all income and property is good. It's good for the nation, and what is good for the nation is good for the people.

But it's not good to tolerate graft or the waste of money or time through inefficiency or poor business operations. The operation of the government, like any business, should be inspected with regularity to avoid these.

Again, the United States government can do big things in a big way because of credit. In addition to current income, it operates on borrowed money—and it's a good credit risk, because never in its entire history has it failed to honor its monetary obligations. The tradition began when it honored the currency issued during the Revolutionary War. The moral character of the United States government is a reflection of the high moral character of its people.

Fair taxes are good because through them a government like that of the United States can maintain military strength to protect the life, freedom, and wealth of its people. It can help all freedom-loving people in their efforts to maintain their freedom. And in helping to supply their needs, it acquires additional wealth. More factories, more machinery, more products, more jobs, mean more tax income.

Taxes are good, but like many good things in life, we may not care for them unless we use reason to see their desirability. As to federal taxes, Congress sets the rules and says: "Save all the taxes you can, but play the game according to the rules. If there is an inequity, we'll change the rules." What can be fairer than that?

The smart businessman does play the game according to the rules. He turns disadvantages into advantages, and in so doing acquires additional wealth. Instead of taking profits in the form of a large personal income (where the taxes graduate up to 91 percent of earnings), he plows them back into his business, and his business grows and grows.

Then, if he needs a large sum of money, he eats his pie and has it too—all according to the rules. He offers a part ownership of his company through a public offering of shares on the open market. And although he owns a smaller percentage of his company, his wealth increases, because the market value of his shares may be worth many times what the sale or liquidating value of his company would be if a portion of his shares were not publicly owned. Remember that the purchaser of shares considers many intangible factors when he buys, such as management and the future.

The investor in these shares also develops wealth. His money makes money for him. For the principal owners or managers of the company are the persons who must do the work to make the money for themselves and build their own equities. As they do so, the value of the shares of the purchaser increases in the same proportion. Then, too, the shareholder may borrow money for whatever purpose he may wish, using the stock as collateral.

The Wealth of Nations

When you compare the rich nations of the world with the poor, it is apparent that the wealth of a nation is not due to natural mineral wealth, oil, lush vegetation, favorable climate, good harbors, and a plentiful supply of inland waters. It is primarily due to the inspired thought, knowledge, know-how, and labor of its people. Natural resources are only *potential* wealth. Just as knowledge is not power, but only *potential* power, natural resources are not wealth until converted.

Before considering how natural resources can be converted by nations that are fortunate enough to have them yet are relatively poor—countries such as India, Mexico, Argentina, and Brazil—let's recognize that there are nations that are not so fortunate but who are on their way to riches—Japan, West Germany, and Puerto Rico, for example. Their progress is due to the positive mental attitude of their governments and people, their knowledge and know-how in manufacturing, financing, marketing, and exporting. Each is employing a success system. Each will continue to move forward.

Now, it isn't difficult to see that in the United States or any other country with rich natural resources, great wealth can be created for the masses of the people by converting its natural resources into wealth through *the success system that never fails,* if:

1. All the raw materials come from the ground within the borders of the nation.
2. Domestic labor is employed to create the finished products.
3. Labor, materials, and all other expenses are paid for in domestic currency.
4. A good credit system prevails, which benefits business, industry, and the consumer.
5. A strong government guarantees enforcement of its laws to preserve the freedom of private enterprise and to protect the life and property rights of each individual equally.
6. The government endeavors to avoid war by being so strong that no unfriendly nation will dare attack it.
7. The attitude of the people is positive and develops pride in personal achievement, which engenders the joy of work, and the desire to make their nation and the rest of the world a better place to live in.

Increased Wealth Through Giving

The United States increased its tangible wealth when surplus food and manufactured goods of all kinds, including war supplies, were sent to help the needy nations throughout the world. It meant more factories, more machinery, more products, more jobs, more homes, and more tax income within the nation. Even though the food and manufactured goods in many instances will never be paid for (since they were sent to help the people help themselves), nonetheless tangible wealth was developed here at home when we shipped abroad. More important, we gave strength and encouragement to our allies and friends, who are willing to forfeit their lives if necessary for their freedom and ours, because through our help they are now in a position to save themselves. Norway, Italy, Greece, West Germany, and Japan are a few outstanding examples.

In addition, the United States and its people have had the courage to help other nations help themselves by sharing the ingredients of *the success system that never fails. Inspiration to action* was brought to these nations by missionaries of various churches, doctors, nurses, scientists, teachers, and businessmen, who also provided *knowledge* and *know-how* as fast as these nations were able and willing to absorb them. We extended them credit and loans, and we purchased their manufactured products so that they, too could more quickly acquire wealth.

Foreign Credit Balances

Fear of an unfavorable foreign monetary credit balance has kept some nations needlessly impoverished. The leaders of these countries could learn from those nations that have acquired wealth.

To every problem there is a satisfactory solution, but one must try to solve the problem with the right mental attitude. Should a well developed nation encounter a serious unfavorable trade balance, it could prudently use moderation in its imports, and it could abandon false pride and temporarily use a system that has proved outstandingly successful for nations that have employed it in good faith: the use of a national barter credit plan instead of gold or silver as a medium of exchange. Thus, if a manufacturing nation needs the products of an agricultural nation, the plan works as follows:

The manufacturing nation agrees to purchase a given amount, say 500 million dollars' worth, of wool, lumber, meat, and other products from the agricultural country. The agricultural country then agrees to purchase a like sum of manufactured goods from the industrial nation. Each nation pays for the products it manufactures or grows in its own currency to its own people. The businessman in the agricultural country pays the agency of his government for the imported manufactured goods, and likewise the wholesaler of meats in the industrial nation pays his government, or its agency, in its own currency.

In short, *wealth is created through the positive mental attitude, education, labor, knowledge, know-how, and moral character of people, under a government that guarantees freedom of private enterprise and respects and protects the life and property rights of each individual. The important ingredients for its acquisition are thought, labor, raw materials, good credit, and fair taxes. Money, or the medium of exchange, must have a recognized and acceptable value.*

Win the Cold War More Quickly

If we want to help the have-not nations of the world acquire wealth, we can *inspire* them to use the *knowledge* and *know-how* of acquiring wealth, which we are willing to share with them.

India gets poorer because of increased population. Reason: more consumers. The United States gets richer because of increased population. Reason: more consumers. The same formula for acquiring wealth in America would develop wealth in India, if it were employed.

And something more: Russia and China can acquire wealth without the conquest of other nations and the enslavement of their people. For they, too, can accumulate great wealth by developing wealth from within, through the use of *the success system that never fails.* But they must understand how modern wealth is created and apply the necessary principles.

You, Wealth, and Opportunity

Keep in mind that if all the gold at Ft. Knox were a myth, the value of the tangible property created through thought, labor, and raw materials in the United States alone would far exceed the value of the world's existing supply of gold and silver.

If you understand the ideas regarding wealth contained in this chapter, then you are ready to apply the principles in your own life.

LITTLE HINGES THAT SWING BIG DOORS

The wealth of a nation depends on the wealth of its people. *You* are part of America's wealth.

You must *understand* the source and operation of wealth before you can acquire it. Why not reread this chapter? Almost certainly, you will catch things you missed before.

15

HOW TO SPARK THE FIRE OF AMBITION

"What do you mean by *hot button?*" I asked.

"Well, it's something common to everyone," said Jack. "To find it you must know what a person wants—what he needs to get it—and how you can help him get it.

"The first thing you must do is to help him to crystallize a need in his mind for something he doesn't have. Then you show him that you have the best thing to fill that need. And when his desire becomes a burning desire, the person's *hot button* has been pushed."

"Do you mean that when you push a person's *hot button,* you motivate him?" I asked.

"Yes," replied Jack, whose personal sales have often exceeded a million dollars a year. He's an authority on how to motivate men and women to become successful in selling. He teaches them how to push the *hot button.*

Jack Lacy is known for his success in training salesmen in sales clinics for the National Sales Executives Clubs. He has trained salesmen for hundreds of corporations throughout the nation. The Jack Lacy Clinic correspondence courses and record albums are known in many parts of the world.

By now you know that the most important ingredient in *the success system that never fails* is *inspiration to action.* Jack Lacy says: "If you want to motivate, push the *hot button!*" And by this,

Jack means the right button to inspire a person to action.

Give Him Something to Live For

Leonard Evans advanced from being one of my salesmen to sales manager. Later he became a district manager of the state of Mississippi. But he maintained a home in Dermott, Arkansas. It seems that when a person gets his toes in the Arkansas mud as a youngster, for some reason he just has to return. There is something about the Arkansas soil that attracts.

Although Leonard succeeded as a sales manager, he became satisfied, and the business leveled off. It was a good business, and Leonard had a good income, but as the national sales manager, I wasn't happy. Time after time, I tried to push the right button to develop a flash of inspiration within Leonard to get him out of the rut he was in. But it seems that each flash of inspiration he did catch was soon extinguished.

Leonard was more than satisfied. But I kept trying. Of course, there was some improvement. But he wasn't keeping pace with our national progress. Then one day I received a letter from Scottie, his wife:

> Dear Mr. Stone:
>
> Leonard has had a severe heart attack. The doctor says he may not live. Leonard has asked me to write you he is resigning.

Had his resignation been submitted when he was in good health, it would have been gladly accepted. *But there is something more to business than making money,* and I wanted Leonard to live. The secret of motivation is to appeal to the emotions as well as to reason. So I sent Leonard a carefully written letter. In it:

- I mentioned that his resignation was rejected—and that his future was ahead of him.
- I suggested that he engage in study, thinking, and planning time.

- Then I spoke of the value of studying the *PMA Science of Success* course, which consists of 17 lessons, and urged him to complete the questionnaire at the end of each lesson—and especially to concentrate on the first question in Lesson One: "What is your definite major objective?"
- I let him know that I'd fly down to Dermott to see him just as soon as he came home from the hospital and was ready to see me.

Experience had taught me *one way to keep a man alive is to give him something to live for.* In my letter, I wrote to Leonard: ". . . we need you, we need you badly; get well quickly, for I have some ambitious plans for you."

And Leonard did live, and he did get well quickly. For he had something to live for; he had realized that *there is something more to life than business and making money.*

When I arrived at his home, he was no longer confined to his bed. He had engaged in study, thinking, planning time. He was inspired with five major objectives:

- To retire on December 31, three years later.
- To double the annual volume of business by then.
- To have tangible wealth of one million dollars.
- To be a builder of men by inspiring, training, and guiding salesmen and sales managers under his supervision to earn large, accelerating incomes and to acquire financial wealth.
- But most of all, to share with others the inspiration and wisdom he had gained from the study of *The Bible* and the *Science of Success* course.

Each of these he fulfilled. The lives of many persons who listened to his speeches on PMA (a positive mental attitude) were changed for the better—salesmen, sales managers, teenagers in high school, businessmen in service clubs, teachers, and members of church groups. They would all agree that Leonard Evans helped make their world a better world in which to live.

How I Motivated Him

Now let's consider some of the factors that motivated Leonard Evans. They are:

1. In Jack Lacy's language, I "helped him crystallize a need in his mind . . . showed him that I had the best thing to fill that need." This was suggestion.
2. There was an appeal to the emotions as well as to reason. I let Leonard know I wanted him, needed him, and had full confidence that his future was ahead of him. He believed me, for I was sincere.
3. While convalescing, he got well quickly because his study, thinking, and planning time were well spent. He had something to look forward to.
4. He had a track to run on, for he studied a self-help correspondence course that has motivated many to high achievement.
5. He answered the questionnaires, each of which was designed to direct his mind in a given channel leading to the development of a positive mental attitude. Thus, when he answered the first question, he came up with five definite major objectives—five desirable aims.
6. I intensified the force of the written suggestions with a personal interview, which eliminated any suspicion he might have had that I was just trying to be nice to a man on his deathbed. Also, I related the story of my friend, Charlie Sammons of Dallas, Texas. Charlie had suffered a heart attack, but he had something to live for. When he recovered, he followed the doctor's orders; he learned to use his mind and let others do the physical work. Outstanding as his achievements were before his heart attack, they were many times greater afterwards. Charlie's doctor says: "He'll live longer, because his heart attack motivated him to take care of his health."

Give Him Opportunity . . . to Make His Dreams Come True

It was Johnie Simmons who had hired Leonard Evans. He hired Felix Goodson, too. I once asked Felix: "Why do you believe that we have been so successful in hiring more outstanding sales managers from Arkansas than from any other state?"

He replied: "I don't know about the others, but when Johnie Simmons interviewed me and gave me an opportunity to earn as much in a day working for you as I was then earning in a week, I saw opportunity. And that was all I needed. For I was willing to work. I could then see how to make the money to make my dreams come true."

He did work, but he worked systematically. He used our *success system that never fails,* and he rose from salesman to sales manager to district manager for West Virginia. He also acquired wealth.

When Felix was a boy, Arkansas mud oozed between his toes as he walked from his father's farm to school. As he passed the white mansion on top of the hill, he would often say to himself: "Some day I'll own this farm and live in that big white mansion on the hill."

Shortly after be became our West Virginia district manager, he did buy the farm with the white mansion on top of the hill. And his thoroughbred cattle were the best in the state.

He proved as a sales manager that he had a love for his fellowmen. For he was truly a builder of men. He was a man of character, and he made men of character. Perhaps that is why I wasn't surprised when, as a comparatively young man, he informed me that he wanted to retire and use his talents to make another dream come true—to become a minister of music and help his church. Now, with his ability as a salesman and businessman, he could also help his denomination raise funds to expand the benefits of its work. This meant years of study, but today he is a minister of music. He is helping his church and trying to make this world a better world in which to live.

So the principle I learned from Felix Goodson was: You can motivate another person to do what you want when you give him an opportunity to get what he wants.

One of the most interesting and easy ways to motivate another person is through the *charm of romance*—that is, to use stories of true experiences to inspire him to action—to appeal to his emotions as well as his reason. That's what I've tried to do throughout this book. But am I *coming through?*

To Motivate . . . Romance

"You're coming through, or *You're not coming through,* are expressions used in teenage gangs," explained Reverend David Wilkerson, the young, slender, boyish-looking "Gang Preacher" of Brooklyn, New York.

I use his story to illustrate how I might *romance* to condition your mind to accept and use this self-motivator I learned from Napoleon Hill: *Every adversity has a seed of an equivalent or greater benefit.* Here's what he told me:

"I was pastoring in a small country church in the hills of Pennsylvania—Coalport. I had heard so much about the crimes of teenage gangs and the drug addiction of teenagers that there were times I couldn't eat. I couldn't sleep. The thing began to possess me. And it became an obsession with me that these boys must be reached.

"I was sitting in my study one day and picked up a copy of *Life* magazine. I saw the picture of seven teenage boys indicted for murder—the murder of Michael Farmer in High Bridge Park in Upper Manhattan. I couldn't forget their faces. They seemed to haunt me. The obsession became stronger."

Then Davey, as his close friends call him, told me how he had driven to New York and attended the trial. He told about the agonizing experiences he felt in hearing the details of the heinous crime committed by the seven accused boys. He told of his compassion and how he wanted to minister to them. And here are his own words, as I recorded them:

"All I felt for these boys was compassion, in spite of what I had heard in the courtroom. As the judge stood to adjourn for the afternoon, I felt a strange urge to stand up—just one of those wild climaxes to an obsession. I had to see that judge, who was going back to his chambers. The guards would be there again. They wouldn't let me see him before, and I knew they wouldn't let me see him now.

"So I took my Bible, so he would know I was a minister, and said: 'Judge Davidson, Your Honor, would you respect me as a minister and let me have an audience with you, please?' He became startled. He ducked down behind the desk and screamed: 'Get him out of here, quick!'

"And all of a sudden the courtroom was turned into an uproar. Two police guards lunged at me and started dragging me down the center aisle. At least 35 individuals jumped up, running out of the courtroom—some screaming, 'Get the cameras—here he comes, get the cameras!'

"And I was to learn to my great surprise that these were reporters. The police frisked me for a gun. The judge's life had been threatened, and I hadn't known that. They thought I was posing as a minister and was going to kill the judge. As I got to the door, my hair was down in my eyes, and I began to weep. I thought the whole thing was a nightmare. I had good intentions, and it seemed that the whole world came crashing down on me in one moment.

"I got to the door, and there was a battery of flashbulbs, NBC television, United Press, INS—and they were all screaming at me to hold the Bible up if I wasn't ashamed of it. And so I told them I wasn't ashamed of the Bible, and that the Word of God was the only answer to this situation.

"So when I held the Bible up, this was the picture that was snapped.

". . . I picked up a paper. It was horrible. It sticks in my memory. I can still see that picture—the two police officers, me with my hair down in my eyes, headlines: SELF-STYLED RADICAL PREACHER INTERRUPTS MURDER TRIAL!"

And then Davey told about the humiliation of returning to Coalport. His father thought he had had a nervous breakdown. The trustees of his church suggested at least a two-week vacation.

"In fact, the organization I was ordained with held a special meeting wanting to lift my papers for bringing reproach on the ministry," he said.

David Wilkerson returned to New York City, and you'll see from his experience an illustration of this self-motivator: *Every adversity has the seed of an equivalent or greater benefit.*

"For," said the young minister, "I walked down 176th street, after parking the car, and I heard somebody call at me: 'Hello there, Dave.'

"I went over and said, 'Do you know me?'

"He said, 'You are the preacher that was kicked out of Mike Farmer's murder trial. You were trying to reach Rul Valdrez and the boys, weren't you?'

"I said, 'Yes.'

"He said, 'Well, I am Tom, president of the Orval gang. Come on over and meet our boys.'

"He took me over and introduced me to the boys . . .

"And they said, 'You're all right. You're one of us.' I didn't understand, until one of the boys said: 'Well, when we saw two cops dragging you out of the courthouse that means that the cops don't like you. And they don't like us. So you're one of us.' And they started calling me 'gang preacher.'"

It was because of his great defeat—being thrown out of the courtroom bodily, front-page notoriety, and humiliation—that David Wilkerson was able to develop empathy with New York's teenage gang leaders and their followers—boys no one else could reach.

For Dave Wilkerson *came through* to the teenage criminals, prostitutes, alcoholics, and narcotic addicts—The Orvals, Dragons, Hell Burners, Mau Maus, Chaplains, GiGis, and others. He inspired them to become decent, law-abiding citizens through a hard-hitting evangelistic approach.

Through his techniques, complete cures are often instantaneous. His success has been so phenomenal that many ministers say, "He performs miracles!" Even some of the worst teenage alcoholics, drug addicts, and vicious and brutal criminals have been inspired to complete their college educations, enter the ministry, and help Dave Wilkerson fulfill his mission in life.

But what does this mean to you?

It doesn't mean a thing unless you are ready.

It doesn't mean a thing unless you can relate, assimilate, and use this principle: *Every adversity has a seed of an equivalent or greater benefit.*

Spark the Fire of Ambition Through The Success System That Never Fails

Now you may ask:

- How can I relate, assimilate and use the principle, *To motivate . . . romance?*
- How do you motivate a person to become ambitious when he is not ambitious?
- How do you inspire anyone to action—to overcome apathy?
- How do you spark the fire of ambition in the first place?
- How do you keep the flame of enthusiasm from being extinguished?

These are the questions that have often been asked me by parents, teachers, ministers, businessmen, sales managers, and youth leaders. And my answer always is: *"Use the success system that never fails.* It consists of three important ingredients: (1) inspiration to action, (2) know-how, and (3) activity knowledge." And then I *romance.* "For example," I might continue, "I hold a class every Wednesday night at the Robert R. McCormick Chicago Boys Club. We have a group of teenage boys who have what they call the Junior Success Club."

Then I tell the person who asked the question, as I have told you, about the value of self-help books, special inspirational movies, and self-help record albums. The Junior Success Club has each of the self-help books mentioned in the *Success Through a Positive Mental Attitude,* as well as those referred to in the book you are now reading. Each boy receives *I Dare You* to start. At a later meeting, each is called upon to tell what the book actually did for him.

At the first meeting two years ago, I said: "This is your club. What would you like to discuss at the next two meetings?"

"How to do better in school and how to get a job," was the response. So the next two sessions started and ended with what has become a custom in opening and closing our meetings.

The president opens with the question: "How is your PMA?"

The group responds with enthusiasm: "Terrific!"

The president then asks: "How do you feel?"

The enthusiastic group response is, "I feel *healthy!* I feel *happy!* I feel *terrific!*"

Before the close of every meeting, I call on each boy to stand and tell (a) what the meeting means to him; (b) what special help he received from the previous meeting, and (c) what specific action he has taken from the principles he has learned.

And then the president repeats the same questions he asked at the opening of the meeting.

How Can I Do Better at School?

I was amazed to find that these boys were more interested in finding out how they could improve themselves at school than in anything else. So I asked what particular subjects they were doing poorly in. Although there were different answers, let's take mathematics as an example. Here's what I did:

1. *Inspiration to Action:* I romanced the thrill—the joy—and the need of each subject. They were told *why* each was so important to *them!*

   Math-stories were told of great mathematicians such as Archimedes and Einstein, mathematics as an aid to thinking logically, and the possibility of communicating with peoples on other planets through mathematical symbols. I showed them how easy it was to learn math by memorizing and understanding the principles or formulas at the beginning of each chapter.

I pointed out that if they knew the principles, they could work any problem employing these principles. In the study of trigonometry at college, I didn't hand in home work, but I did use this system, and I received high marks on every examination. The purpose of working problems is to learn the principle. Why not *learn* the principle? Then you can *do* the problems quickly. You understand exactly what you are doing.

2. *Know-How* and *Knowledge:* The group was asked which teacher from their own high school they would like to have give them instruction right at the McCormick Club. They voted on the teacher they wanted. The professional teacher has the *knowledge* and the *know-how* to teach. He may not have the *know-how* to motivate, but I supplied that. The boys voluntarily studied under the teacher, with whom we had made satisfactory financial arrangements. *What were the results?* In 90 days, one student jumped two grades. (He had been behind two grades.) A seventh-grade student had third-grade reading capacity. In 90 days he attained fifth-grade reading capacity, and by the end of the semester he reached seventh-grade level. Now in high school, he's not at the top in his class, but his homeroom teacher says, "With Dick's positive mental attitude, he's likely to be in the upper 10 percent of his graduating class." Many of the boys are receiving the school system's highest grades.

How to Get a Job

It's understandable that a teenage boy needs money. He wants to earn an honest dollar. In a sense, necessity motivates him. However, I repeated the procedure of the previous week. Here's what was done:

1. *Inspiration to Action:* I romanced the joy of work and the thrill of achievement, then discussed *The Richest Man in Babylon* and gave each the book. Anyone can acquire wealth, if he saves 10 percent of what he earns and invests it wisely. Then and there, we made arrangements to form

an Investment Club.

2. *Know-How* and *Knowledge:* We discussed the several ways a job could be obtained. Each boy volunteered ideas, and I filled in. Among the ideas submitted were: (a) check the want ads and employment agencies, (b) go door-to-door in every store, and (c) go in business for yourself. Sell newspapers, magazines, Christmas cards, or specialties, or make something and sell it. They were told how to approach a prospective employer, how to leave when turned down, and similar techniques.
3. *Instructions:* Everyone who wanted a job was instructed to register with Tom Moore, the assistant director. Tom would have a list of business houses that needed teenage help. My assistant, Art Niemann, made arrangements with the Uptown Chamber of Commerce to canvass every member for available jobs. *What were the results?* One boy was turned down six times, then he got a wonderful job. Every boy who wanted a job got one. Later, if anyone was terminated for any reason, he found a job on his own or came to Tom for advice.

So you see, decent honorable citizens are made, not born; poor students can become good students; the teenager who wants a job can find a job.

And you'll also realize when you read Chapter 16 that "Gifted Men are Made . . . Not Born."

LITTLE HINGES THAT SWING BIG DOORS

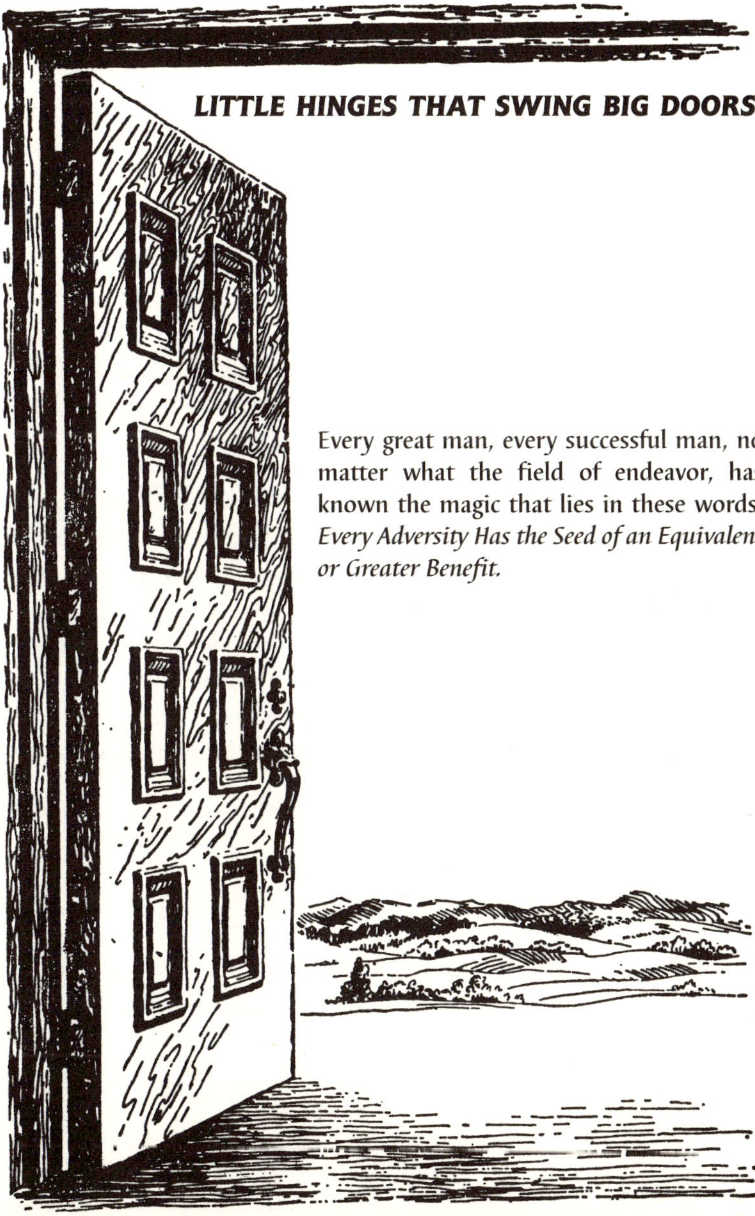

Every great man, every successful man, no matter what the field of endeavor, has known the magic that lies in these words: *Every Adversity Has the Seed of an Equivalent or Greater Benefit.*

16

GIFTED MEN ARE MADE . . . NOT BORN

Are you a gifted person?

Whether your answer is "Yes" or "No," believe me—you are a *potentially gifted person.* And you can be truthfully termed gifted when by performance you use your talents properly. You may not now believe this. So convince yourself as to whether or not you are a *potentially* gifted person.

Why don't you evaluate yourself from the definitions and writings of the experts? It's simple. All you need do is place *Yes, No,* or *?* in the space preceding the check lists found here.

What is a gifted person? Let's see what the experts say. We'll start with definitions and terms that are applicable.

INTELLIGENCE

Webster indicates that intelligence is:

- *The power of meeting any situation,* especially a novel situation, successfully by *proper behavior adjustments.*

_____ Do you exercise this power?

_____ Can you learn to use the power?

_____ Will you use a dictionary to look up every word in this chapter you don't understand?

- The *ability to apprehend* the *interrelationships* of presented *facts* in such a way as to *guide action towards a desired goal.*

  _____ Do you use this ability?

  _____ Can you develop the ability?

- *Success in meeting or solving problems,* especially new or *abstruse problems.*

  _____ Are you experiencing this success?

  _____ Do you believe you can now improve in meeting or solving your problems?

- The *capacity* for *understanding* and for other forms of *adaptive behavior, aptitude in grasping truths, facts,* and *meaning.*

  _____ Do you understand truths, facts, and meaning?

  _____ Can you improve your understanding of truths, facts, and meaning?

Eminent psychologists say *intelligence* is:

- "The ability of an organism to adapt itself adequately to its environment."* (T. L. Engle)

  _____ Do you adapt yourself satisfactorily to your environment?

  _____ Can you learn to adjust better to persons, places, situations, and things?

- "The ability that an individual possesses for meeting new situations or problems."† (Lester and Alice Crowe)

**Psychology—Principles and Application,* World Book Co., 1945.
†*Learning to Live with Others,* D. C. Heath & Co., 1944.

_____ Do you generally meet new situations and problems with the right mental attitude?

_____ Are you willing to try to help yourself meet new situations and problems more intelligently?

- "The ability to see into a problem and work out a solution by applying what one has learned in past experience. Intelligence is not a thing of which you have more or less, but it is a way of acting. A person shows intelligence when he handles a situation intelligently. It is closely related to intellect, which is a comprehensive term for observing, understanding, and thinking . . . Intelligence depends upon knowledge, but it is using knowledge rather than merely having it. We sometimes say of a person that he knows a lot, yet is rather stupid because he makes so little use of what he knows."* (Robert W. Woodworth and Mary Rose Sheehan)

_____ Do you look into a problem and work out a solution by applying what you have learned from experience?

_____ Will you try to recognize your problems and work out a solution by applying what you have learned?

_____ Do you understand what is meant by *"it is a way of acting"?* Is your combined observing, understanding, and thinking satisfactory?

_____ Can you improve in observing, understanding, and thinking?

_____ Do you understand the term *activity knowledge* used in this book?

_____ Do you understand *know-how?*

_____ Do you use the knowledge you have to try to achieve specific goals?

**First Course in Psychology,* Henry Holt & Co., N.Y., 1951.

_____ Do you understand from this definition that *intelligence* is evaluated by: doing . . . applying . . . acting . . . observing . . . understanding . . . thinking . . . using . . . etc?

- William H. Roberts says: "It is important to keep in mind the difference between intelligence and knowledge or information. Intelligence is capacity. It is not information, but the ability to acquire information. It is not skill, but the ability to become skillful. A high intelligence is no guarantee, however, of success either in school or work or in life generally . . ."*

_____ Do you understand that intelligence is capacity—not knowledge, not skill, but the ability to become skillful?

_____ Is it clear that intelligence is no guarantee to success?

_____ Do you see that capacity is latent ability?

- Joseph Tiffin and Frederick B. Knight say: "Intelligence, or intelligent behavior, depends upon (1) clearness of impression, (2) ability to assimilate and retain, (3) fertile imagination, (4) responsiveness to conditions, (5) self-criticism, (6) confidence, and (7) strong motivation." †

_____ Do you believe all these can be developed by you?

_____ Would you say that you have clearness of impression?

_____ Do you have the ability to assimilate and retain?

_____ Do you have a fertile imagination?

_____ Imagination can be developed. Are you willing to try?

_____ Do you react to conditions? Say, for example, something you do offends another. Would you recognize what offends and do something about it?

***Psychology You Can Use*, Harcourt, Brace & Co., 1943.
†*Psychology of Normal People*, D. C. Heath & Co., 1940.

_____ Do you engage in wholesome self-criticism to improve yourself?

_____ Do you have confidence?

_____ Do you have strong motivation to do the thing you ought to do or want to do?

GIFTED • APTITUDE • GENIUS • TALENT

"A gifted child is one whose performance in a valuable line of human activity is consistently or repeatedly remarkable," I heard Dr. Witty say at a lecture I attended. Dr. Paul Andrew Witty is professor of education and director of the Psychological Educational Clinic of Northwestern University.

_____ Have your achievements in some worthwhile activity been consistently or repeatedly remarkable in comparison with others?

Webster's New Collegiate Dictionary published by Merriam gives the following definitions:

1. GIFTED: Endowed by nature with gifts or a gift; talented.

   _____ Do you believe every normal person is so endowed?

2. SYNONYMS FOR GIFT: *Faculty, aptitude, genius, talent, knack,* and *bent* mean a special ability or capacity for a definite work.

   _____ Everyone has a special ability or capacity for a definite work. Have you found yours?

   _____ If you haven't found your special ability, will you try?

3. APTITUDE: Implies a natural liking for some activity and the likelihood of success in it.

   _____ Do you know what activities you have a natural liking for?

4. GENIUS: Inborn mental gift or endowment; talent, extraordinary power of invention or origination of any kind, as a man of *genius.*

_____ Every normal person has inborn mental gifts, endowments, or talents, but everyone doesn't use them. Have you proved by your achievement that you are using yours?

_____ Have you tried to invent or originate anything?

_____ Will you try to engage in creative thinking and applied effort on something specific soon?

5. TALENT: Often contrasted with genius; usually, but not invariably, suggests an inborn gift which depends upon its possessor's industry for development.

_____ Industry and work develop talent. You have the inborn capacity to develop talent. Are you working at it?

Comments on What the Expert Said

In the lecture I previously referred to, Dr. Witty stated:

"Gifted children were superior to their classmates of similar age in size, strength, and general health."

Can you improve your strength and general health? _____

"The educational development of the gifted was generally superior. They did their best work in the fields of reading and language; their poorest attainments were in handwriting and spelling."

Can you increase your skill in reading speed and comprehension and the understanding of semantics? _____

"The gifted pupil is usually remarkable in language development and expression."

Again, these are learned skills. Can you improve in your use of them? _____

"The rapidity with which gifted children learn is an outstanding characteristic which has been commented on again and again by writers in this field."

Can you find a method whereby you can increase the rapidity with which you learn? _____

MOTIVATION IS OF THE UTMOST IMPORTANCE

After the lecture, I asked Dr. Witty what part motivation plays in the development of the gifted child. He agreed that *motivation is of the utmost importance.*

Genius is 1 percent inspiration and 99 percent perspiration, said Thomas Edison. He also stated: *The chief ingredients for success are imagination plus ambition and the will to work.*

Is it true that through motivation you can develop imagination, ambition, and the will to work? _____

In his book, *The Gifted Child,* Dr. Witty reveals the essence of the word *genius.* He writes:

The term "genius" is a definite misnomer for a child or youth. It should be reserved to describe individuals who have already made original contributions of outstanding and lasting worth. Those who test at 180 I.Q. and above, and who are still in their developmental period, are considered as "potential geniuses," and time must elapse to prove whether these youths possess the industry, perseverance, initiative, and originality necessary to earn for them the accolade of "genius."

Inspiration to action develops industry, perseverance, and initiative. It sparks the imagination to originality.

Have you tried to make original contributions of outstanding and lasting worth through self-inspiration? _____

MEET A POTENTIAL GENIUS

If you haven't already done so, fill in every space in the above check list. And when you do, you will discover: *You are a potential genius.*

For, as you have seen in the chapters you have read, and as you will see in the next chapter, "The Power that Changes the Course of Destiny," every living person can use *inspiration to action, know-how,* and *knowledge* to tap the powers of his subconscious mind—powers known and unknown. Napoleon Hill once told me that Thomas Edison, in referring to these powers, used the expression: *unseen forces that come out of the ether.* These unseen forces upon which you can call, as well as the intellectual capacity you have inherited and the mental attitude you may choose to adopt, are not measurable by an I.Q. test.

And in referring to I.Q. tests, Dr. Witty states:

> *If by gifted children we mean those youngsters who give promise of creativity of a high order, it is doubtful if a typical intelligence test is suitable for use in identifying them. For creativity posits originality and originality implies successful management, control, and organization of new materials or experiences. Intelligence tests contain overlearned materials. The content of the intelligence test is patently lacking in situations which disclose originality or creativity.*

YOU CAN RAISE YOUR I.Q.

For many years I have realized that the one thing I.Q. tests do not do is measure intellectual capacity. The construction of these tests overlooks the creative powers of the subconscious mind.

Knowing this, I have been able to motivate individuals to great heights by inspiring them to select an environment that would best develop them towards their objectives and to realize the magnitude of the powers the individual possesses when he uses his conscious mind to affect his subconscious in the desired channels.

> *Children adopted from orphanages into good homes often show an improvement in I.Q. The rise is usually not very great, but may amount to 10 to 20 points . . .*

This is what Robert Woodworth and Mary Rose Sheehan say in *First Course in Psychology.* Also, experiments in adult education indicate that as you increase your vocabulary and reading comprehension, you develop a higher I.Q. rating. One way you can do this is to *keep reading.* Read a minimum of four good books a year, a monthly magazine like *The Reader's Digest,* and your daily morning and evening newspapers. Of the four books, at least one should be in the self-help field.

You might also take a rapid reading course. Many are available, and each is effective, for you must concentrate your attention when you take it; you are inspired to action, or you wouldn't take it; and the course gives you activity knowledge. And that's *the success system that never fails.*

But is there a value in I.Q. tests? The answer is definitely yes. They do measure an individual's preparedness, on the basis of specific standards.

Now that you are aware of your potential powers, let's move to the next chapter, "The Power that Changes the Course of Destiny" and see how you can use it.

LITTLE HINGES THAT SWING BIG DOORS

Your potential is unlimited. It depends on you. How far do you want to go?

Remember what Thomas Edison said: Success is based on *imagination* plus *ambition* and the *will* to work.

17

THE POWER THAT CHANGES THE COURSE OF DESTINY

"Eureka! Eureka!" *I have found it, I have found it,* exclaimed Archimedes, standing in the bathtub.

Archimedes was a great mathematician and inventor of ancient Greece. His friend, the king, had asked his help on an unusual problem. It seems that the king had ordered a new crown made of solid gold. The goldsmith had been given just the right amount of the precious metal. When the finished crown was delivered, the King began to wonder whether it really was solid gold. He had a suspicion that the goldsmith had kept some of the gold for himself and substituted a baser metal.

The king wanted Archimedes to check the purity of the crown, but without damaging it in any way.

So Archimedes engaged in *thinking time.* He thought about his problem for several days without finding any solution, but his subconscious mind was at work all the time. Then one day Archimedes stepped into a bathtub that was filled to the brim. The water poured out over the top. Archimedes stared for a moment, then shouted jubilantly, "Eureka!"

An answer had flashed from his subconscious to his conscious mind, just as the solution to a problem often comes to us unexpectedly when we are relaxing, taking a bath, shaving, listening to music, or awakening from sleep.

Such flashes of inspiration occur in the form of mental images of something you have seen, heard, smelled, tasted, felt, experienced, or thought. And the mental image may be in the form of a symbol that you can easily interpret through the association of ideas. This is especially true when the answer you are looking for comes in a dream.

The thought that came to Archimedes was to take three identical vessels, each containing an equal amount of water, and put the crown in the first jar, the amount of gold the king had supplied the goldsmith into the second, and an equal volume of silver into the third—then to note the difference in the amount of overflow of water from each.

Archimedes, like the man who uses the self-starter *Do it Now!* and immediately gets into action, hurried to test his idea. His experiment proved conclusively that the goldsmith was a cheat. He had used silver as an alloy and kept the balance of the gold for himself. The conclusion was based on the now well-known principle: *A body immersed in a fluid loses as much in weight as the weight of an equal volume of that same fluid.*

Archimedes, like many scientists and inventors we know, wasn't interested in acquiring tangible wealth or operating a business. But if he had been, he could have used exactly the same methods to get his conscious and subconscious mind to work for him. For he knew how to use *the power that changes the course of destiny.*

USE THE POWER THAT CHANGES THE COURSE OF DESTINY

What is this power that can change the course of your destiny?

It's a power that you possess. But like all power, its force can be positive or negative. It can be used for good or evil. It's up to you. The power that changes the course of destiny is—*thought!*

Like all power, it can be latent or apparent, concentrated or diluted, used or unused. It grows with use—the more you think, the more you can think. But you must think with the right mental attitude.

We know that *every effect has a cause.* And *thought* is the first cause of success in any worthwhile achievement. If you don't think, you don't succeed. If your thoughts are based on the wrong premises, you fail to get the right answers.

Archimedes took *thinking time* to solve his problems. And Napoleon Hill employed *thinking time* to find a suitable title for his book.

Use Your Noodle

When Napoleon Hill finished his book, it had the working title: *The Thirteen Steps to Riches.* The publisher, however, wanted a better selling title; he wanted a million-dollar name for the book. He kept calling every day for the new title, but even though Hill had tried about 600 different possibilities, none of them was any good.

Then one day the publisher phoned and said: "I've got to have the title by tomorrow. If you don't have one, I have. It's a humdinger—*Use Your Noodle and Get the Boodle.*"

"You'll ruin me," shouted Hill. "That title is ridiculous."

"Well, that's it, unless you get me a better one by tomorrow morning," responded the publisher.

That night Hill had a talk with his subconscious mind. In a loud voice, he said, "You and I have gone a long way together. You've done a lot of things for me—and some things to me. But I've got to have a million-dollar title, and I've got to have it tonight. Do you understand that?" For several hours, Hill thought; then he went to bed.

About two o'clock, he woke up as though someone had shaken him. As he came out of his sleep, a phrase glowed in his mind. He jumped to his typewriter and wrote it down. Then he grabbed the phone and called the publisher. "We've got it," he shouted, "a million-dollar sales title."

And he was right. For *Think and Grow Rich* has sold millions of copies since that day and has become a classic in the self-help field.

Recently, Napoleon Hill and I had lunch with Dr. Norman Vincent Peale in New York City. In the course of the conversation, Hill mentioned how *Think and Grow Rich* was named, just as I have told it to you here. Dr. Peale, without hesitation, responded:

"You gave the publisher exactly what he asked for . . . didn't you? *Use your noodle* is a slang expression—*to think, Get the boodle* is a slang expression—*to grow rich.*

"Use Your Noodle and Get the Boodle and *Think and Grow Rich* are one and the same thing."

In these stories and others throughout this book, you will observe the use of suggestion, self-suggestion, and auto-suggestion. You'll see how each man's reactions depend upon his previous habits and experiences of thought and action.

Each of us has the power to direct his thoughts. When we direct our thoughts properly, we can control our emotions—and when we control our emotions, we can neutralize any harmful effects of those strong inner urges, such as instincts, passions, and emotions that we have inherited and that so often motivate us to do things we don't quite understand.

We can protect ourselves from future serious wrongdoing by *setting high, inviolable moral standards below which we will not go.*

A Driving Desire Motivated Him to Wrong Action

In the chapter entitled, "The Way of All Flesh," sex, alcohol, deception, and stealing were listed as the four basic causes of failure among salesmen. They are also the cause of failure among men, women and children engaged in any activity. And when one of them is a cause, deception, in one form or another, is generally connected with it.

Let's illustrate with Joe. I'm proud of him; he's a man who won a permanent victory over himself. It happened this way:

Joe is one of my salesmen who was motivated to action at a sales meeting. But he committed a wrongful act because he was a product of habit—the wrong habit. He had not acquired the inviolable standard of honesty. When competing in an incentive program, instead of trying to achieve the honors given to those who won them in an honorable manner, he was motivated to try to steal the hero's crown.

In an aggressive sales organization—where there is dynamic enthusiasm, constant drive, and push to break sales records—when the sales manager holds a sales meeting, he appeals to the reason and emotion of his salesmen.

At the meeting Joe attended, I set very high aims for the organization, and for each individual. At such a meeting, the salesman believes he can achieve the high goal set for him. After the meeting, he gets into action, and the high goals set by the organization are achieved, because—*the subconscious mind transmutes a driving desire into reality when the individual believes it is attainable.*

After this particular meeting, Joe brought in more sales per day than any other representative in the entire United States. The sales record seemed phenomenal. Each of the hundreds of insurance applications he brought in was fully paid for. At the end of the incentive program, it appeared that Joe had won all the top honors and highest awards. He was the fair-haired boy.

His Moral Code Didn't Stop Him

I brought him to sales meetings in many parts of the country, and Joe would tell in minute detail exactly how he achieved his success. His stories seemed so sincere and convincing that they were believable. Joe was promoted to the position of sales manager in another territory. But when the renewals came due for servicing, we found that, like the goldsmith, Joe was a cheat. He had deceived the management. He had stolen the hero's crown. But worst of all, Joe had deceived himself. And the more he lied in telling about his supposed success, the more he began to believe it. That's the way the subconscious mind works.

Low standards hadn't stopped him from deception; high standards would have.

In an effort to help Joe, I required that he pay a price: He gave back all the rewards, was deprived of his honors, and was disgraced among his fellow-workers, because the deception became known when the true winners were honored.

I asked Joe to leave the organization until he could prove that he had found himself. Because hope is one of the greatest motivators, he was given hope that when he did find himself he could rejoin the sales force. I advised him to seek professional psychiatric treatment and to send me a report with regularity. Also, he was urged to get help where help can always be found by anyone who is searching for it—from his church.

After this experience, we made it a practice to inspect all sales after an incentive program before making awards. Joe seemed to everyone to be a man of character, yet his actions were unbelievable. To win recognition, he had actually paid the net premium due the company out of his own pocket.

Now there are many men like Joe whose moral codes don't stop them. They do wrong and are unable to offer any reason for it. But the true reason is that they didn't *develop high, inviolable standards below which they would never go.*

High Standards Keep Him from Crime

Now here was a problem. It bothered me so I kept searching for the answers.

What's the reason for such deception? How can we avoid its recurrence? How can I help Joe and others like him? My thoughts were concentrated on the specific problem. I directed them as you can direct your thoughts, by asking myself questions. The answers came to me because of my experience in solving problems by relating principles contained in the materials I had learned and read and associating them with the problem at hand, just as Archimedes' answer came to him because he was familiar with mathematics and interrelated physical laws.

I was a student of Emil Coué's famous *Self-Mastery Through Conscious Autosuggestion,* and the term *conscious autosuggestion* is synonymous with the term *self-suggestion* used in this book.

Dr. Emil Coué, as you know, won world renown for his success in helping people to help themselves to cure illnesses and maintain good physical, mental, and moral health through affirmations, which I term self-motivators. His most famous was: *Day by day in every way I am getting better and better.*

I was also aware of experiments in hypnosis where the subject, hypnotized, was handed an imaginary knife, told that a dummy was an enemy who was going to injure him, and given the command: "Stab him!" But as the subject was ready to stab what he believed was a living person with what he believed was a real knife, he would stop. His subconscious mind wouldn't let him commit murder.

Why? Because the individual had an inviolable standard so ingrained in his subconscious mind that his subconscious mind refused to act in response to a suggestion below that standard. High standards kept him from crime.

But an individual who has already stabbed a man or committed murder, and who is uninhibited in this respect when motivated, would not hesitate to do under a state of hypnosis what he would willingly do if he were conscious.

High, Inviolable Standards Repel Evil Suggestions

It was while engaging in thinking time that the answers I was looking for became crystal clear:

1. What's the reason for such deception? Here's what I concluded:

    - Joe had attended a dynamic, enthusiastic sales meeting in which the energized power of the suggestion that he achieve high sales goals in the incentive program aroused his emotions. And a person who is highly emotionalized is at that time particularly susceptible to suggestions desirable to him. Joe was told and believed he would achieve high sales goals.
    - Joe had not developed high inviolable standards of honesty below which he would not go to achieve his objec-

tives. He wouldn't steal money, but he would steal the hero's crown. His conscience would not prevent him from deception in reporting and paying for sales he didn't make. For he had established the habit of deception, first in trivial things, then in more serious matters.

2. How can we avoid its recurrence?

   - Condition the minds of those attending a sales meeting by emphasizing the importance of honesty and integrity. Specifically recommend the use of these self-motivators:

     Have the courage to face the truth.
     Be truthful.
   - Gear editorials in bulletin releases to motivate salesmen to develop high, inviolable standards of honesty and integrity.
   - Let everyone know that his work will be inspected, for it is a known fact that men may not do what you *expect,* unless you *inspect.*

3. How can I help Joe and others like him? Here's how I helped him:

   - Joe had taken a salaried job where he wouldn't be tempted, in line with a suggestion I had made to him. I wrote and encouraged him to keep up the good work he was doing on his job for I had heard from both him and his psychiatrist.
   - He was urged to memorize the two self-motivators: *Have the courage to face the truth* and *Be truthful.* He was to repeat these many times a day, particularly in the morning and evening, for 10 days. Then, when he was tempted to lie or deceive, he was immediately to do the right thing when one of these self-motivators flashed from his subconscious to his conscious mind.
   - The editorials I had written to motivate the reader to develop high, inviolable standards of honesty and integrity were sent to him.

- A year later, when he and his psychiatrist both informed me that Joe was ready, I rehired him after a personal interview. I let him know how proud I was that he had won a personal victory.

The discovery of the necessity of developing high, inviolable standards below which you will not go regardless of external influence was a thrilling and wonderful experience. For it led to additional techniques to help persons in all walks of life, especially children and teenagers, to help themselves.

To me, this is one of the true riches of life.

You read in Chapter 12 about the use of suggestion with the teenager. With children, as you are probably aware, when you consistently sow seeds of suggestion with statements such as: "You're bad; you'll never be any good; you'll never amount to anything," children will respond by being bad, and never being good, and never amounting to anything.

With others, of course, there may be a reverse reaction. If a child develops the habit of being contrary, he may say to himself, "I'll show you!" for if the child has acquired the habit of thinking *I can* rather than *I can't,* then negative suggestions often cause a reverse reaction.

In my work with the Chicago Boys Clubs and my association with such movements as Teen Age Evangelism in Brooklyn and the House of Correction in Chicago, I have become aware of the impact of suggestion in helping so-called problem children. When such a child does something that is good, and you sow seeds of good thoughts, he immediately responds favorably.

Here are a few seeds of good thoughts: "You're improving. Every day you're getting better. I'm proud of you."

How to Develop the Power That Changes the Course of Your Destiny

Now we have seen:

- The power of thought to change the course of destiny.

- The importance of suggestion, self-suggestion, and autosuggestion.
- The interrelationship of the conscious and subconscious mind.

We have also seen that the power or process of thinking helps us solve problems. Thought applies to an idea expressed or unexpressed that comes into your mind as a result of reflection, and reflection takes time.

The purpose of this chapter is to encourage you to employ study, thinking, and planning time daily, and to develop and use the power that can change the course of your destiny. For, as Dr. Alexis Carrel says: *To make thought itself the goal of thought is a kind of mental perversion.* Thought must be followed through by action.

Now you can see that if you employed study, thinking, and planning time daily, you could develop and use the power that can change the course of your destiny. But you may not know how.

So when you read Chapter 19, entitled "The Success Indicator Brings Success," you will find the story of George Severance and his Social Time Recorder, and you will learn how to develop your own time recorder, which will guarantee you success if you use it daily as instructed. It will aid you to increase your power to develop *inspiration to action* at will and to find the *knowledge* necessary to acquire *know-how* in any activity in which you may be interested.

But first let's take a look at the *true riches of life.* In Chapter 18, you'll read quotations from letters I received from well-known persons in answer to the question: "What are the true riches of life?" And you'll read the story of a man who has acquired these riches.

LITTLE HINGES THAT SWING BIG DOORS

Thought is the most tremendous force in the universe.

Think kind thoughts . . .
you become kind.

Think happy thoughts . . .
you become happy.

Think success . . .
you become successful.

Think good thoughts . . .
you become good.

Think evil thoughts . . .
you become evil.

Think sickness . . .
you become sick.

Think health . . .
you become healthy.

YOU BECOME WHAT YOU THINK!

18

THE TRUE RICHES OF LIFE

"Hello, Jack," said a voice on the other end of the wire at 7:30 one morning. This telephone call started a chain of events that changed the life of Jack Stephens, a young businessman.

The voice belonged to Harold Steele, the executive director of a boy's club in Atlanta, Georgia. There was a note of serious urgency as Harold explained:

"My car won't start, Jack, and I'll be unable to keep an important appointment: I promised to pick up a four-year-old boy and his mother at eight this morning and take them to the hospital. The boy is in the last stages of leukemia, and I am informed that at the very most he has only a few days to live. Could you help me out and drive the boy to the hospital this morning? Their home is just a few blocks from you."

At eight that morning, the mother of the boy was sitting in the front seat of Jack's car. The child was so weak that he was lying down, his head in his mother's lap, his little feet resting on Jack's right leg. After starting the motor, Jack glanced down at the youngster, who was staring at him. Their eyes met.

"Are you God?" the boy asked.

Jack hesitated, then answered softly, "No, son. Why do you ask?"

"Mother said God would come soon and take me away with Him."

"And six days later, God did come to take the child with Him," Jack told me.

The course of Jack Stephen's life was changed. For the picture of the boy lying with his head in his mother's lap, the eyes of the helpless child, and the question "Are you God?" were constantly with him. They created a deep, emotional impression that forced Jack Stephens to take action.

Today Jack Stephens is actively engaged in a lifetime career, helping boys in Atlanta grow into healthy, decent, patriotic American citizens. For he is director of the Joseph B. Whitehead Memorial Boys Club.

Ever since Jack Stephens told me his story, I have thought of it often. For it is the story of the power of thought. Everyone has it: power to think and do good or evil.

"Are you God?"

No one will ask you this question. But you, like Jack Stephens, may have the urge to seek *the true riches* of life as you conceive them to be. For there are many such riches from which you can choose.

What Are the True Riches of Life?

At a recent meeting of the board of directors of the Boys Clubs of America, I asked General Robert E. Wood:

"If someone should ask you for publication, 'What are the true riches of life?' what would your answer be?"

Without hesitation, he replied: "A happy marriage and a happy home."

When I arrived home, a happy thought occurred to me: Why not ask the same question of some other eminent people—persons who have had the chance to choose whatever they wanted from life. So I asked people like J. Edgar Hoover, Mrs. Franklin Delano Roosevelt, and Captain Eddie Rickenbacker, who are, I feel, three of the most highly esteemed persons in our country today; also the governors of the several states. Following are some of the replies I received. Together, the ideas add up to a picture of *real* success for anyone.

J. Edgar Hoover:

"I believe one of the true riches of life lies in the knowledge that through service to our Nation and mankind we help preserve our precious heritage and protect our sacred freedoms."

Eleanor Roosevelt:

"The true richness of life lies, I think, in a sense of having fulfilled some needs of others."

Eddie Rickenbacker:

"Help the American youth."

S. Ernest Vandiver,
Governor of the State of Georgia:

"When I visited the Georgia State Mental Hospital at Milledgeville in conjunction with a vast program of mental health reforms, which I had recently approved, I looked down upon a sea of faces which for many years had reflected no hope; they had reflected only resignation to a semi-life in a 'human warehouse.' But on the day I looked into these faces, I saw hope—an eager, grasping, newly-awakened type of hope. To me, this was one of the greatest riches of life.

"A person in public office has unlimited opportunity for winning the true riches of life, perhaps more so than in any other profession."

Michael V. DiSalle,
Governor of the State of Ohio:

"During the days when I was the oldest of seven children, my mother and father had considerable difficulty in making both ends meet. But during those days we learned through them that no matter how little you had, you were fortunate to share it with others."

Buford Ellington,
Governor of the State of Tennessee:

"One of the true riches is a friend. A friend is always near. He rejoices in your good fortune; he shares your disappointments; and your problems become his problems.

"One is never poor, even though his clothes may be worn and his purse empty, if he still has the love and understanding of loyal friends."

John Anderson, Jr.,
Governor of the State of Kansas:

"Perhaps the most important thing in a man's life is to be loved and respected by his fellow man."

Ernest F. Hollings,
Governor of the State of South Carolina:

"The real riches of a man's life can best be obtained through public service. This is not necessarily to mean only political service."

John Dempsey,
Governor of the State of Connecticut:

"The true riches of life are experienced in the feeling of satisfaction that comes from having served your fellow man. The man who seeks to make such service his primary goal almost certainly will have a happy marriage, a happy home, and all the other things that we associate with 'the true riches of life.'"

Matthew E. Welsh,
Governor of the State of Indiana:

"I personally think that faith, a happy home, and challenging work are the motivating factors for a happy life."

Otto Kerner,
Governor of the State of Illinois:

"In my judgment, the greatest wealth any man can amass in this life is the enduring reward of serving his fellow men. It is only through self-forgetful activity for others that we come at length to discover who we are."

Elmer L. Andersen,
Governor of the State of Minnesota:

"The happiness and success of one's children."

Norman A. Erbe,
Governor of the State of Iowa:

"To me, the true riches of life include the privilege to work at those tasks which will live as beneficial accomplishments for mankind and the satisfaction of knowing that I have helped in the progress of the completion of these tasks."

Albert D. Rosellini,
Governor of the State of Washington:

"I agree with Aristotle in that learning is the greatest of pleasures and with the founders of our nation who believed in liberty under the law. To this one might add health, a happy home, and the opportunity to work with and serve others in his community."

Archie Gubbrud,
Governor of the State of South Dakota:

"*Health and contentment.* Perhaps this reply is trite. But upon reflection it seems to me to be the ultimate in physical and mental aspiration."

J. Millard Tawes,
Governor of the State of Maryland:

"In my humble opinion I would say the following: God in His Heaven; the Constitution of the United States; and the greatness of Mother Nature."

Farris Bryant,
Governor of the State of Florida:

"The knowledge that I did my part is one of the true riches of life."

Elbert N. Carvel,
Governor of the State of Delaware:

"1. Robust physical and mental health.

"2. The opportunity and desire to accumulate knowledge from a broad well of wisdom.

"3. The full utilization of our talents for the welfare of all mankind."

Richard J. Hughes,
Governor of the State of New Jersey:

"To me, the true riches of life are a happy family, close and faithful friendships, and a strong enduring faith. The extent to which a man is blessed with each of these and is aware of them as blessings determines the richness of his everyday life."

Jack R. Gage,
Governor of the State of Wyoming:

"In the riches of life, health has to come first, then the privilege of working at an occupation you enjoy, which, if you work hard, will enable you to honestly enjoy your recreation and leisure. Conversely, with no hard work, nothing else is fun."

F. Ray Keyser, Jr.,
Governor of the State of Vermont:

"There can be but one answer, the motivation of seeking and enjoying the eternal peace of the principles of happiness."

"What are the true riches of life?" I asked Stanley, my barber at The Orrington Hotel in Evanston, Illinois. Stanley thought for a long time. And here's what he had to say:

"Togetherness . . . goodness . . . searching . . . and the joy of finding."

What would your answer be?

THE FINE ARTS AND THE TRUE RICHES OF LIFE

Among *the true riches of life* are those that appeal to the imagination and the sense of beauty: painting, drawing, sculpture, architecture, poetry, music, dancing, acting, and the like. These are included in the fine arts. And to many these make life worth living. They bring relaxation, contentment, and joy, stimulate creative thinking, and motivate persons of all ages and in all walks of life.

It was a love of music that motivated a little girl in pigtails, too poor to go to the National Music Camp at Interlochen, to achieve so much for so many when she finally got there. She shared a part of her time and talents that made the dream of a great man and thousands of children become a reality. Here's what she says:

"When I was in pigtails and tooting a tenor saxophone in a small-town Missouri school band, my most cherished dream, like that of thousands of other small fry musicians in America, was to spend a summer at that fabulous place in the Michigan north woods which I knew only as Interlochen.

"To all of us then, Interlochen was a magic word, a summer camp where kids who loved music could go and play music to their heart's content. And to most of us it was beyond reach, a futile childhood dream which back in those Depression years we knew in our hearts could never be fulfilled."

This is Norma Lee Browning, a feature writer for the Chicago *Tribune*. One day, she and her husband, Russell Ogg, were having dinner at my home. She read to us parts of the manuscript of her new book on Joseph E. Maddy and Interlochen. A title had not as yet been selected, and the manuscript had not been edited. As she read, she interrupted herself with comments as ideas flashed into her mind. At one point, she said: *Life has a way of compensating for disappointments and linking up a chain of unexpected events like a shining string of pearls.*

Then she continued to read. One story in the manuscript was about her feelings when she lost a chance to win a scholarship to go to the National Music Camp at Interlochen. Here's the way it read:

"During my junior year in high school—1932—something happened that hit me like a jolt. A little girl named Eleanor Cisco, who was a year behind me in school and who played the clarinet, was chosen to go to Interlochen.

"Eleanor was first chair clarinetist in our school band and orchestra. Her brother played the cornet, and her mother was a fine pianist and director of our church orchestra. I was happy for

Eleanor but also secretly crushed that I had not been chosen for Interlochen. I felt I was as good on the saxophone as she was on the clarinet. My music teacher tactfully explained a few facts of life—and music—to me. I think this was when I first began to realize that in the world of good music, the saxophone is not exactly an indispensable instrument. Besides, Eleanor could play the piano as well as clarinet; she had been offered a scholarship to Interlochen. And there was little hope that I would ever be offered a scholarship—as a saxophonist.

"Eleanor came back from Interlochen with glowing reports of the National Music Camp that made us all envious. We all had heard about the camp before, but this was the first time anyone from our hometown had ever been there. Though I realized there was no chance that I would ever get to go to Interlochen, this experience made a deep impression on me and perhaps was a motivating factor in my future life.

"And this is why: because of my love of music, because of that one word *Interlochen*—a place I had never seen and knew nothing about, but which made such a deep impression one me—and because I knew that I was not good enough to go there, I secretly, stubbornly, determinedly made up my mind that someday I *would* be good enough to go there. In spite of the dark insinuations about my saxophone, I practiced even harder. I determined that I was going to be a musician. I started saving my money to go to college—*to study music.*"

Once again she stopped reading and said:

"But before I graduated from high school my music teacher told me that I could write poetry much better than I could play the saxophone, and she wisely advised me to study journalism. This I did."

Norma Lee Browning finished college, married her college sweetheart, Russell Ogg (now a well known photographer), and the two of them set out for New York and points beyond as a writer-photographer team.

"In the summer of 1941," said Norma Lee, "Russ and I were driving in northern Michigan on an assignment for *Reader's Digest.*

Suddenly in front of us loomed a roadside sign that rang a bittersweet bell. It said:

Interlochen
National Music Camp
Turn Left

"With a sudden surge of nostalgia, I exclaimed: 'I've *got* to see that place. I just want to see if it's as beautiful as I always dreamed it was.'"

It was everything she had dreamed of as a little girl, and more. She describes it beautifully in her new book.

Today, the chain of unexpected events has completed its circle. Ironically, the little girl whose family was too poor to send her to Interlochen and whose tenor sax didn't make the grade in winning a scholarship was one of the first to be invited on the faculty of the new Interlochen Academy of Fine Arts. She is not teaching music, but she is teaching creative writing for the gifted youngsters there.

Through her influence as a writer, Norma Lee Browning has done more for Interlochen Academy of Fine Arts than anyone else, except Dr. Maddy. For she has attracted hundreds of thousands of dollars to help build and support this school for gifted children.

It was Norma Lee Browning who introduced me to one of the true riches of life—meeting and becoming a close personal friend of one of America's great men, Dr. Joseph E. Maddy.

He Shares the Love of Music and Finds True Riches

Did you ever meet a person for the first time and immediately feel that it would be a privilege to have him as a close friend? That's the way I felt about Dr. Joseph Maddy when I first met him, and that's the way I feel about him now that I know him well. For he is a man of character with a positive mental attitude, a man of action who knows what he wants and goes after it—and gets it.

Fay, his wife, is a symbol of everything a good wife or mother should be. Music, Fay, and a driving desire to develop great musicians in America—to share a part of his love for music with all mankind—constantly motivate this man to ever-greater achievement. Dr. Maddy loves to talk, and everyone who meets him loves to listen. For he tells story after story of the great musicians of our time.

In her new book, Norma Lee Browning shows how Dr. Maddy shares the love of music and finds true riches, but here I'd like to share with you bits of his philosophy and his activities as he related them to me. For I believe you will get the feel of his *success system that never fails: inspiration to action, know-how,* and *activity knowledge.* The following are a few notes from the many I jotted down as I listened to him:

"My purpose in life has been to try to make music a part of our educational system."

"My beliefs have been founded on experience."

"Motivation is the main requirement in teaching music. If we have proper motivation, we succeed. If we don't, we fail."

"The try-out system we have developed at Interlochen, well known in the musical world, is the greatest motivator there is to inspire music students to try to excel. For each one has an opportunity to be recognized for his work on a competitive basis."

"Why I entered the field of music education is rather difficult to explain. I just wanted to teach. My father and mother were both school teachers. I felt that I had a knack for teaching. And another thing that got me to enter the field of music education was that I have always had a hankering to play every musical instrument I ever saw."

I once asked Joe, as his friends call him: "What is the difference between the technique of teaching developed by you and that used in Germany and other European countries?"

"The European method is the mechanical method," he replied. "Tedious hours are spent to master thoroughly the working of the instrument itself. Each person is taught individually—not by class instruction.

"I use the motivational method. First, I try to inspire the students in a class with the love and appreciation of music itself. Then a simple, popular song is played after which each student picks out the notes on his own instrument.

"Everyone has had the experience of hearing a popular song or melody, and then the next morning singing or humming it. My students merely convert the tune that is in their minds to the sound from their instruments.

"A common expression for this is 'playing by ear.'

"The students are motivated because it's fun. Then it is a very simple matter to motivate them to perfect their techniques."

This is how Dr. Maddy developed what is known as the "Universal Teacher" method, the basic teaching technique in the United States. Students in large classes, with every type of instrument, learn at the same time. Every member of the group is kept busy. Thousands and thousands of young people play musical instruments today, and play them well, because they learn through the motivational system rather than the so-called mechanical system.

Dr. Maddy says: "My contribution, in collaboration with Dr. T.P. Geddings, is the most important thing I've done, for I made it possible for us to have symphony orchestras in all the small towns in the United States, and to teach all instruments in any size school.

"In Europe they still train the soloist," he continued. "Over here, we train the orchestra, and we have 1,400 symphony orchestras, which is 80 percent of all the symphony orchestras in the world. That's the way we train at the National Music Camp at Interlochen, and that's what we will do at the Academy also."

Dr. Joseph E. Maddy is the person to whom I referred in closing the last chapter as having the true riches of life. For he employs his power to think and do good . . . has a happy marriage and a happy home . . . renders a service to our nation and mankind . . . fulfills some of the needs of others . . . helps to build character in American youth . . . inspires hope . . . shares with others . . . is enriched by the friendship of many loyal friends . . . is loved and respected by his fellow men . . . is engaged in a challenging work that he loves . . . has succeeded in a true self-forgetful activity . . .

finds happiness in the success of his children . . . thrills to learning something new . . . possesses good health and contentment, without letting contentment keep him from further progress. In brief, Dr. Maddy has acquired many of life's true riches.

There are those who have high objectives, but fail. For they don't even start, or they go the first mile and quit. Perhaps they go the second mile—but they don't go on to the end of the road. Yet to get to your destination, whatever it may be, it is necessary to go to the end.

There is nothing to stop you. For you are blessed with freedom of choice in a land of unlimited opportunity, under a government that makes the true riches of life available to all who seek them. As a reminder of these riches, listen to what the great American Herbert Hoover has to say:

> Under our unique American system, we have given more opportunities to every boy and girl than any other government . . . But more important than all, we, more than most nations, respect the individual rights and personal dignity of our citizens. . . .
>
> The outstanding spiritual distinction of our philosophy from the other (Communism) is compassion. It's the noblest expression of man. . . .
>
> I believe not only that religious faith will be victorious, but that it is vital to mankind that it shall be . . . .
>
> From their religious faith, the Founding Fathers enunciated the most fundamental law of human progress since the Sermon on the Mount, when they stated that man received from the Creator certain inalienable rights and that these rights should be protected from the encroachment of others by law and justice. . . .
>
> One of the riches of American life is the vast reservoir of leadership in the people. . . .

> It (Freedom) is a thing of the spirit. Men must be free to worship, to think, to hold opinions, to speak without fear. They must be free to challenge wrong and oppression with surety of justice. Freedom conceives that the mind and spirit of man can be free only if he be free to pattern his own life, to develop his own talents, free to earn, to spend, to save, to acquire property as the security of his old age and his family....

> Certainly it is true that the objects of organized society are to assure justice, freedom, respect for the dignity of man and the improvement and security in living.*

And it is fitting that this chapter end with another statement of Herbert Hoover:

> Might I suggest that there are already some old and trusted codes of ethics? There are the Ten Commandments, the Sermon on the Mount, and the rules of the game which we learned at our mother's knee. Can a nation live if these are not the guides of public life? Think it over.*

And after you "think it over," you will be ready for the next chapter: "The Success Indicator Brings Success."

**Addresses Upon the American Road,* Stanford University Press, Stanford, California.

LITTLE HINGES THAT SWING BIG DOORS

What does the phrase "true riches of life" mean to you? Crystallize your thoughts by answering the question in the space below. You may be surprised at the way your mind starts to churn.

Part V

THE SEARCH ENDS

19

THE SUCCESS INDICATOR BRINGS SUCCESS

You can't fail!

I repeat: You can't fail—when you *follow the instructions* outlined in this chapter. It tells you:

- What a *Success Indicator* is.
- How to make one.
- How you can use your very own.
- Why the *Success Indicator* brings success.

And when you use your *Success Indicator*—you will motivate yourself to high achievement . . . eliminate bad habits and acquire good ones . . . get out of debt . . . save money . . . acquire wealth, health, happiness . . . and find many of the true riches of life. I guarantee it!

Prove it, you may think.

I will prove it if you will do just one thing for me. Make up your *Success Indicator* and use it daily, as described later in this chapter. Then you'll begin to see concrete proof; you'll begin to notice important changes in yourself. Try it. You have everything to gain and nothing to lose. But you have much to lose if, through inertia, apathy, or laziness, you don't try. Then you'll never know what you've missed.

The principles on which the *Success Indicator* is based have brought only good to the countless thousands who have used them—famous statesmen, philosophers, members of the clergy, persons in all walks of life.

But first let's read the letter from Edward R. Dewey on Leading Indicators, referred to in Chapter 11, for it, too, can have a tremendous impact on your life.

Leading Indicators

Do you need to know what's ahead for business? There are many ways in which you can do this. One way is through the use of "Leading Indicators."

A *leading indicator* is anything that happens ahead of something else. A black cloud would be a leading indicator of rain. Falling leaves provide a leading indicator of winter. Toy rabbits everywhere are a leading indicator of Easter. In all instances, the indicator comes ahead of *(leads)* the event in which you are interested.

Certain business figures tend to go up or down before other business figures. That is, they tend to reach a maximum and start to turn down (or reach a minimum and start to turn up) before business in general goes the same way.

"New Orders for Durable Goods," is one well-known leading indicator. Orders decline, then production declines; then there are layoffs; then those involved reduce spending; then retail stores sales fall off; then retailers reduce orders; etc., etc.

Other leading indicators are "Hours Worked in Manufacturing," "The Number of New Incorporations," "Stock Prices," "Construction Contracts," "Failures."

"Failures" (either the *number* of failures, or better yet, the liabilities of failures), operate in reverse. That is, when failures go up it's a bad sign, when they go down, it's a good sign.

The Geisinger Indicator

There are special combinations and interrelationships of business figures that give even better (and earlier) forewarning of business turns than the leading indicators generally known. One of these special combinations was discovered by Robert Geisinger of Troy, Ohio. It is known as the Geisinger Indicator. It usually turns about nine months before the turns in industrial production. ("Industrial production" is a measure of the volume of things produced by industry.)

There are only three people in the whole world who know how the Geisinger Indicator is put together: Bob Geisinger, Miss Gertrude Shirk, editor of *Cycles Magazine,** and myself.

Cycles Magazine publishes the Geisinger Indicator every month to help its subscribers out-guess the future of general business (industrial production).

How to Relate and Assimilate

Throughout this book, you've read the oft-repeated expression: *relate and assimilate.* And because the obvious is not always seen, let's see how you might relate, assimilate, and use the principles in Ned Dewey's letter on Leading Indicators.

Do you want to know what's ahead in your business, family, social or personal life (physical, mental, and moral)?

Remember: *A leading indicator is anything that happens ahead of something else. In all instances, the indicator comes ahead of (leads) the event in which you are interested.*

But you must have *knowledge* and *know-how* to interpret the meaning of what you observe. If you don't know that rain clouds precede rain, that falling leaves precede winter, or that the sale of Easter toys precedes Easter, these leading indicators will be meaningless to you. Similarly, if you don't know that man is a creature of habit, you will not realize that acts of stealing make him a thief, that telling lies makes him a liar, telling the truth makes him truthful.

Because it's easy to determine which characteristics are leading

*Foundation for the Study of Cycles, Inc., 124 South Highland Avenue, Pittsburgh, Pa. 15206.

indicators of good character and which are not, you have the ability to choose those that will help you become the person you want to be. But to react to a leading indicator, you must think.

You see something happen. Then, from experience and through inductive reasoning, you can logically infer what is going to result. Now, when you lack experience, your logic may be based on wrong premises, so your conclusions will be wrong. That's why it pays to listen to the voice of experience until you have sufficient experience of your own.

You may see a given result. Through experience and deductive reasoning, you can discover the cause. When you know the cause, then you are aware of the leading indicator for that same result in the future.

A simple illustration: If one of my new salesmen has the right mental attitude, that is a leading indicator. If he learns the theoretical work taught in our sales school, that is a leading indicator. If he employs the principles he has learned, that, too, is a leading indicator. Each indicates that he will succeed as a salesman for my company.

When I first met George Severance, I observed that he was a man of character, had a positive mental attitude, loved his work, and was an expert. From these facts, I could logically infer that he was successful in his chosen field.

His Social Time Recorder and the Success System That Never Fails

Perhaps you recall that in Chapter 3, I related how George Severance developed a *Social Time Recorder* and became a self-builder.

Now, for the first time, George's secret of success is revealed to you:

"The big problem in life with nearly everyone," George told me, "can be illustrated by salesmen who don't keep a record of the amount of actual *selling time* they are spending in sales work. These salesmen don't realize the monetary value of the *selling time* they waste. In fact, they don't know where they are going in life, or how to get where they think they want to go—all because they don't have a time recorder."

"Well, how did you solve this problem for yourself?" I inquired.

"First of all, if you want to make an improvement in your daily life, you must certainly know some of the errors that are creeping into your daily performance. Knowing these errors makes you conscious of self-improvement to start with. That's what my Social Time Recorder does for me. It helps me to *accomplish more—by working less.*"

"And why is this?" I asked.

"Well, you have to have specific objectives in life. President Wilson used to say: '*Without a vision, the people perish.*' And without a direction, you don't know where you're going. *You must have some purpose in life.*

"For what's going to happen to us tomorrow depends on what we are doing today and planning for tomorrow. That's why I like to know how I am performing each day so that I can prepare for the next."

"Now, George, tell me," I said. "Exactly how do you use your Social Time Recorder?"

"Keep in mind that the card I developed for myself fits my life like a glove. But anyone can *use exactly the same principles* that I employed and design his own *Time Recorder.* It can motivate him to achieve success in any activity that he may choose. Of course, *he must use it daily.*

"As you can see, I have on this card: *Office Detail, Lunch or Dinner, Meetings, Idle Chatter, Extra Time on Interviews, Sports, Family Duties, and Late Hours.*

"Now, let's discuss sports, for example. I have always been an avid sportsman. Early in my selling career I got interested in ping-pong and squash, so I found a club where a group of fellows were experts at these games. We'd meet at twelve, and the first thing you know, I was playing until three o'clock in the afternoon."

"How did this show up on your Social Time Recorder?"

"On the line marked *Sports,* I'd write '2 hours' in the column headed *Wasted Time.* Then at the end of the month I'd make a tally.

And I found I'd spent as many as 25 hours playing ping-pong or squash during *selling time.* I soon realized that I had to do something about it. Don't misunderstand me. I still play ping-pong and squash, but only during time I've set aside for *play time.*"

"How did your Social Time Recorder motivate you to do something about eliminating this waste of *selling time?*" I asked.

"Well, on the card I have boxes entitled *Needed Improvements—Business* and *Personal.* In the personal column I'd mark, 'Eliminate ping-pong and squash during *selling time!*' I'd abbreviate this statement in the form of a code, so if someone else picked up my card, he wouldn't be aware of my personal faults.

"As *I completed a new card each day,* any encroachment on my *selling time* from these sports would be forcibly brought to my attention, and I'd take corrective action. At the end of the month, I'd see all the hours stolen from *selling time* in sports. This would motivate me to do something about it."

"Where does the total show up on your Social Time Recorder?" I asked.

"To tally the total at the end of the month, I'd make a special card merely by changing the word 'day' to 'month' on the first line of side one of my Social Time Recorder (see Fig. 3) and insert the sum of all time spent in the proper places."

"What effect would this have on you?"

"The daily writing of 'Eliminate ping-pong and squash!' under the heading *Needed Improvements* obviously would affect my subconscious mind. I wanted to succeed, and in due course, I developed the habit of converting wasted selling time into profitable selling time. I also engaged in sports, but during my play time."

"George, am I correct in concluding that certain listings on side one of your card pertain to time that might be *an infringement on selling time?* Specifically:

- *Idle Chatter* means such things as selling time wasted in visiting over a cup of coffee?
- *Extra Time Interv.* Means unnecessary time spent in pro-

longed interviews?

- *Family Duties* refers to running errands or shopping for the family during selling time?

"And is it correct that *Late Hours* means time lost from your home and family unnecessarily after business meetings, and that the abbreviation *Obj.* stands for 'Objective' and *M* indicates thousands of dollars of life insurance?"

"You're absolutely right," said George.

"Why the subheading *Evening?*" I asked.

"In my business, it's necessary to make some evening calls. With my Social Time Recorder, I have reduced this work to a maximum of two nights a week instead of six. On such occasions, however, I will shorten my business day so I have plenty of time for my family, recreation, and study. Each of these is most important for a truly successful life."

Then I continued: "On side two of your card (Fig. 4), you list the names of persons you intend to call on. *Time See* indicates the *time* of your appointment. And under *Pres. Pros.* you show the time you actually spent in the presence of the prospect. Under *Sales Calls, Sub* means subsequent calls. Is this correct?"

"Yes, and *I differentiate between sales calls and sales interviews.* There are many times when I make a call and don't try to make a sale; I may be just seeking information or making arrangements for a sales call. You will also see the notation *Att. Close.* This gives me a check on the number of times I *attempted* to close.

"If you don't make any attempt to close, you aren't going to make any sales.

"Of course, *Amt. App.* means the amount of life insurance sold. The heading *Other Time—Ser.* stands for *service calls.*

"I get a lot of prospects from service calls and list the number under *Pros.*

"Under *Club* I also list the number of business prospects, for I'll accept an invitation to play golf during business hours if by so doing I know I can line up good prospects. I make this part of my business."

Then I asked, "Do you list new names under *Replacement for Prospect List?*"

"Yes," George responded. "Just like a fellow in the timber business. If you chop down one tree, you've got to plant another tree. Because if you don't have any replacements, it isn't going to be long before you are out of business.

"I sell almost 95 percent on my first sales call, because I prepare for each sales call in my previous sales interviews. I never make more than three sales calls on one prospect. For I have the courage to tear up old prospect cards. I just don't want to waste my *selling time.*"

"What about the two lines of squares at the bottom of side two?"

"These are important. You have to have some goals, and you must be able to see the progress being made. As I *work out each new card daily,* I have specific objectives for that day.

"When I review the cards I have completed over a period of a month, it's like seeing a movie newsreel of what has actually taken place. At first, I was ashamed of what I saw. Because I was, I did something about it."

Don't Expect What You Don't Inspect

Epictetus said: *The road to hell is paved with good intentions.* For he knew the binding power of habits once formed and the difficulty of changing them. George Severance knows it, too. So did Frank Bettger. So did Benjamin Franklin. And so do you.

I say, and Epictetus would agree: The road to heaven is paved with good intentions when you follow through with action and thus acquire new, good habits to replace old bad ones.

You may be *inspired to desirable action* to fulfill your good intentions, but you may lack the necessary *knowledge,* or you may neglect to use the required *skills* if you have them, and thus you may fail to develop new habit patterns.

But Epictetus, Franklin, Severance, and Bettger knew what to do and how to do it. For each developed and used his own *success*

SIDE ONE — **SOCIAL TIME RECORDER**

KNOWING MAKES ONE CONSCIOUS OF SELF-IMPROVEMENT

SOCIAL TIME - RECORDER

Name ______________________ Day __________ Date ______________

Total Hours Wasted _______ Was the day a Social Success Yes ___ No ___ Working schedule

	Useful Time	Wasted Time	Needed Improvements	Weekly Objective	Objective	Actual
1 Office Detail			BUSINESS	M	Starting Time	
2 Lunch or Dinner						
3 Meetings				Monthly Objective	Quitting Time	
4 Idle Chatter						
1 Extra Time Interv.			PERSONAL	M	Evening	
2 Sports						
3 Family Duties				Yearly Objective		
4 Late Hours					Study & Planning	
SAVINGS — YOUR KEY TO INDEPENDENCE				M		
Obj. ____ Actual ____						

CHARACTER AND PERSONALITY TRAITS

Positives to Accentuate	Negatives to Eliminate
1	1
2	2
3	3

Figure 3

SIDE TWO — **SALES TIME RECORDER**

TOMORROW'S SUCCESS DEPENDS UPON TODAY'S PERFORMANCE

SALES TIME CONTROL

CALLS	SELLING TIME		SALES CALLS			Sales Interviews			RESULTS		OTHER TIME				
	Time See	Pres. Pros.	1st	2nd	SUB	1st	2nd	SUB	Att. Close	Amt. App.	SER.	PROS.	CLUB	TEL.	Lunch

REPLACEMENTS FOR PROSPECT LIST

	NAME	ADDRESS	AGE	INCOME	CHILDREN
1					
2					

Eve. Appts. ☐	Travel Time ☐	Selling Hours Field ☐	Selling Hours-Office ☐	No. Appts. Needed for Mo. ☐
Obj. ☐	Obj. ☐	Obj. ☐	Obj. ☐	Obj. ☐

Figure 4

indicator to help him to carry out his intentions every day. You, too, can make a *success indicator* especially designed for you.

What is a *success indicator?* For George Severance, it is his Social Time Recorder and Sales Time Control; for Benjamin Franklin, a little book. In his *Autobiography,* Franklin wrote:

> I made a little book, in which I allotted a page for each of the (13) virtues. I rul'd each page with red ink, so as to have seven columns, one for each day of the week, marking each column with a letter for the day. I cross'd these columns with thirteen red lines, marking the beginning of each line with the first letter of one of the virtues, on which line, and in its proper column. I might mark, by a little black spot, every fault I found upon examination to have been committed respecting that virtue upon that day.

And the pages Franklin drew looked like this:

HUMILITY							
Imitate Jesus and Socrates							
	S	M	T	W	T	F	S
T							
S	*	*				*	
O	*	*	*		*	*	*
R			*				*
F			*	*			
I			*		*		
S	*	*		*			
J		*			*		
M			*	*			*
C	*					*	
T			*		*		
C		*			*	*	
H							

In his book, *How I Raised Myself from Failure to Success in Selling,* Frank Bettger told exactly how he used Franklin's principle. Instead of a book, he used thirteen cards which he, like George Severance, found to be more convenient than a notebook. Like George Severance and Benjamin Franklin, he placed a self-motivator at the top of each card. On his first card—"Enthusiasm"—the self-motivator was: *To be enthusiastic—act enthusiastic.*

These men used their success indicators for several purposes, one of which was to check their own activity for each day. A successful business organization considers it mandatory to inspect work performance with regularity, yet it's unusual for a person to inspect his own habits daily. But herein lies a secret of success:

Don't expect what you don't inspect.

You can readily see that you will live up to your New Year's resolutions much more effectively if you check on *yourself* every day and keep trying.

Now, before offering suggestions that will be helpful to you in designing your own success indicator, let's consider how important *inspection* really is. For you must have faith in yourself and others, but faith should not be blind.

"La Fé"

"La Fé," the painting reproduced in this chapter, was created in tempera colors by the famous Spanish painter, José Gausachs, professor of Los Bellas Artes Dominicanos of Santo Domingo. Take a good look at the photograph of this painting. What do you see?

I see a concept of faith—a terrific force arising in the Caribbean Sea—feminine and strong, moving forward high in the heavens, facing all manner of men on earth. Are both eyes closed, or is one partially open? No one but you, not even José Gausachs, can answer that question for you. Look at the eyes and decide for yourself.

Faith is that which is believed—complete confidence in someone or something, even someone or something that may be open to question or suspicion. Blind faith, with both eyes permanently closed, lacks discernment and demonstrates unwillingness to understand. Such faith is often without reason or discrimination. It is the mother of ignorance and the frequent cause of misery and disaster.

Isn't faith strengthened by having one eye closed and one partially opened—be it faith in an individual, an idea, or a philosophy? Isn't it effective when those whom you want to influence are not absolutely certain whether one eye is partially open when both appear to be closed?

You often read the anguished laments of a mother whose teenage son is accused of theft or some other crime: "He was always such a good boy; he never did anything wrong before." What would have happened if this mother had kept one eye partially open instead of both eyes closed?

To keep one eye partially open to inspect doesn't in itself indicate the slightest degree of distrust. But doing so strengthens, protects, and guarantees the preservation and effectiveness of faith, in every relationship where faith is imperative for harmony and happiness.

Have faith in yourself and others, but don't blind yourself to reality. Others need not know with any degree of certainty whether—like the eyes in the painting, "La Fé"—both eyes are closed or one is partially open. They, like you, must make their own decision and act accordingly.

Be Honest With Yourself

"If you are an honest person, when you make a promise to another person, you will live up to it. But it's just as important that you *be honest with yourself.* So when you make a promise to yourself, live up to that promise. And don't make a promise in the first place unless you intend to fulfill it," says George Severance.

It's Up to You

Now make a solemn promise:
I promise myself that I will:

1. Begin to design my own success indicator before I go to bed tonight.
2. Spend at least 30 minutes each day for the next 30 days in study, thinking, and planning time—in concentrated effort on self-improvement—to get the most out of my success indicator.
3. Immediately start a new 30-day series if any day I should fail to live up to my promise of a half an hour devoted to this form of self-improvement.
4. Ask for divine guidance each time I begin my half hour of self-improvement, and thank Divine Power for my specific blessings. (Enumerate.)

The following suggestions may aid you:

- Start with a pencil and piece of paper. Later, when you have developed the form that is effective, have it mimeographed or printed. George Severance's cards are printed, but he started with just a sheet of paper.
- There should be a self-motivator on the first line. This can be changed at regular intervals, but not more frequently than weekly.
- Give a suitable title, such as "My Success Indicator."
- If you find it difficult to originate a design, you might copy what is applicable from the forms in this chapter.
- Have suitable spaces so that you can check either the fulfillment of an objective or momentary failure.
- You may prefer to have a form indicating relative progress.
- Indicate the positive characteristics you wish to acquire. I recommend that instead of indicating negatives, you phrase your statements in the positive. Illustration: If your weakness is deception, instead of listing the negative "Eliminate

Deception," write down "Be Truthful" or "Truthfulness."

- Because the fire of enthusiasm can become extinguished unless it is refueled, try to read some self-help material for at least five minutes each day.

Now you must think for you. Only you have the power to direct your thoughts and control your emotions. Therefore, you must design your own forms for this program to be effective. For it's through self-effort that you receive self-benefits.

LITTLE HINGES THAT SWING BIG DOORS

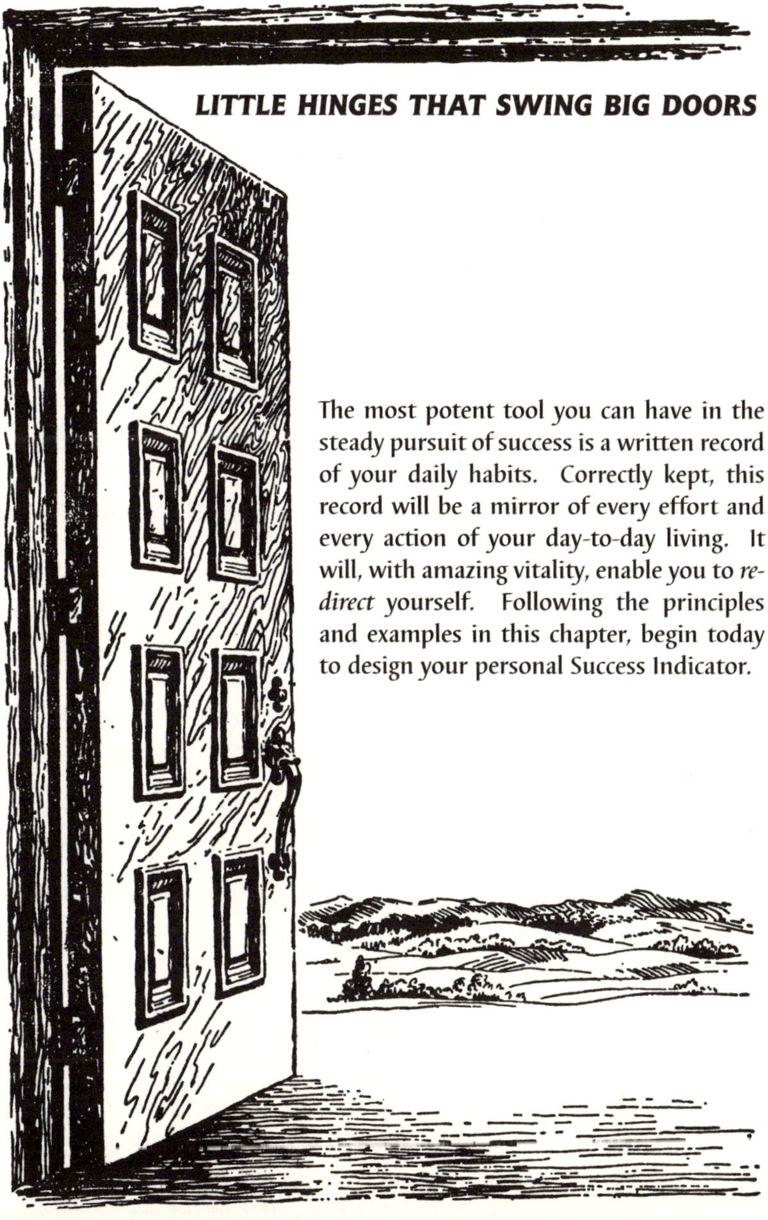

The most potent tool you can have in the steady pursuit of success is a written record of your daily habits. Correctly kept, this record will be a mirror of every effort and every action of your day-to-day living. It will, with amazing vitality, enable you to *re-direct* yourself. Following the principles and examples in this chapter, begin today to design your personal Success Indicator.

20

THE AUTHOR REVIEWS HIS OWN WORK

"A small drop of ink makes thousands, perhaps millions think," wrote Byron in *Don Juan.*

And that's what I thought as I began to write the manuscript for this book. For its purpose is to motivate the reader:

1. To learn and use three simple, easily understood concepts that must be used by any person for continuous success in any human activity. Herein lies the essence of this work. For the person who uses these three ingredients in combination in any specific activity cannot fail.
   - *Inspiration to action:* that which motivates you to act because you want to.
   - *Know-how:* the particular techniques and skills that consistently get results for you when applied. It is the proper application of knowledge. *Know-how* becomes *habit* through actual repetitive *experience.*
   - *Activity knowledge:* knowledge of the activity, service, product, methods, techniques, and skills with which you are particularly concerned.
2. To strive day by day to continue his education and thus expand his horizon.
3. To help himself become a better person and constantly strive to make his world better for himself and others.

4. To learn to develop the habit of recognizing, understanding, relating, assimilating, and using principles from his reading, the people he meets, and his everyday experiences.
5. To acquire financial wealth and business success, even though the *spotlight is on the true riches of life.*
6. To preserve and protect his inheritance as an American.
7. To feel, live and act with a dynamic philosophy resulting from the action of striving to live up to the precepts of the religious teachings of his own church.
8. To seek and find the true riches of life.

Again: *A drop of ink makes thousands, perhaps millions, think.* And a self-help book has changed the lives of countless thousands for the better. Take Fuller Duke, for example.

My Mind Has Been Opened

Fuller was a successful salesman, and he became a successful sales manager for me before he went blind. Like all our representatives, he received self-help books and record albums, such as "The System That Never Fails."* Fuller is happily married, the father of six fine boys and five wonderful girls.

And something more: Fuller Duke has a living religious faith. This has been proved many times in the past, and it has again been evidenced in the present by the letter he recently sent me, a portion of which is as follows:

"I had the services of one of the best eye specialists in the country. He exerted every effort to save my vision and was very upset at the final examination to find that further surgery or treatment would be without avail.

"Now as to my thinking about my future: Bearing in mind that every adversity carries with it the seed of an equivalent or greater benefit, and using 'The System That Never Fails,' I was *inspired to action* and immediately set forth to acquire the necessary *know-how* and *activity knowledge* to ascertain what, if any, limitations are

*Businessmen's Record Club, 415 N. Dearborn St., Chicago 10, Ill.

to be mine. I was thrilled to discover that this is only a detour on the road to my ultimate goal.

"Since last Thursday, I have talked to many professional men, executives, and business people, and learned that by attending school for three months I can learn Braille and how to travel alone—in short, lead a normal life. I have been doing a lot of brainstorming, and my thoughts are all positive. . . .

"To be sure, I will not cease to search for a cure. I hope, like George Campbell in *Success Through a Positive Mental Attitude,* that I, too, can demonstrate my positive mental attitude by proving that I am still capable of attaining success.

"It is my firm belief that the age of miracles has not passed, and if it be the will of the Almighty, the prayers of my family and friends will not go unanswered.

"Even though my eyes have been closed . . . my mind has been opened!"

The way you and I can keep our minds open is to continue our education.

Expand Your Horizon

"Education is what we are trying to do in our American way of life to develop the finest in each individual. We are attempting to develop in the individual his intellectual, physical, moral and spiritual well being," says Dr. K. Richard Johnson, president of the National College of Education in Evanston, Illinois.

And Paul Molloy, in his humorous but down-to-earth book *And Then There Were Eight,** tells us:

> ". . . the true training of the child does not start at school or church; it begins at the knees of the mother."
>
> ". . . if parents and children bumped into each other more often, they'd be less inclined to drop one another later on."
>
> ". . . I don't know what the child-guidance experts would say about this, but we've operated on the theory that a child bright

*Doubleday & Company, New York.

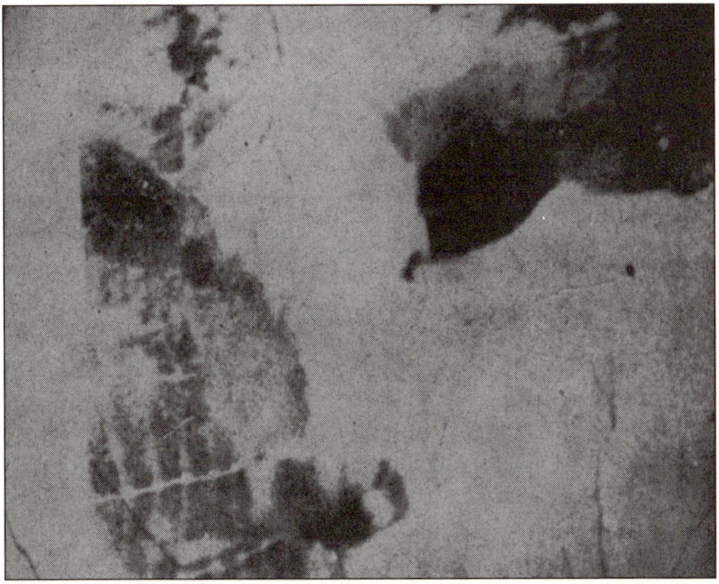

WHAT IS IT?

This fascinating picture is not an illustration. It is an actual, distinct photograph of a familiar subject. *Can you see it????*

(see over)

The object in the picture is a cow. The head of the cow is staring straight out at you from the center of the photograph, its two black ears framing the white face. The picture is widely used by the Optometric Extension Program Foundation to demonstrate the difference between *eyesight* and *vision.* What is the difference? Vision, the Foundation states, is the ability to get meaning from eyesight.

The picture may also help to impress you with a fact of supreme importance—there is a difference between *reading* and *understanding.* What is that difference? Understanding is the ability to get *meaning* from reading—to comprehend the full force of the written word. The more you are able to do this, the more valuable will be the time you spend with this book.

You probably did not immediately see the cow in the picture the first time you looked. Isn't it probable, then, that you have missed much of the *meaning* in these pages, after only one reading? This book should be re-read and studied until it yields up *all* its powerful ideas.

enough to reject turnips when there are cookies on the table is almost bright enough to begin picking up after himself."

And I, for one, would rather recommend the advice of the man who has the knowledge and know-how of raising children than the advice of the child guidance expert who tells how to raise children even though he has none of his own to raise.

Self-Help Books Changed His Life

And that's why I felt warranted to write this book. For I have the experience, knowledge, and know-how to motivate persons in all walks of life.

One way to motivate people is to introduce them to a self-help book. I *romance* the value of any particular book I recommend by telling true stories of how it has helped others. This technique has been especially effective in reaching teenage boys and girls through Boys Clubs, high schools, colleges, and penal institutions.

Francis McKay is a social worker in the House of Correction in Chicago. He's a student of the *PMA Science of Success* course, and he's been taught how to motivate others through self-help books. Here's part of a letter that inspired me when I received it from one of his teenage charges not so long ago. This boy had learned how to relate and assimilate principles that could change the course of his life for the better:

> Gentlemen:
>
> I have just finished reading your book *Success Through a Positive Mental Attitude.* I want to thank you for writing such a book. . . .
>
> I can honestly say that the book inspired me and changed my way of thinking. It has shown me that "Where there's a will, there's a way."
>
> You see I am 19 years of age, and the "Problem Child" and "Charlie Ward" that you mentioned in your book is myself, looking into a mirror, and seeing them as they were. I also took pride in being recognized as #1 bad boy of the

gang. Because of that pride, my environment, and my associates, I have been going to reform schools and institutions such as this for the past four years.

I know now it's time to grow up and leave my associates and make something of myself . . .

When the years pass and I am living and working like a respectable human should, I will look back and remember the social worker and the books. I know I can make good, and with God's help, I will.

My philosophy on life used to be "Live for Today, Forget Tomorrow;" My outlook has changed to "Live for Tomorrow."

I will never forget those words, for I believe in them. *What the mind conceives and believes, it can achieve.*

The Disciplinarian with the Kind Heart

Arthur Ward is superintendent of the House of Correction in Chicago. He is known as the disciplinarian with the kind heart.

More than one-third of the inmates are alcoholics—as is Ward himself. But through the inspiration of his wife and the parish priest, he developed the courage and strength to say "No" to temptations to drink. And because he is a self-builder, he knows how to inspire and build those who are afflicted with the same misfortune he overcame.

He knows that *hope* is the magic ingredient in motivation, so he has developed a philosophy called *Operation Hope.* When men and women leave the House of Correction, they have pride in their appearance and an inspirational philosophy in their hearts. For under *Operation Hope,* each has been given suitable clothing and an opportunity to learn success principles from the *PMA Science of Success* course and other inspirational materials.

"I guess you would say that the theme *Operation Hope* has been the story of my life. To me, this symbolizes the true riches of life—the reward that comes from helping others play the game of life in the best and fullest possible manner," says Ward.

And what do others have to say on this matter? Here are additional answers to the questions: "What are the true riches of life?"

General David Sarnoff:

"While it's true that you can get happiness and peace and serenity from being at the lower end of the ladder, it is also true that you cannot enjoy the ecstasy of achievement. Success, in a generally accepted sense of the term, means the opportunity to experience and to realize to the maximum the forces that are within us."

John A. Notte, Jr.,
Governor of the State of Rhode Island & Providence Plantations:

"It seems to me that the 'true riches' are the spirit, and are derived from good family life, inner strength that comes from one's faith purposefully practiced, and the maintenance of high ideals in day-to-day personal conduct."

Price Daniel,
Governor of the State of Texas:

"Our success in life depends entirely upon what we do on this earth for our fellow man. This is the test which the Master says will be applied in the final day of judgment. In His words, 'Inasmuch as ye have done it to these, the least of My brethren, ye have done it unto Me.'"

Mark O. Hatfield,
Governor of the State of Oregon:

"It immediately occurred to me that these riches are not found in the material. Neither are they found in a philosophy, but they are found in a Person. Saint Paul wrote to the church at Colosse, 'in Jesus Christ lie hidden all God's treasures of wisdom and knowledge.' I've found in my personal life that this is true. In my relationship with this Person is found true riches—the treasure of god's wisdom. All else of value springs from this."

Sister Joan Margaret, Directress,
St. Vincent's School for Handicapped Children,
Pour-au-Prince, Haiti:

"You asked about the 'true riches of life.' Very simple: love of God and love of one's neighbor. It just goes straight back to the Bible. I firmly believe that: 'Whatsoever things are true, whatsoever thing are honest, whatsoever things are just, whatsoever things are pure, whatsoever things are lovely, whatsoever things are of good report, if there be any virtue and if there be any praise, think on these things.' (Phil. 4:8)"

I don't know Sister Joan Margaret's age . . . I don't know what she looks like . . . but I do know that she has found the true riches of life. This American girl is doing so much for crippled Haitian children that she is a symbol to me of all the good women who are devoting their loves to the service of the church. She has a great love for all people, and a special mercy for the sick and the crippled.

Another American girl who has found the true riches of life in Port-au-Prince is Lavinia Williams Yarborough, a famous dancer who heads the Haitian Institute of the Dance.

Because I Love My People

Lavinia recently wrote me: "I first started to work with Sister Joan Margaret in 1954 during Hurricane Hazel. She did a tremendous job, flying to various parts of Haiti to help carry food and clothing to the victims. On one of these trips, she found a six-month-old girl who was the sole survivor of her village. She brought the child to Port-au-Prince and nursed her to health. She had been sick and starving.

"I told Sister that I would start giving the child exercises when she became three years old to develop her body. She was very tiny for her age, but you should see her now—a beautiful, healthy, normal child, who is still dancing.

"I also work with the deaf and dumb. One of my trainees at St. Vincent's is a deaf mute and is teaching dancing at Sister Joan's. I take as students some of the more talented mutes who dance in my concerts. No one would ever recognize them for deaf and dumb, since I have never distinguished them myself from the normal children. I now have four mutes as students, all of whom are superb. I also work with Sister Joan's recovered polio victims. These children study ballet to strengthen their limbs. I also have other children from St. Vincent's."

Little Hinges That Swing Big Doors

This chapter is a review of the entire book. In it, you feel the undercurrents flowing throughout. The spotlight has been thrown on the true riches of life. For in seeking them you can also find monetary wealth and success.

In a speech, Governor Price Daniel of Texas gave the following illustration: "A South American leader and visitor who many years ago was asked why the material progress of North America had so far outstripped that of South America, replied: *'The people who settled North America came here seeking God. Those who came to South America were in search of gold.'*"

The wife of one of my sales managers in Waco, Texas, Naomi Nyberg, is writing a book titled, "Little Hinges That Swing Big Doors." The title kept going through my mind like a melody, so I asked Naomi if I might have permission to use it as a chapter or subheading, and she enthusiastically and graciously gave me the privilege of sharing this thought with you.

So, at the end of each chapter you have seen "Little Hinges That Swing Big Doors." The open door symbolized faith in your fellow man, your vision of the world without . . . and within is the hiding place, so obvious it wouldn't be seen.

The Hiding Place . . .

There is an old Hindu legend stating that when the gods were making the world, they said: "Where can we hide the most valuable of treasures, so that they will not be lost? How can we hide them so that the lust and greed of men will not steal or destroy them? What can we do to be assured that these riches will be carried on from generation to generation for the benefit of all mankind?"

So in their wisdom they selected a hiding place that was so obvious it wouldn't be seen. And there they placed the true riches of life, endowed with the magic power of perpetual self-replenishment. In this hiding place these treasures can be found by every living person in every land who follows *the success system that never fails.*

LITTLE HINGES THAT SWING BIG DOORS

The True Riches of Life

Are Hidden in the

Hearts and Minds of Men

INDEX

Shirk, Gertrude, 221

ABOUT THE AUTHOR

W. Clement Stone began his phenomenal selling career as a newsboy in his home city of Chicago. At twenty he formed his own sales organization for accident and health insurance. He was so successful in this venture that he decided to put aside early ambitions to practice law and concentrate instead on the expansion of his business. In addition to other activities, he was president of Chicago Boys Clubs and a member of the Board of Directors of Boys Clubs of America. He was also a board member of National Music Camp and Interlochen Academy of Fine Arts. Mr. Stone was Chairman of the Board of The American Foundation of Religion and Psychiatry and The Foundation for the Study of Cycles.

W. Clement Stone was President of Combined Insurance Company of America . . . Combined American Insurance Company . . . The First National Casualty Company and Hearthstone Insurance Company of Massachusetts, as well as editor and publisher of *Success unlimited* magazine and a director of Alberto-Culver Company. He co-authored, with Napoleon Hill, *Success Through A Positive Mental Attitude* (Prentice-Hall, 1960).